A Spinster's Last Stand

Book 3 of Lady Knights series

Cara Maxwell

Dragonblade Publishing, Inc. is an imprint of Kathryn Le Veque Novels, Inc.
P.O. Box 23
Moreno Valley, CA 92556
ceo@dragonbladepublishing.com

Produced in the United States of America

First Edition September 2023
Trade Paperback Edition

ARE YOU SIGNED UP FOR DRAGONBLADE'S BLOG?

You'll get the latest news and information on exclusive giveaways, exclusive excerpts, coming releases, sales, free books, cover reveals and more.

Check out our complete list of authors, too!

No spam, no junk. That's a promise!

Sign Up Here

www.dragonbladepublishing.com

Dearest Reader;

Thank you for your support of a small press. At Dragonblade Publishing, we strive to bring you the highest quality Historical Romance from some of the best authors in the business. Without your support, there is no 'us', so we sincerely hope you adore these stories and find some new favorite authors along the way.

Happy Reading!

CEO, Dragonblade Publishing

**Additional Dragonblade books by
Author Cara Maxwell**

The Lady Knights Series
In Bed with a Blackguard (Book 1)
Lost to Lady Scandal (Book 2)
A Spinster's Last Stand (Book 3)

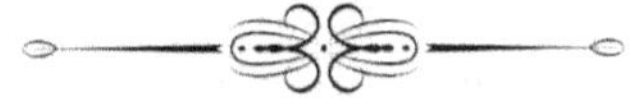

CHAPTER ONE

August 1817
Essex, England

EVEN SHE DID not deserve this.

She'd botched her last quest—she'd offer no argument or defense on that front. For six months, Ethelreda McGovern had little more to do than sit on her arse and ruminate about all the ways she'd bungled things for herself, for her friends, and for her queen.

Six months without an assignment… Red had thought that was her punishment.

But she was wrong.

So, so terribly wrong.

The quest she'd been assigned by the Duchess of Guilford was so much worse.

Isolation she could handle, even if she was a normally gregarious person. Even in a backwater Essex village there was plenty of conversation to be had. After two months, Red knew the name and life story of every single person in the village. More importantly, they knew her. If anyone cared to inquire, there would be dozens of people here to give glowing descriptions of Ethelreda Trudeau, a down-on-her-luck governess living frugally between postings. The villagers knew her so well, they could hardly remember a time when she had not lived among them.

Exactly as she'd intended.

But the final summons from Oxley Park had arrived that afternoon—as well as a parcel from the duchess herself.

Red glared at the book sitting across the table from her while she toyed with her solitary supper. The bespectacled woman etched upon the front seemed to stare at her. Mocking her.

Miss Plimpton's Guide for the Modern Governess.

If she had to wipe a nose, she was going to be ill.

A gentle knock spared her the image of snot and tears. "Miss Trudeau?"

Stubbornly refusing to look at Miss Plimpton's odious book, Red crossed to the door and fixed a soft smile upon her face.

"Good evening, Anna," she said to the other young woman, who was framed in the doorway with one armful of fresh linens and the other balancing a discarded serving tray.

"Have you finished with your supper? May I take the tray— Oh, I beg your pardon, miss."

Red swung her eyes accusingly to the nearly untouched platter of food she'd abandoned seconds before.

The small inn's sole maid shifted under her burdens. "Is there something amiss with the food?" she asked. Though Red could see clearly enough that if there was, Anna did not particularly want to know about it.

She forced the bright smile she'd worn thousands of times in London ballrooms to her face. "Not at all! I am too excited to eat. I have finally secured a posting!"

Anna's mouth tightened. "How lovely, Miss Trudeau. Will you be leaving us soon, then?"

Red pretended not to notice the wobble of the tray as the maid's arm quivered. Anna was irritable at the best of times; this evening, she was particularly sour.

"Oh yes, right away!" Red exclaimed. She even rubbed her hands together, as if she could not contain the excitement.

"I shall just tell Mrs. Crawford, then, shall I?" Anna cast a not-so-subtle glance toward the stairwell behind her, where the innkeeper's wife would be minding the dining room below.

Red jumped, a hand to her bosom, artifice uncracked. "Oh dear, do not let me keep you! All of that looks quite heavy!"

"Aye, 'tis," Anna mumbled, waiting for no further invitation before swinging for the stairs.

Red waited at the open door, listening to every grumble the woman muttered to herself. Each word was a reassurance that she'd played her part well. The maid was well and truly annoyed with her, and sure to complain to Mrs. Crawford, the cook, and anyone else within earshot, that Miss Trudeau had kept her standing with her arms full to spout on about her new posting.

By midday tomorrow, the rest of the village would know Ethelreda's news. Since they all knew how desperate she was for the posting, none would question when she disappeared without a proper goodbye. Just as she had floated into town, she would slip out. Nothing more than a pleasant memory the villagers might think of now and again. No one they would worry over or try to seek out. Exactly as she'd intended.

At least she could do something right.

As she sank back down into the chair before her untouched food, Red glared at the book. The Duchess of Guilford had not even bothered to enclose a note with the parcel. The message was clear enough—do not muck this up.

Shoving her supper aside, Red snatched up the book and opened to the first page of text. She was indisputably the worst lady knight for this quest. Crying children made her want to scream and cry herself. Reclusive former soldiers... Well, all men were much the same for Red. Best kept at a distance. At least there was no chance of any romantic entanglement, as seemed to be the trend for young English governesses.

She would manage. She had to.

And if things went awry... Red stroked the handle of her parasol, always at her side. If things went wrong, she'd stab first and ask questions later.

Two months ago
London

RED SHOVED A bit of fruitcake into her mouth to avoid having to fake a smile. Or speak with anyone. She'd been hovering in the corner for the entire wedding breakfast, even as guests stood and began swirling around the McGovern home, congratulating the newly married couple and the family that had gathered around them.

Her mother looked particularly relieved. The youngest of her daughters was finally married. To a duke, no less. It was quite a coup for the fourth daughter of a second son himself, whose own father had been a mere baron.

As Red chewed her fruitcake, her eyes tracked her father across the room. For the first time in more than ten years, his shoulders were relaxed. He laughed freely at whatever tepid joke her sister Elizabeth's husband offered. That was enough to garner a real smile from Red's clenched cheeks.

The younger McGovern sisters had made advantageous marriages, one and all. Most of it was due to Elizabeth's husband, who was now repeating his jape to a larger audience. Red let her face soften as she watched; for all that he might lack in wit, he made up for in generosity. Elizabeth's husband had provided substantial dowries for both of the younger McGovern girls, Annabelle and Mary Jane. They were both now well and happily married.

Young Mary Jane had said her vows to the Duke of Hartwell that very morning at St. George's. Which meant that, finally, Ethelreda was free.

She'd spent each Season since her debut thinking about how she would manage to see her younger sisters suitably settled. That she was unmarried registered not at all; she did not want to be married. She wanted the autonomy of spinsterhood and the fulfillment of her work.

So why did her freedom taste like sour fruitcake?

"Sip a bit of champagne, dear. You look peaked."

Red nearly choked on her fruitcake. But she did manage to get a hand out in time to catch the glass of champagne the Duchess of Guilford shoved into it.

"Your Grace," she said, swallowing hard. "We are honored by your presence."

The dark-haired duchess sipped her own champagne, eyes fixed on the crowded parlor. Red darted a glance. The duchess—Miranda—always looked so damn queenly. The threads of gray at her temples only heightened the effect, pulled back from her face rather than teased to hide the signs of aging. She wore them proudly. How many times had Red stared at her own face in the mirror and tried to emulate that look of regal detachment?

She settled instead for pursing her lips.

"You sister has made a spectacular match. Your family must be very proud," Miranda commented.

"We are honored to count the Duke of Hartwell among us." Red was honored. Well, perhaps more relieved than honored. But the duke was a kind man—and he adored her sister. So she could say she was honored and not balk.

"I heard a rumor that the duke gifted your mother with several rare paintings as part of his courtship of your sister," the duchess said. Quiet, but calculated to be so. Loud enough that they might be heard by the two or three guests nearest them. So no one would think it odd when Red answered:

"I would be most pleased to show you, Your Grace."

"How kind of you, Miss McGovern."

It was a charade they'd played out a dozen times. Red took Miranda's now-empty glass and met the eye of the footman who stood at attention in the corner. The duchess turned away, stopping to exchange paltry greetings with several other guests before making her way to the foyer where Red now waited. Without any haste, without any cause for suspicion or notice, the two women slipped out of the fray.

The paintings were in the library, where Red's mother preferred to take her afternoon tea and enjoy the afternoon light upon her treasures. The room also conveniently boasted a Bramah lock, courtesy of Red herself. She'd posed it to her father as a novelty—the lock was famously unpickable. That it provided Red with a secure place within her home to conduct her work… Her family need never know such details.

Despite the contrived ploy, Miranda drifted toward the three paintings on the southern wall and leaned in to examine them. "True masterpieces," she murmured.

"Do you think I would have let my mother hang forgeries?" Red hedged her annoyance with false amusement.

The tightening around Miranda's lips was the only indication she saw through that façade. "I have a quest for you."

Years of training kept Red from any more than a sharp inhale followed by a carefully controlled exhale. Inside, her heart was thudding. She wanted to dance and jump and cry for joy. Finally, a quest.

The corner of Miranda's mouth twitched. "I expected rather more excitement."

Red's mouth fell open. She could feel the color climbing her cheeks. All it took was that tiny opening, and her emotions surged out.

"There it is," the duchess said, a knowing smile now curving her lips.

"I cannot stay away for long; my mother will miss me. She has grand aspirations of marrying me off to one of the Duke of Hartwell's friends. Tell me," Red said, more entreaty than demand.

"Your mother shall have to give over those notions, I am afraid. You are going to Essex."

Red's heart began to hammer harder inside her chest. "What is in Essex?"

"Sir George Caldwell, late of His Majesty's Fifth Regiment of

Foot." As she spoke, Miranda drifted to the next painting, as if she were casually commenting upon the masterpieces rather than a potentially dangerous quest.

"Was he at Waterloo?" Red's mind was already flicking through possibilities, summoning what she knew of the final days of the French conflict.

"Yes. Which is precisely why you are being sent to Oxley Park."

"Oxley Park," she repeated, turning over the name in her mouth. "I am not familiar with it. Nor the family name. I take that to mean he does not spend much time in London?"

"Correct." Miranda nodded. "For once, this is rather to your benefit. He will not know your family or your background."

"Am I to assume a new identity?" Red bit her lip to keep it from quivering. She was a trained lady knight, sharp as a well-honed blade. She should not be unnerved by the notion of playing at someone she was not. She had done it before.

But usually that sort of thing was left to Dominique. Red *used* her societal connections in her work, rather than hiding them.

"Yes. You will leave in two days and travel to Essex," Miranda said.

"Two days?" Red blinked. "My mother—"

"I have already put it in her ear. My sister, Lady Danner, needs a companion for a rather arduous tour of the Low Countries. You will be accompanying her."

Red digested that knowledge as quickly as she could, knowing her time with the duchess was running out. She would need to return to the party soon, and there were still vital questions left unanswered—especially if she was to depart in only two days.

"Once I arrive at Oxley Park, what role—"

"You are not going to Oxley Park. Not directly. You will spend the next several months establishing your identity, until you ultimately go to take up your post." As she spoke, the duchess reached into an expertly concealed pocket in the folds of her gown.

Red had long suspected Miranda still favored the older fashions for particularly this reason—the voluminous pockets could hide any manner of secrets. Unlike the slimmer silhouettes currently in fashion, which made hiding even a penknife a challenge. Red twirled the parasol at her side.

The duchess's hand emerged, long fingers curled around a thick sheaf of papers. Excitement and anxiety thrummed through Red's chest, before twining around her spine and spiking through her legs.

She accepted the packet, wanting nothing more than to sink into one of the well-worn armchairs and read every word, eschewing the celebrations beyond. But instead, she crossed to a bookcase on the far side of the room, rearranging several books to reveal a narrow wooden box with another one of those unpickable locks. As she slid the key from her bodice and secured the documents to peruse later, she put her final set of questions to the duchess.

"What am I looking for and who am I to be?"

"We have received intelligence from our officers in France that one of Napoleon's most dangerous assassins has escaped and taken refuge in England. Antoine Legrand. There is some reason to believe he may seek out Caldwell."

"Why—"

"That is what I want you to deduce. Why would Legrand come to Essex, and why Caldwell? Legrand is considered the most dangerous, one of Napoleon's inner circle. Even serving as his personal assassin when needs be."

That was why she'd been tasked with this quest, Red realized. Of all the lady knights, she was the best equipped to handle herself in dangerous hand-to-hand combat. She gripped the curved handle of her parasol a little tighter.

"There is every possibility that Legrand has already arrived in Essex and assumed a post in Caldwell's household. From your position, you will have access to the entire staff. Trust no one. Not even Caldwell himself."

Red was used to that—self-reliance. She'd been the savior of her family for years, cleverly steering her younger sisters to advantageous matches even when they lacked the dowries to support them. As a lady knight, the people she trusted could be counted on one freckled hand: her other lady knights, and the woman standing before her now.

But one sentence from Miranda's explanation snagged in her mind. *From your position, you will have access to the entire staff.* There were precious few roles she might assume that fit that criterion…

"What is the post?"

Miranda sighed heavily, letting no hint of amusement or remorse show on her regal face as she said, "You shall be governess to Sir Caldwell's two young children."

Red's grip on the parasol was the only thing that kept her upright.

CHAPTER TWO

August 1817
Oxley Park, Essex

"HELL AND DAMNATION—EVELINE!"

George leapt from the too-small chair, his knee hitting the table on the way up, and seconds later sent the entire thing careening sideways. Dishes hit the floor with a vicious crash, the thick rug not nearly enough to save the teapot or its companions.

"Ooooooww," Archie wailed, loud enough to wake the dead.

George snatched the child up, expecting to find blood pouring from his body. He held him aloft, searching for injuries and finding none.

"What are you bawling about?" If the child had a response, George did not hear it. Eveline was tugging at his arm. He managed to get his hand up a second before the tea towel hit his face. He thunked the little boy down on his bed before rounding on his daughter. "Eveline—"

"I am sorry, Father! Here, let me help—"

"You have done enough!" he thundered.

The girl shrank away immediately, fleeing toward the hallway.

"Eveline, don't you dare—" But she was already gone.

Hell and damnation, indeed.

He'd put his foot in it now. It could very well take him hours to find her now, so clever was she at hiding herself away in some corner of the house.

Archie's screeches had ebbed to pitiful whimpers. And George's trousers were covered in tea.

At least it had not been hot.

It had taken him so long to corral his two children to actually sit down for a spot of afternoon tea that the pot the maid had delivered had cooled completely. Now, the entire spread was on the floor.

"What the hell am I doing?" he growled under his breath.

Archie whimpered in response.

Two months, he'd been managing this nonsense. Three, really, if he counted from when Miss Swan had left them. In the dead of night, the damn woman. Afraid to give him her notice in person, she'd fled in the dark. Whether that reflected on him or his children…

Mrs. Johnson, his housekeeper, had not lasted a week before demanding she resume the duties she was hired for or leave his employ entirely.

He could command an entire infantry battalion, but he could not manage two children? It was utterly ridiculous.

He caught a glimpse of himself in the mirror above Eveline's dressing table—necktie loose, hair in similar disarray. Perhaps he ought to start wearing his uniform. That might get his children into proper form.

George settled for straightening himself in the mirror as best he could, retying the neckcloth and the club of hair at the nape of his neck. When he straightened once more, at least he looked the part of military composure, for all that he did not feel it.

A streak of red caught his eye—a smear down his right cheek.

Suddenly the face that stared back was not his own. The dark brown was not the wood paneling of the nursery, but the dirt and mud. That face—*the face*…

Blazing-hot rage lanced through him. He had to get to McGovern, had to help him—

There was blood everywhere. His hands, his face, even soaking his trousers. So much blood. None of it his own—

"Fa… Father?"

The tiny, quivering voice cut through the darkness that entrapped his mind.

Slowly, painfully slowly, the waking nightmare faded. The light from the afternoon sun filtered in through the open drapes. The bedsprings squeaked as little Archie shifted his weight.

It was not blood on his trousers, but tea. Not blood streaking his face, but raspberry preserves from the overturned tea service.

He was not on a battlefield.

But looking around the destroyed nursery, he might as well have been.

Stalking across the room, George yanked on the bellpull to summon the maid. He righted the table and the small chairs with mechanical efficiency, setting them well clear of the disaster on the floor. Then he turned on Archie, whose cheeks were still smeared, but tears no longer actively flowed.

"At attention, soldier," he ordered Archie, setting the boy on his feet. "Sit in that chair until I come back." Archie followed the direction of his pointed finger, but did not move. "Hut, Hut!"

The child jumped into motion, nearly tripping over his feet. But when George turned back, notebook and quill pen in hand, the boy had managed to maneuver himself into the seat.

George dropped the writing materials onto the table. "Write your alphabet. Again and again. Until I find your sister. Or I give up and come back," he grumbled.

He paused in the door long enough to watch Archie tentatively reach for the notebook, cracking it open and flipping through to a blank page. With a sharp nod of satisfaction, George turned into the corridor.

He made a mental tally of all Eveline's favorite hiding places, at least those he'd discovered in the past few months. He'd start with the ones on the first floor... Perhaps luck would be with him. Though after the day—nay, year—he'd had, George had no reason to believe that it would be.

She was not in the guest room armoire, nor the cupboard in the servants' stairwell. He swept through the suite of rooms that had once belonged to his younger sister, but Eveline was not beneath the rose and cream duvet. When he reached the last suite of apartments before the wide staircase...

"Anywhere but here," he murmured to himself.

It took him several minutes to muster the courage to reach for the door handle, which was polished even in disuse. But something pricked his intuition. A second later, he heard it. The subtle *click*, back in the direction from whence he'd come.

Ten long steps and he was reaching for a different door—the one on the waist of the defunct grandfather clock that stood sentinel at the end of the corridor. In the half-second it took him to open it, a dozen thoughts collided in his mind:

Was he such a terrible father? To drive his daughter to hide from him in such a tiny, close space? What would her mother have said... Or his own mother? Perhaps he ought to send them to Elsie. But that would mean admitting defeat.

He tugged the waist door open, expecting to find tears and sadness. Instead, hellfire and condemnation stared out at him. She may be folded inside the tight space, but Eveline's dark eyes danced with ire that he'd seen matched only in his own reflection. And perhaps in his younger sister Elsie's from time to time, when he'd played an unusually cruel jape upon her.

"Your ever-growing list of hideouts is impressive," he said, admiring the way she'd managed to maneuver her body into the same. She was slight for a nine-year-old, otherwise she would not have managed it.

Eveline stared up at him, her pert little mouth tight. George could practically see the cogs turning in her sharp mind. If he gave her long enough, she would come up with some retort that would necessitate that he swat her bottom. Best to act before such lengths became necessary.

He held out his hand, and he was more than a little surprised when she took it. George had expected her to swat it away—as her mother would have done. But Eveline was not her mother. As her little hand was enveloped inside of his, that could not have been clearer to him.

The pain rose in his chest, burning through the martial resolve he'd secured into place.

No. He could not let it get control again.

He tugged her to her feet and then pulled his hand away, fixing both his arms in rigid, straight lines at his sides. "To the nursery," he ordered her.

Eveline swallowed, rebellion flashing in her eyes for the briefest moment. Then she stalked down the hall back to nursery, her steps as measured as an infantryman. She did not look back over her shoulder.

George did not allow himself to tarry in the hall. A good soldier was efficient. A good leader led by example. When he stalked back inside the nursery, Archie was still writing his alphabet—or at least something that resembled an alphabet. Eveline stood behind her child-sized chair, back stiff, awaiting further orders.

"Eveline. Notebook. Practice the math tables I set for you yesterday."

The spirit that had shone in her eyes inside the grandfather clock had not deserted her, but she followed her father's edicts, fetching her supplies from the shelf and assuming a seat alongside her younger brother.

"We shall drill in our studies for forty minutes." George crossed to the mantel and tapped the clock there. "Then we shall have a ten-minute walk through the garden, and then back for reading."

Eveline's eyes widened. Beside her, Archie whimpered. George thought he saw Eveline snake a hand over to her brother's knee, but he could not be certain.

He would let it slip. For now.

"Hut, hut!" He clapped his hands twice in rapid succession. "Begin."

Both dark-haired heads dropped to their work. For the first time in months, George felt satisfaction begin to bloom in his chest. When the maid entered a few minutes later to clear up the ruined tea, the children hardly glanced her way.

Yes, he would manage just fine. Finally, he'd found a way to control his children—by calling upon his military training. He could keep things in hand until Miss Ethelreda Trudeau arrived.

Ethelreda—what a hideous name. Of a different century—or two—entirely. But that was for the best. It seemed his children required a very firm hand, and a steely-haired relic of the past century was exactly the sort of governess who would not abscond in the dark of night.

"Father…" Eveline said tentatively, chancing a glance over her shoulder at him.

George did not have the energy to suppress his sigh. "Yes, Eveline?"

"I am hungry."

TRUE TO THE portrait of a struggling governess, Red begged a ride in a farmer's wagon out of the village. In exchange for an apple from his knapsack, she recited bits of poetry. Lucky that she'd happened upon a literature-loving chap. Most men she met learned to read solely so they could parse the horse-racing program.

But she was forced to bid adieu to the bibliophile farmer when she arrived at the outskirts of Braintree. He was bound for Colchester; Oxley Park was two miles in the opposite direction.

No matter. Red hefted her valise under one arm, sprang open her parasol, and set off. Two miles was ten thousand, five hundred and sixty opportunities to plan her approach to the mysterious Sir George Caldwell and his brood.

Did two children constitute a brood? Her own family of four sisters certainly had. Red supposed that it depended upon the children themselves. Though after months without a governess, she'd best keep her expectations on the ground.

She did suffer a twinge of guilt at that. The Duchess of Guilford had told her she would ensure no other governess took up the post at Oxley Park—so that by the time Red's name was put forward, Sir George would be desperate to take her on.

To whom had the children's care fallen during the intervening months? A housekeeper, most likely. Red knew little of Sir George Caldwell other than the facts of his military background, the dates of his marriage, and the births of his children. And the death of his wife.

But in any case, she doubted Caldwell himself would tend his children. He had not even been present for most of their young lives.

She could manage two children.

I can, I can, I can, Red chanted to herself with each step down the country road turned dusty by summer's heat.

Three years she'd been a lady knight. In that time, she'd been responsible for six new residents of Newgate, dismantled one criminal enterprise using the *ton*'s unsuspecting dames to embezzle money, and taken down men twice her size and strength with the sharp blade of her rapier.

Two children, however wild, must be manageable.

She passed the one-mile mark. She of course knew the length of her own steps, and had been counting in the recesses of her mind. This last mile would be spent on thoughts of actual importance, Red decided. Antoine Legrand.

The reason she'd been posted as a governess, of all things.

The dossier that the Duchess of Guilford had slipped into her hand at her sister's wedding breakfast painted a chilling picture— an assassin who liked to play with his prizes before slaughtering them. Red had understood then why she'd been selected for this quest. If it came to a physical altercation, she was the most likely to emerge alive.

She fingered the handle of her parasol instinctively, while her mind catalogued the other weapons concealed on her person— her throwing knives, tucked into her ornate, heavily appliqued bodice; the wickedly curved dagger secured around her upper thigh with a specially crafted garter.

Of course, all of it was for naught until she deduced who Legrand was within the household. The physical description had been painfully bare—dark hair and brown eyes. Medium height. That sketch of details fit half the male population of England. Depending on the size of Oxley Park, she may have to evaluate dozens of servants.

That prospect, as well as the weight of her valise, pressed down upon her as she trudged through the final quarter mile. She was thankful for the shade of trees, which thickened as she approached the tall stone pillars that she inferred would mark the entrance to Oxley Park's grounds. But no amount of shade would remedy the trails of sweat rolling down her back, between her breasts, and along her thighs.

She ought to have worn breeches—there was even a pair tucked away in her valise. At this rate, the insides of her thighs would be red and raw.

Pain was nothing but a distraction, Red reminded herself.

A distraction that had her nearly walking straight past the gateway of Oxley Park. Red caught herself, using her forward inertia to spin on her heels and face the house. Even at a distance, the house was large. And it was quite a distance.

She squared her shoulders and stared down the long drive-way to Oxley Park. Her lower lip did not quiver at the half-mile-long drive. It did *not*.

Nor did her chest sink as she considered the number of serv-ants it would take to run an estate of this size.

She would be here for *months*.

CHAPTER THREE

*T*HE STINGER OF *the apis mellifera is barbed, making it a particularly efficient tool for dissuading interlopers.*

His head was pounding.

Ever since his return, he could read for no more than an hour before his gaze began to blur and the thumping in his head would begin. The thumping was always a precursor to something worse. The first time, he'd yelled so loudly that Mrs. Yates had come running. The second time, he'd knocked over an armchair. At least that had been at night, when the rest of the house slumbered. So no one had witnessed his humiliation. His utter lack of control.

If his head was pounding, he must put the treatise away. Or suffer the consequences.

Which could not happen, today of all days. Not when the new governess was set to arrive—finally. He could not risk running the woman off.

George snapped the book closed, marking it with a scrap of paper where he'd scribbled a few notes. Then he neatly tucked it away, where neither of his children could happen upon it. He'd learned the necessity of that only two days after returning to Oxley Park.

However, when he stood, the pounding began anew.

It was not in his head, he realized.

But on the door.

"Mrs. Yates?" he called, crossing the study. It was oddly positioned near the front of the house, a quirk of his father's. If it had been in the rear, like in most country houses, he'd likely never have heard the knocking at all.

"Cross?" he tried, entering the foyer. "Where the hell is my staff?" George grumbled to himself. *What have the children done with them*—his first and most uncharitable thought. *Perhaps they are hiding from me, like Eveline*—the second.

He ought to learn a whistle for them as well…

Whoever was pounding at the door chose that moment to try the door for themselves—at the exact moment that George gave up on his staff and opened it. The body stumbled through, falling against him, wet and hot and cursing.

George shoved her back, desperate to get the blood off him, to get away from the heat and fetid smell of death and decay that filled his nostrils.

"I beg your pardon, sir!" she cried, and a sharp clang rang through the tiled foyer as she slammed her parasol onto the floor—whether in indignation or to keep her balance after being so unceremoniously manhandled, he was not sure.

She.

Not a bloody, injured body. A woman—slick with sweat, cheeks flushed with the afternoon heat. Standing straight, uninjured, and looking thoroughly put out.

"Please excuse me," he managed, voice hollow. "Miss…"

"Miss Ethelreda Trudeau," she huffed, punctuating her introduction with another harsh rap of her parasol against encaustic tiles.

"You… You are Miss Trudeau?" George curled his hands to fists instead of raking them through his hair. He thought he'd curbed the habit. Even with his fists at his sides, he could imagine the blood and gore upon them that day at Waterloo. He blinked, and the vision was gone.

"Indeed, I am. I have come to serve as governess to Sir Caldwell and his children. Would you be so kind as to fetch them?" she said pointedly, looking him over from tip to toe.

She knew, George realized. He was not quite certain what it was about her posture or her tone that gave her away, but his instincts spoke clearly enough. She knew who he was, but was making a show of pretending she did not. Why? Because of the mishap and perceived slight?

"I am Sir George Caldwell," he said, military steel returning to his voice.

The woman lifted a hand to her bosom—her very generous bosom, he could not fail to note—and made a little mewl of surprise.

"I beg your pardon once again, sir. It has not been common practice in the households I have worked in before this for the master of the house to answer the door."

Saucy chit.

The thought shocked him. When was the last time he'd noticed a woman enough to even note such a thing? Worse, instead of it deterring him, he felt something stirring within his gut. And lower. Something that had not been awakened in a long time. Since before his wife's death. Before Waterloo. Before everything had gone to hell.

"It is not common practice in this household either, I assure you. I have no notion where Mrs. Yates and Cross have gotten to," he ground out.

"I am glad to hear it, sir." She nodded sharply and turned an assessing eye around the foyer, gaze scanning the attached rooms and the wide staircase before landing back on him. "Oxley Park is quite impressive. You must employ a veritable army of servants to keep it running. And yet none of them are in sight."

Whether it was the mention of the army, the quip about his servants that set him on edge, or the slight quiver of her lower lip as she turned her clever blue eyes back to him, George was certain of one thing: Miss Ethelreda Trudeau was going to be trouble.

The question was—would she be more trouble than she was worth?

Only time would tell.

"I shall summon the children." With that, he pulled a cast-iron, military-style whistle from the interior pocket of his waistcoat and blew three distinct, sharp notes.

Almost instantaneously, the sound of chairs scraping and doors opening reached his ears.

It was quite ingenious, really. The sound carried throughout the house and could easily summon the children from the nursery or if they were walking in the gardens. He ought to have thought of it sooner. It would have made the past three months considerably less hellish.

It worked on a rowdy battalion, and it seemed to work just as well on children.

George was quite proud of himself and his innovation, until he swung his gaze back to Miss Trudeau. Her eyes had gone wider still, stuck somewhere between disbelief and horror.

"Did you just summon your children with a whistle?" Her coppery eyebrows, several shades darker than the bright red tresses of her hair, rose expectantly.

"The house is too large for yelling," he countered.

"And you are too frail for walking?"

George blinked. His inferiors would never—

But she did not consider herself his inferior. Even as footsteps rang out in the corridor above, signaling the approach of the children, his eyes stayed on Miss Trudeau, assessing her once again.

She was everything he ever looked for in a woman—back in the days when he'd done the looking. Soft curves brimming at the constraints of her gown, as if the rounded beauty could not be contained by trappings as simple as silk and taffeta. Christ, her breasts... Did the freckles that covered her moon-white neck extend to those gloriously full orbs, swelling above the neckline of her gown with every haughty breath?

The wide set of her hips... Her gown fell in a loose column from where it was gathered below her bust. Looser than the frocks he'd seen on the women in the village parading about, and frustratingly efficient at concealing the curve of hip and leg beneath.

Efficient. That was what he was supposed to be. An army colonel. In control at all times.

Never mind that soldiers were known for their lusty proclivities.

His eyes snapped back to her face. Her eyebrows were still raised, but now knitted tightly together as she glowered at him. Oh yes, she'd seen his wandering gaze. The glare she fixed him with was not precisely angry or disapproving. In fact, she looked a tad confused, but—

"Sir! I apologize for my delay! Young Mr. Bronson has taken ill, and I was arranging to have his duties seen to. I am most ashamed—"

"No need, Cross," George said, stepping away to make room for the older gentleman.

Cross swept in, murmuring his apologies to Miss Trudeau and relieving her of her valise.

"Cross, speak with Mrs. Yates and have the staff assembled. I'd rather introduce Miss Trudeau to everyone all in one go."

"Of course, sir, as you wish." Cross hurried away, intercepting Mrs. Yates near the stairs, where she was shoving the children the last few steps into the foyer.

George motioned them forward. He was pleased to see they were neatly turned out. The orders he'd issued that morning had been diligently followed, he saw with a flush of satisfaction. He turned proudly to the red-haired vixen who'd appeared on his doorstep.

"Miss Trudeau, I present my children. Eveline Isobel Caldwell, age nine. Archibald Christian Caldwell, age five." He'd have preferred if each of them stepped forward when he said their names, but he was satisfied by the straight posture and clear eyes.

No tears sparkled in them. And if that was mischief in Eveline's…
No, she would not dare.

Miss Trudeau executed a polite, graceful curtsey that was distinctly reassuring. Perhaps her show of sauce and temper had merely been due to their unfortunate meeting. She may not be the steely-eyed matron he had expected, but she could do well enough. It would take a bit of steel to manage his children, as he'd learned well enough himself.

"Good afternoon, Miss Isobel, Master Archibald," she said, nodding to each of them in turn. "I am certain we shall get along grandly."

Eveline met the woman's eyes. At all of nine years old, his daughter had the heart of a soldier. But Miss Trudeau's blue eyes yielded no weakness. His headstrong daughter may very well have met her match.

No sooner had the thought entered his mind than Eveline opened her mouth to speak.

"Back to your schedule," George said sharply, cutting her off.

Whatever his daughter's first words were for her governess, George decided he would rather not hear them. There was too high a likelihood of something impertinent. Best to let the two of them sort things out among themselves, without his intervention. A commander had to be in control of his own troops, so to speak.

The children disappeared up the stairs, making it about half-way up before losing their decorum and degrading to an all-out scramble. George held back his flinch as he turned back to Miss Trudeau—who was watching him, rather than the children, with intense interest.

He cleared his throat, attempting to straighten his spine, but already finding it stiff as a ramrod. "I shall give you a copy of their schedule."

"If you like." Her red head bobbed. "However, I shall most likely change it completely."

The retort was on George's lips before he could think, but he swallowed it back down. She was the governess, after all—

employed to look after the children and do such things as create a schedule for their daily learning and tasks. But the sparkle in Miss Trudeau's eyes begged him to challenge her.

Instead, he put a different challenge forward.

"Every governess I have contracted has left within a day, or else never appeared at all." He raked his gaze over Miss Trudeau's soft curves, so at odds with the steel in her spine and face. "I trust I can depend on a bit more from you, Miss Trudeau?"

The corner of her full mouth twitched. A movement so slight, George would have missed it if he had not already been staring at her lips.

Staring at her lips, hell and damnation.

"Is something wrong with the children?" those lips asked sweetly.

"Why should there be something wrong with the children?" George shifted forward half a step, instantly defensive. Even though he *knew* his children were hellions. "There is certainly something wrong with the governesses."

There was that twitch again.

Was she wearing rouge? How could her lips be so perfectly pink?

The scuffle of footsteps spared him his own deleterious line of thinking, as the household staff began to assemble in a line along the perimeter of the foyer.

He lifted the whistle, still clasped in his hand, to his mouth. "If you hear this sound—"

"That will not be necessary, sir."

Those eyes held his with such distinct, direct challenge that George found himself lowering the whistle.

What might it be like to challenge that wit, to meet her iron will with his own and see who was the victor? Those clear, knowing blue eyes of hers… They seemed to mock him, as if she were reading his thoughts and daring him to go toe to toe with her.

Saucy chit, indeed.

Chapter Four

"THERE IS A lovely set of rooms set aside for you," Mrs. Yates explained as she led Red up the staircase. Wide enough to accommodate a team of horses, should one ever decide to climb up to the first floor of Oxley Park.

Red wondered how the servants' stairwell fared in comparison and, for the first time, felt a bit of gratitude for the position the duchess had secured for her within Sir Caldwell's household. If she'd been relegated to playacting as a maid, she would have learned exactly how tight the narrow servant stairwell clung to her ample backside.

"You have your own bedchamber and small sitting room, which adjoins the children's nursery on the other side."

She kept the smile fixed upon her face, even as she inwardly cringed.

What were the odds there was a lock between the children's apartments and her own? Red was not prepared to wager much on that particular possibility.

"Do the children attend supper with their father?" she asked instead, further calculating her odds of having a bit of time to herself before she officially assumed her duties.

"Not ordinarily."

"Is he often in residence?"

"Not ordinarily."

Red tucked that bit of information away. It would certainly make her investigations easier if she did not have the surly Sir Caldwell lingering about. Something about the gentleman unnerved her.

Not his military bearing… Though the fact that he'd even entertained the notion of summoning her with a whistle was laughable. She would be sneaking into his rooms and stealing that particular item away posthaste.

"Here we are."

Mrs. Yates held open a door intricately carved with a motif of Tudor roses. Ethelreda smiled despite herself. Her mother, with her absurd obsession for English history, had named her after one of the alleged illegitimate daughters of Henry VIII. It was rather fitting that these were to be her rooms.

They were lovely, as was every part of Oxley Park that she had seen. Whoever had initially decorated the manor house had invested in timeless, sturdy furnishings. And Red had attended enough *ton* parties in her decade of Seasons to know that in recent years, someone else had seen to having the décor updated with modern fashions.

But otherwise, the rooms were unremarkable.

Which Red would use to her advantage—when she rid herself of Mrs. Yates.

"I shall assume my duties with the children in the morning," Red said, infusing her tone and eyes with the air of regal command the Duchess of Guilford wielded to such success. "Please have my supper sent up to my room. I am rather tired. In future, I will dine with the children."

Mrs. Yates's unkempt gray-brown eyebrows knitted together, rather like a caterpillar in motion above her matching gray-brown eyes. But Red met her gaze and lifted her chin, issuing the woman a silent dare to challenge her.

If the militaristic Sir George Caldwell had not risen to the challenge, she doubted his housekeeper would.

A second later, Red's gamble was rewarded.

"As you wish, Miss Trudeau." Mrs. Yates did not bow, but it was hardly necessary. She retreated, closing the door behind her.

That was what Red had wanted.

Her valise had already been delivered, set neatly on the bench at the foot of the four-poster bed. Red flicked open the latch, retrieving a ball of twine from the bottom of the luggage, and set to work.

Four entrances—the door to the corridor, the one connecting her parlor and the nursery, and two windows. She laid a clever trap at each. From the direction of the children, the door would trigger a petite bell when it opened. It was more a precaution than anything else; she'd hear footsteps from the parlor long before the bell sang.

The windows were another easy matter. No one ought to be opening them other than her. If they did, they'd be hit quite hard with the paperweight she'd rigged there.

The door to the hallway was the most difficult. There was no lock upon it, and to insist upon having one installed would only garner suspicion. No one ought to come tumbling through her door without notice, but the possibility of a wayward maid bringing tea or fresh linens was not nil.

But nor did she want to render said maid unconscious.

Ten minutes later, Red was satisfied with the choice she'd made. A clever bit of work with the twine would cause the door the catch, holding up whoever entered momentarily. Long enough for Red to hide away whatever she was working on that she did not wish to be seen.

Finally, with all those trappings in place, she settled at the little writing desk tucked up against the wall. The notion of taking it all apart again whenever she wanted to leave her rooms was already an annoyance nagging away at her, but there was nothing for it. The traps did not have to be laid all of the time, only when she was conducting sensitive work.

An entirely different array of snares would be put in place when she departed her rooms each day—the ones that would tell her whether her apartments were searched in her absence.

It was already half past five o'clock. Assuming that Oxley Park kept country hours, her supper would arrive soon. She needed to make her list and secure it before that.

It took her a few moments to recall the memory tool she'd used as she filtered down the long line of introductions in the foyer. But by the time she'd laid out her quill pen and parchment, she had it top of mind—*SLY GRACES*.

Shelley, Mrs., cook

Louisa, kitchen maid

Yates, Mrs., housekeeper

Gerald, footman

Rooney, footman

Alice, housemaid

Cross, butler

Ellis, valet

Sara, housemaid

She stared at the list for several long moments, before dipping her quill again and appending one more name.

George Caldwell, former soldier

The Duchess of Guilford had not explicitly said that Sir Caldwell was a suspect, but the subtext was there all the same. He met the general description for Antoine Legrand, though that description itself was worth near to nothing. He had been at Waterloo, and he had only recently returned to the estate. It was just possible—on the periphery of probability—that George Caldwell and Antoine Legrand were one and the same.

If they weren't—and for some reason, Red found herself earnestly hoping they were not—then it was still within the realm of possibility that Sir Caldwell was aiding Legrand in some way.

Many men had suffered on that battlefield. Thousands had

lost their lives. The ones who survived were not the same merry men who'd sailed away from England's gray shores. Red knew it as well as anyone—she had lost her own cousin at Waterloo.

There was no accounting for what a man might do to save himself or someone he loved.

Setting aside her quill pen, Red carefully folded the list and stood.

As she did, her feet and legs screamed in protest. Particularly that abused patch between her thighs. She ought to make a trip down to the kitchens and see about a salve of some kind. Thoughts already several steps ahead, Red rifled through her valise with her free hand until she came up with a singular truffle. A gift she'd acquired just before leaving London with the express intent of ingratiating herself with Oxley Park's kitchen staff.

What should she have brought to ingratiate herself with Oxley Park's master?

Perhaps if she'd been wearing a redcoat, he'd have found her more tractable.

Pfft. She owed tractability to no man.

But even so, George Caldwell was a puzzle she'd been turning over in her mind since she stepped—or rather, fell—over his threshold.

She'd known instantly who he was. His stiff bearing screamed of military service, and he possessed none of the reticence of a servant. One minute he'd practically had her in his arms, and the next he'd nearly shoved her onto her bottom. If it had not been for her parasol, her thighs would not be the only part of her body boasting an injury.

The whole encounter had left her reeling, though she did think she'd made a good job of not letting it show. When she'd fallen into him, her heart began this terrible stuttering cadence that she'd never experienced before, even when fully exerted from fencing with the duchess.

Just as quickly, when he'd pushed her away, a cool hollowness had taken over.

Then there were those eyes of his, sharp and intelligent, and utterly infuriating in the way he watched her, expecting her to obey his every word.

Red had never been so put out by a man in her entire life. That included the six men she'd landed permanently in cells in Newgate Prison.

She removed her special book from her valise, then unlocked it and stored the list inside before relocking and shelving the book with several others already waiting above the mantel. Then Red's bosom began to quiver most queerly.

At least her senses were still working.

She heard the maid's footsteps in the hallway in plenty of time to disable her snares and open the door to accept her supper tray with a complacent smile upon her face.

However, even after eating her meal, bathing, and settling into the comfortable bed with *Miss Plimpton's Guide for the Modern Governess* as her companion, she could not account for the slight tremble of her bottom lip.

Nor the way her ears strained to hear the voices of the children settling in for the night, listening for a sharp, authoritative voice.

THE COPPERY SCENT invaded his nostrils with demonic ferocity, driving him from darkness to a field bathed in blood.

So much blood.

It was his fault. He ought to be the one lying dead, blood draining from his face, his abdomen. Each beat of his heart pumping his lifeblood away through the gaping hole in his chest… No, no, he could not watch.

It was not him. It was young McGovern.

The lad's face was clear even in the dark, through the swirling smoke.

But in a flash of gunpowder, he was far away. McGovern lay on the field, twenty yards away. Gasping for each breath. If only George could get to him, stop the bleeding…

Yet when he looked down, he was covered. Bodies, covering his legs and holding him in place. He strained against them as yet another fell, and another. Until he was gasping for breath himself, the boy's cries echoing in his ears.

George hauled himself up. He'd fallen asleep sitting in his study.

A nightmare. Only a nightmare.

"No, no, please, please, make it stop! I am dying! I know I am dying!" Pleas for mercy morphed into animalistic screams.

He turned, reaching for the voice, knowing it even as it cleaved into his soul and ripped his insides to shreds. Not his study, for there was a bed behind him. Her bed. Just as it had been—

No. More blood. So much more blood than the first time.

She actually was dying.

But there was no one. No midwives or servants or even the bawling of an infant. Just the dark-haired beauty, arching her full belly toward the drapes of the four-poster bed, screaming in brutal agony.

It was too loud, too hoarse. Not a woman's scream at all, but his own.

He crashed to his knees, clawing and crawling for the bed, certain that if only he could reach it he could save her—

"Sir Caldwell!"

"Sir, my lord—"

"Papa…"

"Has this happened before?"

"Well… Yes, but—"

So many voices. Yelling, arguing, whimpering. So many voices flooding his pounding head, chest, lungs. His entire body burned and vibrated with rage and horror. He was going to succumb, to beat himself or something or someone—

"Colonel Caldwell!"

The voice was foreign, but the command struck home.

George cracked his eyes open, just enough to glimpse the scene. Then he slammed them shut once again.

Miss Trudeau hovered in the doorway, the children braced behind her. Her arms were stretched across the opening, keeping them from their raging father. But the terror in Eveline's eyes… George could not bring himself to look again.

"Leave me," he whispered, his voice a hoarse rasp.

"Cross, fetch some brandy. Water it heavily. Too much alcohol will—"

"Leave me," he growled, pushing off the bed. The sheets were a tattered mess, his chest bare. An animal. He was no better than an animal.

The pity in Miss Trudeau's eyes speared through him. The pain in Eveline's was worse.

He forced him to meet those storm-cloud-blue eyes—to make his plea.

She seemed to understand, lowering her arms and catching the children by the shoulders. Whatever she said, he did not hear. Only the hard reverberation as the door slammed and he collapsed once more.

RED SUPPOSED SHE technically had assumed her governess duties in the morning. Though a two o'clock screaming alarm bell was not precisely what she'd envisioned.

She ushered the children back into their nursery. Before she could intervene, Eveline had tucked Archie into bed and then climbed in next to him. By the time Red closed the door behind them, Eveline had rolled away, presenting her new governess with nothing more than her dark head of hair.

Red stood in the middle of the spacious nursery still drenched in darkness, unsure of what to do. A screaming, violent soldier? That had not perturbed Red at all. Two children who were in obvious need of her comfort, but did not want it... She had no notion how to manage that scenario.

The glint in Eveline's eyes in the hallway, the pain as she'd watched her father writhe and struggle with his demons... The child needed *someone*. That much was clear. As was the fact that the two of them would have it out at some juncture. Red could spot another dominant female with a hunter's predisposition for scent and instinct.

After several moments of silence, she settled for murmuring, "My door is unlocked if you have need of me," before retreating to her own quarters. She did not set any of the snares she'd hastily untangled minutes before.

She doubted she would hear from either child before dawn. This was not the first time such a scene had transpired.

As she settled back into her blankets, Red found her thoughts floating back down the hallway, toward the master suite. Sir George would be awake for a very long time. Red may not know the exact shape of the nightmares that haunted them, but she recognized the color and coda nonetheless.

The feral look in his eyes, the sheen of sweat coating his thickly muscled chest and arms... Red shivered. Her own heart, which had been remarkably calm thus far, began to flutter as she sorted through the images in her mind, fitting them against her dossier on Sir George and trying to make sense of how it might all be connected to her quest. Such firm muscle corded in every inch of his body...

Red's mouth was dry. She reached for the glass of water she'd set near the bed while she contemplated.

He must keep up some sort of physical regimen here at Oxley Park in order to maintain the muscle he'd built during his soldiering. She must study his routine, if she were to get a sense of the man. Did he include fencing and swordplay?

An uncomfortable heat flooded her body as she pictured him

standing across from her, blades in each of their hands, his shirt missing, as it had been that evening.

Red threw back the covers and stalked to the window, removing her trap from the nearest one and shoving it open several inches. She would finagle a method for leaving it open while also ensuring she could keep away unwanted intruders in the morning. The excitement of the evening had left her brain uncharacteristically blurred and her insides quivering with heat.

It must be the unusual challenge presented by the children, she decided as she settled back against her pillows. Two snotty enigmas. That was certainly the reason for this unusual upset.

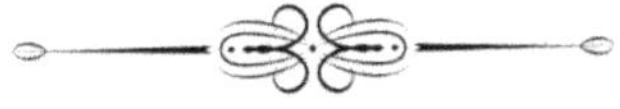

CHAPTER FIVE

"HE IS GONE." Red shook her head, once, twice, certain she must still be asleep. Or perhaps someone had poisoned her. "What can you possibly mean by that?"

Alice, the maid who'd brought up the breakfast, began to melt under Red's scrutiny. Her shoulders slumped and she glanced behind her toward the door. Red forced herself to calm. This one required gentleness, rather than a firm hand.

"I apologize for my harsh tone, Alice," Red said. If she'd been the lady of the house, or a member of the family, she would have patted her hand comfortingly. But it would not have the same effect coming from the governess, who in reality was a servant as well. "You know this house better than I. I am a newcomer to Oxley Park. I was surprised when you told me that Sir George had departed." She let those words percolate for a moment, waiting to see if the maid would relax. "Is it usual, for Sir George to take such sudden journeys?"

Alice was still wary, shifting her weight between her feet. But she answered without a tremble in her voice. "It has happened before," she confirmed.

Red wanted to scream. Instead, she asked, "And how long does Sir George stay away?"

"A week or two, at least. Last time he was gone for a month."

A month. What was Sir George Caldwell doing away from

home for a month? He had two young children! What could possibly possess him to be so irresponsible?

Unless it had something to do with Legrand. That was why she was here, Red reminded herself. Not to be a governess. Well, yes, to pose as a governess. But her real quest was to identify Legrand, determine why the French assassin was at Oxley Park, and detain him and any accomplices.

If she had to wipe a few noses along the way… She would do it. But not with a smile on her face, mind.

"Do you require anything else, Miss Trudeau?" Alice asked from the doorway, ready to bolt.

Red could hardly blame her. She was not relishing telling the children. From the little she knew of Eveline Caldwell, Red thought that Alice had the right of it—trying to get as far away from the nursery as possible.

Unfortunately, Red had no such luxury. She squared her shoulders and turned to face the children, who had already begun eating. She determinedly ignored the flapping butterfly in her stomach. She put criminals into Newgate and could best anyone with a sword. She was not intimidated by two children.

She pulled out her chair, perching dubiously on the wooden contraption. It was built for children. Perhaps a delicately boned young woman. Certainly not for a buxom spinster nearing thirty. Even so, Red arranged herself with grace, as her mother had taught her long before she'd become a lady knight. Then she turned her sharp eyes upon her charges.

"First rule: you do not take a bite until everyone in the party is seated."

Archie froze, a soft-boiled egg halfway in his mouth. Eveline paused, her tea halfway to her mouth. She did not look up at her governess. Then she lifted it the rest of the way and drank.

Red was already formulating a strategy in her mind. Eveline, all of nine years old, was a worthy adversary. Perhaps even more so *because* she was nine years old. She was not hindered by the worries of an adult. Which made her even more volatile.

"Put the egg down, Archie," Red instructed the boy.

He, at least, was willing. He stared up at her with big, dark eyes. A bit like a puppy, eager to please. She'd have no trouble with him, Red realized. He was a young boy, so he'd be given to impishness, of course. But he was starved for affection. If she gave him that, he'd do anything for her.

Eveline chose that moment to set down her teacup. Red did not think it was because of her instruction, but rather fortuitous timing. But she was not going to let the opportunity pass. "Very good," she said, nodding at each of the children in turn.

Archie smiled. Eveline glared. Red supposed she should accustom herself to that.

"Before we continue with our etiquette instruction, I must tell you that I've been informed your father has been called away on business." It was not what she'd been told. But Red was a good liar. She'd made a career of it.

She expected Archie to cry or Eveline to flip the child-size table.

But instead, they did nothing.

The two children sat in silence. Archie stared at his plate. Eveline turned in her seat so she could look pointedly out the window.

Red had expected tantrums and tears? This was so much worse. For not the first time, her heart hurt for them. Whatever tragedies had befallen the Caldwell household—the loss of their mother, their father's absences and his evident distress—the children were suffering because of it.

Red had been privileged, she knew, to have a happy and safe childhood. If there was less money than everyone would have liked, at least there was a profusion of love and warmth. She had only to look at the restrained pain, the practiced pain, written on Archie and Eveline's faces to know that the alternative was so much worse.

"Ahem." She stood, tossing her napkin aside, plate, utensils, and teacup untouched. "We shall skip our etiquette lesson for the day. I'll have the kitchen prepare us a hamper. We are going out."

Archie perked up at that. "Out where?"

Red sidled around the table so she stood between Eveline and the window. She swung her arm out to indicate the vista beyond. "Oxley Park. I have only just arrived. I am in need of a tour. Will you two be my guides?"

Archie was already on his feet, percolating with excitement. Eveline had switched from looking out the window to staring at her tea. Anything to avoid making eye contact with her governess. Red did not blame her. But nor would she let her sit and stew the day away. Red reached for the bellpull so she could request the children's outdoor clothes and a hamper.

She'd worry about etiquette and setting a schedule later—in the afternoon, or tomorrow, even. Today, she had to do something to help the children. If she could get a look at the estate that would be her home—and her base of investigation for the foreseeable future—all the better.

THE GARDENS WERE lovely, the stables adequately stocked with horseflesh and enough grooms to make Red's head ache. She'd been filing away name after name using her memory devices, but she knew it would take another trip around the grounds to confirm she'd remembered correctly.

But the summer house. The summer house was absolutely gorgeous.

Nestled about halfway between the manor and the two stone pillars that marked the entrance to the estate, the octagonal building was bordered on one side by a pond and the other by thick brush and bushes. The landscape was turning gold with the last remnants of summer. The sunshine bounced off the floor-to-ceiling windows of the summer house then reflected back the swaying grasses until everything was gilded in gold.

Red was in absolute awe.

It would be the perfect place to practice her swordplay, far enough from the main drive that no one would stumble upon her, especially if she made a point of coming very early in the morning. Even now, with the parasol extended over her shoulder, she itched to pull her rapier free and execute a few graceful moves. To stretch her body…

"Stop it! You shall get mud on my dress!"

"It is just mud!"

"You are—"

"Stop squabbling," Red commanded, catching Archie by the hand as they walked the path that curved around the perimeter of the building. "It is not ladylike to lift your voice above normal speaking volume, Eveline." Archie snickered. "*You* are a gentleman. Gentlemen do not shout at ladies, ever." He hung his head, for all of three seconds, before he tried to skip away after a grasshopper. Red held him tight. "How many sides does the summer house have?"

Archie looked between her and the building. He shrugged.

"Eight," Eveline said from behind her. Red was tempted to smack the sass out of her voice, but she knew that would do little good for either of them.

"What is the name for an eight-sided shape, Archie?" Red asked as they continued. The path edged away from the building to skirt around the picturesque pond that bordered three of those eight sides.

"A pentagon?" He nudged a foot into the mud at the edge of the path.

Eveline snorted.

"Unladylike," Red said over her shoulder, not bothering to look at Eveline's face. Two could sass. "Penta is the prefix meaning five or last," Red explained. "We shall start with the Greek, since I prefer it to Latin. Mono for one, di for two, tri for three, tetra for four, penta for five, hexa for six, hepta for seven, and octo for eight. Therefore, an eight-sided figure would be…?"

Archie nudged his boot around. Red held back her reprimand.

He was thinking. Boots could be cleaned.

"Octagon," he said quietly.

Unexpected pride surged through her. She squeezed Archie's shoulder. "Marvelous."

The smile he turned up to her melted her heart. Maybe, just maybe, she'd be willing to wipe his nose. It was a rather adorable nose, in a very sweet face.

Behind them, Eveline muttered something under her breath. That was not a face Red was particularly fond of.

Red tugged Archie away from the water's edge, continuing along the path. There was a split up ahead. She paused, following the divergent trail. It disappeared up over the hill, with the view beyond blocked by the dense brush.

"What is that way?" she asked, calculating whether it was worth their time. They'd already exhausted the contents of the hamper she carried over her arm, and she doubted the children would last much longer without sustenance. It was almost teatime.

"Nothing," Eveline said sharply, stepping around Red and Archie. She strode down the other path, back in the direction of the manor.

Red bit her lip to keep in the words she wanted to hurl at the irritating girl. She was the adult, she reminded herself. At twenty-eight, she was old enough to be her mother. Although she felt more like a resentful elder sister.

They'd walked miles in their explorations of Oxley Park. The girl was entitled to be tired and hungry. Besides, Red knew she was a forceful presence. Not everyone took to her immediately. Especially someone like Eveline, who had every reason to keep outsiders at a distance.

Red settled for smiling down at Archie and nodding to indicate they ought to follow his sister. They'd made it almost back to the main path when Archie spotted the puddle.

"Look at that," he said, coming to stand, complete awe etched in every line of his little face.

To his credit, it was a rather impressive puddle. Right where the smaller path they'd been on joined with the larger one, it was at least a yard and a half wide, the edges extending into the brush on either side of the path. The paths had sloped away toward this spot, funneling the rainwater from the night before down from all the surrounding areas to this one spot.

Red tightened her grip on Archie's hand just in time to keep him from darting forward.

"Please!" he wailed, twisting his arm.

Red opened her mouth to respond, but it was Eveline's acerbic voice that cut through the sunshine.

"Have you taken leave of your senses? Father has insisted on hiring this spinster to teach us etiquette, and instead of behaving yourself and proving we are just fine on our own, you are acting like a heathen! It is no wonder that Father is always away. He wants done with us!"

Red expected Archie to crumble. But perhaps that only proved how little she knew about children.

"You are the meanest, most disgusting pretend lady ever! You are not a lady!" Archie screamed. For a child of five, it was impressive. And it was clear he knew his target well, because Eveline wilted where she stood.

Before she realized what she was saying, before her own heart could break for the two of them, Red opened her mouth and words started tumbling out.

"We shall compromise. We will all jump in together!"

Both children stilled—Eveline halfway to shoving past them on the path to go back the way they'd come, and Archie a half step away from the puddle's edge. They both turned to her, gaping.

Well, in for a penny, in for a pound, as her father liked to say.

"But we must do it properly. We will return to the nursery and change into our oldest, dingiest clothing. Then we shall return here and each have a go at jumping in. We'll measure the reach of the splatter to determine who created the biggest splash."

Eveline stared at her as if she'd grown three extra heads.

Archie, meanwhile, looked ready to fall down on the ground and worship at her feet.

"Yes," he breathed, as if he could hardly believe his good fortune. "Yes, yes, yes!" He began jumping up and down with each word.

"It shall be a mathematics lesson," Red warned, catching his hand. But he was only half listening. Eveline, for her part, must have been stunned beyond words. It was the only way to account for how she fell into a docile line behind them and followed back to the manor.

⊷⊱⊰⊶

"WAIT, WAIT, WAIT, you must wait long enough for us to establish the parameters of the experiment!" Red grabbed Archie by the shoulder to hold him back.

An hour after they'd originally come upon the massive puddle, the trio now stood on the other side of it, on the main path, contemplating. What was going through Archie's mind was clear enough—jump. Eveline was more difficult. She was silent.

Red preferred her that way. Especially after her outburst earlier. Though she did not blame Eveline for her saltiness, she wasn't particularly desirous of being subjected to more of it.

"What unit of measurement shall we use?" Red asked, keeping her grip on Archie firm.

"We haven't brought a wooden rule," Archie said, calming slightly. Red did not drop her guard or relax her hold.

"We have not," she agreed. "We shall have to use another unit of measurement. Fingers, hands, feet—which seems most appropriate?"

"Fingers!" Archie yelled, scooping up a handful of mud jubilantly.

"Fingers shall take all day."

Both Red and Archie's heads snapped up. Several feet away, near the far edge of the puddle, Eveline stood. Red nodded.

"Continue," she urged.

"Measuring by fingers will take too long. It is a big puddle, and there will be significant splatter. Especially when Miss Trudeau has her turn."

Red ignored the jab.

"So what would you suggest?" she asked.

"Feet, so I do not have to get my hands dirty."

"But you'll get dirty already when you jump in the puddle," Archie reminded her, squelching the mud from one hand to another. Red did not allow herself to regret this decision; it was far too late for that.

At least Sir George was not in residence. If he came across this folly, she'd surely be released from duty. Miss Plimpton would have an apoplexy.

"I am not jumping in the puddle." Eveline accentuated her statement by spinning on her heel, striding to the farthest part of the path she could occupy while remaining in view, and crossing her arms.

"Never mind her," Red said, rubbing Archie's shoulder. "We shall measure the splatter using our feet, then. Your feet, rather than mine. Actually, we'll do both and then compare," she decided. It would be a good opportunity to speak about relative lengths and different types of nonstandard measurement.

"Then I can go?" Archie vibrated with anticipation.

Red could not contain her smile. "Yes, go."

"Yippee!"

The five-year-old plunged into the center of the puddle in one gargantuan leap. Red was impressed by how far he managed to splatter the water. Leaning down, she positioned one of the rocks she'd collected on their walk back to the pond. "This will mark your spot. Now come out so I can have my turn."

It took her two more tries to extricate the still-splashing Archie. When he was standing firmly beside his rock, covered in mud to her waist already, Red positioned herself. She glanced over her shoulder to Eveline.

"Are you certain, Eveline? You could very well beat your

brother," she said, trying to entice the girl with competition.

Red could not see Eveline's face clearly through the glint of late-afternoon sun, but she did see her shake her dark head.

"Well enough," Red sighed. "Here I go!"

Her splash was more like a tidal wave. And her feet did not land in the middle of the puddle, but her bottom did.

"Are you all right? Miss Trudeau!" Archie bellowed. Then the next moment, he was in the puddle with her, offering her an arm up.

Spitting mud, Red took his hand and tried. But she lost her footing, and in the next second, she'd pulled them both back down. Archie landed atop her, knocking the wind from her chest. His little body was shaking. Red flipped him over, searching for injury—only to find his mud-smeared face wide with a grin and his chest shaking with laughter.

Red's own smile bubbled over, first into a chuckle at the ridiculousness of it all, her faux lesson gone awry. Then in uncontrollable laughter.

"You two look ridiculous," Eveline decreed from the edge of the puddle. She'd come closer, Red realized, probably to check that they actually were both all right.

"You could join us," Red invited again.

"Certainly not."

"Oh, come on, Eveline! You don't always have to pretend to be a lady!" Archie cried. With that prescient statement, he slung a wave of mud in his sister's direction.

Eveline stared down at the wide swath of brown on her chest. Archie ignored her, already bored with her lack of reaction. But Red watched and waited. Finally, Eveline's head lifted and her gaze landed on her brother.

"I will make you pay for that!" she yelled, charging into the puddle. Red scooted to the side to avoid the flailing of limbs and mud, but it was no use. They were all covered from head to toe.

But by the time they crawled out, they were laughing. Even Eveline.

Red had won the first battle.

CHAPTER SIX

September 1817
Essex, England

D ARKNESS CLOAKED HIS soul. But even George was not desperate enough to travel alone by night.

But as soon as the black began to soften, the rays of dawn little more than a whispered promise, he rose from his rented bed and began to dress.

He ate breakfast only to pass the time. Even so, it was barely light when the sleepy groom led his mount from the ramshackle stable. George knew the exhaustion lining his own eyes was worse, and the reason he avoided the mirror most mornings.

Sleep had eluded him. Since that night at Oxley Park.

He'd had nightmares before. They were his most steadfast of companions. But a fit loud enough to wake the entire house… Removing himself had seemed the kindest solution for all.

He flicked the half-awake groom a ha'penny as he rode out of the inn's dooryard. A hard hour's ride and he'd be passing through the twin towers welcoming him back to Oxley Park. The children would likely still be abed, having inherited their late mother's penchant for sleeping late. Unless Miss Trudeau had changed their routine…

That was the other reason he had not been sleeping.

Or rather—*she.*

She'd come to him first in the throes of a nightmare. He was on a battlefield—it always began on a battlefield. But instead of image after image of resounding horror, a flash of white had drawn his eye. There on the edge of that muddy, bloody field, at the edge of his very mind, stood Miss Ethelreda Trudeau. A glowing vision in naught but her night rail.

He'd awoken with his head free of terrors and his hand on his cock.

George had stayed away another full week on the strength of that folly alone.

Yet it seemed even a month was not enough to banish Miss Trudeau's fulsome curves from his imagination. And he could not abandon Oxley Park indefinitely.

He was, for some unknown reason, conflating the image of Miss Trudeau in her nightclothes with an unattainable notion of salvation.

George knew there was no redemption waiting for him. Not after what he had done.

But still she came to him in his dreams, again and again. His mind remembered what his eyes had missed in the terror of that night.

Her nightgown brushed her shins, revealing creamy white calves. Strong. Made for wrapping around a man's waist. That spinster's nightgown, fastened with a white ribbon at her throat, so proper and matronly. Yet it did nothing to hide the glorious globes of her breasts, free of stays and satin, pressing forward and begging for his touch.

Despite the biting cold of the autumn morning, he shifted uncomfortably in the saddle, heat flooding his groin.

"Hell and damnation," he cursed wickedly, slowing his mount. He could not very well gallop with a raging erection.

He would not be reduced to pleasuring himself on the roadside. To imaginings of his children's governess, no less. Therein lay the true irony of his predicament. In the weeks he'd been away, George had never once worried about Miss Trudeau deserting her post. He had known the woman less than a day, and yet the steel in her voice that matched her spine spoke to something deep within his soul. He knew when he returned to Oxley Park, Miss Trudeau would be there with his children in hand.

She would be there, he amended.

What inroads she might have made with Eveline and Archie… He shuddered to think. Either they would be at one another's throats or thick as thieves. George was not sure which prospect was more worrying.

Briefly, an image of Miss Trudeau in the nursery, both children huddled around her while she read aloud, entered his mind.

George laughed. The image suited neither his children nor Miss Trudeau.

Though she *was* a governess, with sterling references. He supposed she would be reading with them, no matter how incongruous the notion.

It took another mile for his ardor to cool sufficiently for him to nudge his mount into anything more than a walk. By the time he passed between the towering stone pillars welcoming him to Oxley Park, more than an hour had passed and the sun was nearly up. The children might still be abed, but the staff would be awake and about their duties. Certainly enough to meet him.

But instead of steering his horse toward the imposing manor house nestled between the distant hills, George found himself turning at the first track shooting off from the main drive. He was not avoiding the children. Surely. But a certain buxom redhead…

So, of course, it must have been fate that steered him along the western curve of the property and into view of the summer house. Where a flash of red caught his eye.

Distinctive, rich red. Not copper. Not blonde.

Unmistakable even through the glass panes of the summer house.

Without meaning to, George eased up on the reins. His destination had been the apiaries beyond. His gaze even flicked up over the peaked gray roof of the summer house, to where the hives waited. If he listened closely enough, he often felt he could hear the distant buzzing long before they came into sight.

But he was not listening for bees just now.

All of his focus narrowed on the octagonal building, glass doors thrown open to welcome in the brisk autumn air, and the swirling body of Miss Ethelreda Trudeau. There was a flash of light as he reined in, sliding to the ground in a dismount so easy that he hardly noted the action until the sharp thud of his own feet hitting the packed dirt roused him.

But he did not have time to wonder at the peculiar glint, because as he stepped forward, he was trapped by two sea-blue eyes. They pinned him in place as effectively as a bayonet pressed to his throat once had upon the battlefield.

Her chest rose and fell rapidly, as if she'd been running or tussling with—

No.

It was an inappropriate thought. Besides which, there were no young men in sight.

But he could not stop himself from saying: "It is quite early to venture out on your own, Miss Trudeau."

Her coppery eyebrows, a few shades darker than the curls pinned atop her head, rose up her forehead. The hair at the nape of her neck was slightly darker as well, and at her temples. Perspiration, he realized, gut clenching.

But Miss Trudeau had understood his question clearly enough. "I find it quite useful to enjoy one's own company. It is the only presence one can always depend upon."

Her blow was as sharp and swift as the bayonet he'd imagined earlier.

He *could* be depended upon, he almost said. But he kept the bitterness from his voice and said instead: "Your role, however, necessitates company."

She snorted, shaking out her arms and straightening her

bodice. She clasped a parasol in her left hand, her fingers toying with the curved handle as she spoke—a hint of amusement in her voice. "Your children sleep shamefully late. I could take my morning constitutional and host a wedding breakfast before they crawl from their coverlets."

"They take after their mother," he said before he could bite down upon the impulse. Somehow, mentioning her here in Miss Trudeau's presence felt like a violation. To whom and of what, he could not say.

But Miss Trudeau did not ask about his late wife. She merely inclined her head, slanting her eyes at him as she looked him up and down. Her breathing was returning to normal, her breasts now rising slowly with each even breath. But that did not make them any less glorious.

"Sir George?" She cleared her throat.

He coughed, a strangled mirror of the sound she'd made seconds before. "How are the children?" he asked hoarsely.

Her bosom bounced with her soundless chuckle. George was presented with a glorious view of her derriere as she walked to one of the settees arranged against the walls of the summer house and collected a shawl. Regret—when she picked it up. Relief—when she draped it over her arm rather than her shoulders.

Leaving that expanse of creamy, freckled skin on display to him.

"Sir George," she said again, her voice firm—forcing his eyes up to her face rather than at her bosom. Her eyes were intent, questioning.

Christ, she'd realized what he was about. He was going to lose another governess, this time for nothing less than his own uncontrollable lust. He ought to have visited a brothel if his manhood was becoming this untamable—

"The children are well enough. Archie is quite deficient in his reading skills for a child of five. Eveline, however, is quite advanced. I would like to add Greek to her language instruction, if you are amenable. She's quite mastered French."

George blinked. Twice.

Reading. Greek. The children.

"Would Latin be more appropriate?" he asked, voice a bit more even. But Miss Trudeau must have noted the strain in it, for she frowned.

"If you desire it, sir. Either would be acceptable. Though I rather think Eveline will enjoy reading the classics in their original form."

She might as well have been speaking another language—one he was not proficient in. German, perhaps. His lust-addled mind was completely incapable of comprehension.

Miss Trudeau, however, was not amused.

She crossed her arms over her body, her parasol sticking out at a sharp angle, akin to a sword. She looked like nothing more than a fierce warrior girding herself for battle.

"Sir George," she said for a third time, patience nowhere near her tone. "We are speaking of your children. I would appreciate your full attention."

His head snapped up. "You have it."

Only years of military precision and scolding from his superiors kept the flush from his face. This was not the military, and Miss Trudeau was not his superior. But the comparison felt too valid to dismiss.

"Very well." With a flick of her wrist, she was ushering him out of the summer house and closing the doors behind her, latching them into place. "Eveline struggles more with mathematics, but I believe it is simply due to lack of sufficient instruction. I shall see it remedied—"

Her words fell from her lips.

Her beautiful, luscious lips.

The lips that were now only a foot from his.

She'd closed up the summer house, turning to face him, not realizing how close they stood to one another on the narrow path that led down to the picturesque garden retreat. The bright blooms of spring had faded to golden stems as autumn descended on Essex, framing the walk with a riot of gold and brown and red. Colors perfectly suited to complement Miss Ethelreda Trudeau—governess, iron-willed maiden, and siren.

George was vaguely aware of the horse shifting its weight on its hooves behind him, pinning them in—his mount on one side, the closed glass doors of the summer house on the other. No escape for Miss Trudeau, who had no notion what was about to happen.

No escape for Sir George Caldwell, who lost complete control of his good sense and lowered his lips to hers.

SO THIS IS what a kiss feels like.

Wet.

And hot, and delicious. Those thoughts weren't even fully formed within her head, but rather swirling colors of emotion and feeling she could not hope to process. Not while George's lips were pressed to hers.

No wonder Jacquetta and Dominique were always kissing their way through their quests. It was absolutely intoxicating. And that was before he traced his tongue along the seam of her lips and she opened for him instinctively.

Oh.

Oh, yes.

This was even better.

Red had no notion what to do with her tongue, but George seemed more than satisfied to do the work himself, curling his tongue around hers, tracing the inside of her lips. It ought to have been a disgusting intrusion, but rather than feeling repulsed, Red found her tongue edging its way past his lips to take a taste of her own.

Nutmeg and tea. How peculiar.

Yet she could not help herself from delving deeper and taking more. He hummed against her lips, creating the most delicious friction that sent shivers down her spine. Her hand tightened on the hilt of her parasol, tight enough to break the inlaid handle if she were not careful.

Careful. The word flashed through her mind, its image written in bold strokes on an otherwise empty canvas.

This was the opposite of careful. This was complete and utter foolhardiness.

Red dragged herself back, pressing her back flat against the doors to the summer house, hard enough she was sure she'd have the grid pattern of the glass panes etched upon her back. But she did not care for physical pain; she'd learned long ago to box it up and shove it to the back of her mind, where it would not cloud rational thinking. Rationality was essential to her work.

She was supposed to be chasing a goddamned French assassin—not letting the master of the house kiss her senseless.

For his part, George's expression was nothing short of horrified.

Which was both a relief to Red, but also a bit discomfiting. Had she really been so terrible at kissing?

"Miss Trudeau, I apologize. I have no notion what came over me. It shall never happen again." He met her eyes directly as he spoke.

Not a coward, for all that he'd run away after that ghastly nighttime display several weeks before.

Red traced her fingertip over the handle of her parasol, caressing the outline of the fox artfully wrought there. Tail, snout, paws. It calmed her nerves enough for her to nod sharply and say:

"We will not speak of it."

George's throat bobbed as he swallowed. Red found herself noticing the elegant curve of his throat, wondering what color the beard would be if he ever let it grow. Being a military man, she doubted stubble was ever a part of his uniform.

"Very well," he huffed.

She was still pinned between him and the summer house. Flicking her eyes meaningfully over his shoulder, she tried to communicate without words—

George's eyes widened, and his shoulder dropped back against the horse, shoving it back. The poor animal huffed his distaste, but allowed his rump to travel back into the golden grasses.

Red stepped around them adroitly, as swift and sure as the steps of swordplay she'd been executing in the summer house moments before George stumbled upon her. She'd have to ensure she kept the doors closed from now on, lest her prowess with the rapier be discovered. She had an excuse ready, but it was thin, and she'd rather not have to use it.

"I must return to the nursery. The children's lessons begin promptly at nine o'clock. I will not allow them to waste away the entire morning." She was shocked at how easily the command came into her voice, where it regarded children, at least. She'd never had any trouble ordering around adults.

"Of course." George caught the halter of his mount, but instead of turning to follow her down the path, he pointed his horse toward the narrow track that circled the summer house.

"Aren't you coming to greet the children?" Red frowned, calling to mind the map she'd constructed of Oxley Park and its grounds. To her knowledge, the path she stood on was the most direct route back to the manor house.

But to her utter shock, George shook his head. "I must see to the bees."

"Bees."

"Honeybees."

She shook her head, not understanding. What did honeybees have to do with anything?

"There is an apiary beyond the summer house."

She glanced over his shoulder, through the shoulder-high foliage, to try to see beyond the unique octagonal roof of the summer house. But there was nothing she could discern, though she knew the undulating hills of the grounds did extend for another half-mile or so beyond.

But she had not bothered to keep the surprise and confusion

from her face, and George answered them both.

"I keep an apiary. Several hives," he said.

"I know what an apiary is."

"Of course."

"Why do you keep one? You do not take honey in your tea?" Red bit down on her own tongue viciously. Just because she had noticed the fact did not mean she should remark upon it. Indeed, George was staring at her quite curiously.

Ignoring the fact that he had not answered her question, she hurried on.

"Shall I bring the children to you there?" She could not keep the cringe from her voice. She was already imagining tending to bee stings, could practically hear Eveline's feral sobs.

"Certainly not," George scoffed.

Even as relief coursed through her, another emotion reared up. "But sir, the children have not seen you for weeks—"

"The apiary is no place for children." He spun on his heel with military precision, that warrior's grace lurking beneath his gentlemanly veneer. None of the confusion she'd seen in his eyes earlier, seconds before he kissed her, marred his handsome features.

Red could not help but wonder how he was with a sword, and her mind filled with fantasies of crossing blades—

This was precisely why she was still unmarried. She fantasized about swordplay rather than flirtatious repartee. Though now that she'd been kissed, perhaps her fantasies would take on a different shade and shape.

But none of this was about her and her fantasies, whatever they may be.

"Supper, then?" she asked, catching him on the threshold.

Red watched as his shoulders knitted together, tension in every muscle. "Yes."

"I will tell the children," she said, turning her back upon him without a farewell. But she paused a few yards down the lane, tossing a last rejoinder over her shoulder. "Do not desert them again."

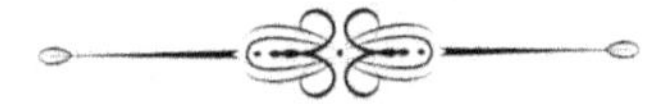

CHAPTER SEVEN

Eveline Isobel Caldwell had all the makings of a fine lady
knight.

She was wicked smart, ascertaining every principle Red laid
before her in little more than the time it took her governess to
explain it. Her penchant for hiding was unparalleled. The child
could teach classes to the other lady knights on how to conceal
oneself quickly and completely.

Most of all, she was patient.

Red knew the accord between them was tenuous at best.
Eveline obeyed her new governess, but only insofar as she could
not be specifically called insolent.

In those first few days after George's flight, she'd been happy
enough with the détente between them. But the flashes of ire in
the young girl's eyes were unmistakable, even to someone not
trained to notice every detail.

An implosion was coming, that much was certain. Whether it
would be initiated by Eveline herself or by some event that
tripped the girl's herculean efforts at repressing her emotions,
time would only tell.

Red would not be the one to give in, that much was certain.
She would not be tricked into hysterics by a child. Even if she
suspected that was precisely what had happened to George, what
had prompted him to take up military tactics to control two small

children.

The only exception to Eveline's innocuous maneuvering was reading. Red suspected if the girl had possessed the ability, she would have tried to find a way to subsume that directive as well. But once Eveline opened a book, she was lost to anything but the words on the page.

Which accounted for the fact that when Red strolled into the nursery, Eveline's plate was untouched. Ignored except for the trail of egg that led from the edge of Eveline's plate to Archie's. The younger Caldwell was munching happily, two portions of eggs nearly gone into his bottomless stomach.

"Good morning," Red said as she stepped in, setting aside her parasol and gloves as she made to join them in breaking their fast.

Archie opened his mouth—

"Young Master Caldwell, please remember what we discussed about speaking when one's mouth is full," Red said, settling into her seat.

She'd had the child-sized table replaced her second day in residence. A woman of her stature and furniture of that size were incongruous.

"Eveline, please put your book down. I wish to speak with you both."

The girl's dark eyes appeared over the top of the book. She inched it down, inch by agonizingly slow inch, until her entire face was revealed. She could still look down and read the words. Compliance, but only in the narrowest construction of the word.

"Your father has returned."

Red knew better than to expect a reaction from them. Where their father was concerned, the two children had trained themselves to expect nothing. It was a way to avoid being disappointed. While she wished it wasn't so, it was a reflection of the situation in the Caldwell household.

"From now on, we shall join him each night for supper rather than dining here in the nursery. It will be an opportunity for you both to practice the skills we've been studying."

Eveline stared at her book, though her eyes did not move from side to side. Archie was looking at her, those big, round eyes asking a hundred questions, none of which Red had the answer for.

Instead, she said, "We shall begin tonight."

Eveline's book snapped down on the table. *Here it is*, Red thought, steeling her nerves. But instead, Eveline stood and walked to the bellpull.

"We had best get on with our lessons," she said, giving it a vicious yank.

Just like that, the tension was broken. Archie returned to stuffing as much food into his mouth as he could manage before the maid arrived to clear the table, and Eveline retrieved her workbook.

But Red could sense the gathering storm.

Sir George has no notion what is coming for him.

MISS ETHELREDA TRUDEAU was a miracle worker. She ought to be sainted. Using no harsh orders, no military whistles, and seemingly nothing but her own wit, she'd managed to corral his children into presentability.

Archie was himself in miniature. As he watched his son in the middle of the large table, sipping his soup—albeit a bit loudly— George remembered sitting in that very same spot across from his own sister.

Eveline was the image of her mother. George could think on it no more than that.

His daughter wore a white dress with a pink sash and a matching bow in her dark hair. She was very much the lady he'd hoped she would become under proper tutelage, using her silverware correctly and sitting straight. She wasn't speaking much, which was not like her. But perhaps she was feeling shy. That was his fault—he'd been away for weeks.

Miss Trudeau was as good as her word, pretending as if nothing untoward had passed between them. She'd donned a dark pewter gown that was rather severe on her soft features, as if to remind him that there nothing improper could occur between them. At least, nothing further.

George did not need reminding. All of that had been a mistake, and one he would never repeat. He needed to focus on the children. They needed him, as Miss Trudeau had so sharply pointed out earlier in the afternoon. She hadn't said as many words, but the reproval was there nonetheless. And while he didn't feel the need to please her, precisely, George did know that he did not want to be on the receiving end of her displeasure.

Of that, he was quite certain.

Which was also what forced the words out of him. Miss Trudeau fixed him with a glare from the other end of the long table, message clear enough—*speak*.

"Your dress is very nice, Eveline," he said, immediately followed by a sip of claret.

His daughter did not look up from her plate. Miss Trudeau turned that lethal stare upon her eldest charge, but to no avail. Eveline was not looking at her either. So she took more direct action. She cleared her throat. Loudly.

Eveline raised her chin with agonizing slowness. She looked to her governess, who smiled and tilted her head meaningfully in his direction. Then, with the same lack of haste, Eveline looked to her father.

"Thank you." Her chin dropped once again.

Miss Trudeau was clutching her spoon like a weapon. George did not know whether he was the intended victim or his daughter. Either way, he turned to Archie, his son, whose own spoon was at that moment being loaded with peas.

"Archibald." The child leapt in his seat, scattering peas across the table and onto the floor. George shoved down his cringe. He did not dare look to the other end of the table. He was gifted a momentary reprieve by the arrival of the next course.

Once the footmen stepped away, he tried again with Archie. "Miss Trudeau tells me you've been giving special attention to your reading."

Archie's dark eyes turned owlish. "Yes, sir." He toyed with a rogue pea near the edge of his plate.

"Tell me about something you have read." George tried to soften his words, but they sounded like a command nonetheless. Which was precisely how Archie responded—as one would to an order.

"Miss Trudeau has been reading to me about the jungle, sir."

Right, George remembered. Because Archie wasn't reading yet himself. *I'm an idiot. Miss Trudeau told me as much only this afternoon.*

"That sounds fascinating," he said. Anther drink of wine was warranted. A deep drink. Archie returned to his peas.

Which was when Miss Trudeau decided she'd had enough of his ineptitude at reconnecting with his own children. "Archie, you are meant to eat your supper, not play with it."

George watched Archie straighten, but he also saw the covert flick of his son's wrist. He wondered if Miss Trudeau had. But George had no chance to intervene, because she turned those demanding blue eyes upon him last.

"Perhaps you can share with the children something about your travels and what took you away from Oxley Park," she proposed, flicking a springy curl over her shoulder. She raised one eyebrow in challenge.

Hiding from you. Hiding from them.

The truth would not suffice. Nor could he bring himself to lie to his children. He'd told enough lies and half-truths over the past few years.

"There is nothing interesting to report," he said.

Miss Trudeau's wine glass was halfway to her lips. He watched her hand still, saw the frustration and attempt to maintain her composure as she forced herself to take another drink and shrug dismissively.

She then directed her attention to the table's third occupant. "Eveline, tell your father about the books you've read while he's been away. Your daughter is a voracious reader."

"I see." He turned to Eveline. Books—he could talk about books. He was well read. Admittedly, his favored texts were probably not that appealing to a nine-year-old girl. But he'd manage. "What are you reading now?"

Eveline lifted her chin, this time more speedily. Her expression was difficult to read, it often was, but George thought he saw interest in her little furrowed brow.

"I have just begun *The Mysteries of Udolpho*," she said quietly.

George blinked. "Isn't that rather inappropriate for a girl of your age?"

Miss Trudeau's wine glass hit the table with a thud. "She is enjoying it."

"Yes, but there are graphic depictions—I did not read Mrs. Radcliffe until I was at Harrow." George remembered the book well. He could not imagine his quiet daughter reading the descriptions—

"She is reading at a very high level for nine years old. Certainly the equal of most of the chaps I've met in attendance at Eton and Harrow," Miss Trudeau put in.

George shook his head. "I do not think—"

Archie chose that moment to launch the missiles he'd been covertly collecting in his hand under the table.

The peas sailed across the table in a spectacular arc, hitting their mark with stunning efficiency. They bounced off Eveline's face and chest, and one even landed with a *plop!* in her glass.

"You little beast!" She launched her napkin across the table, upending a goblet of water, sending a tidal wave over Archie's chest.

George shot to his feet, knowing he had to intervene. "Eveline, there is no—"

"Me? You are scolding *me*?" she shrieked, shoving back the chair. "You don't know anything about me! You do not even know that I like to read! Or that *this* is the sort of thing *he* does at every single meal! Because you are never here! Even when you are, you are always with your stupid bees!"

Miss Trudeau's chair scraped as she stood hastily, surely to insert herself, force Eveline to apologize—

But Eveline flew from the room, giving him no chance to retort. There was no retort, really. Nothing he could say to that. Because she'd spoken the truth, as much as he did not want to hear it.

Miss Trudeau was half a beat behind her. Throwing her napkin down on her chair, she whirled for the doorway. But she paused on the threshold, turning to glare at him with vitriol as fierce as Eveline's.

"I hope you are satisfied with yourself," she spat. The next part she must have meant to speak under her breath, but it echoed through the near-empty room. "It seems I will be wiping noses tonight after all."

Then she was gone, leaving him alone with a wide-eyed Archie, who had a heaping serving of his own guilt.

CHAPTER EIGHT

MORE THAN ANYTHING, Red regretted not bringing a flask of Jacquetta's cognac with her on this quest. Claret was served with supper, but it wasn't nearly potent enough to dull the edge of her—

Her what?

Temper? She'd certainly wanted to bash George over the head with a skillet after his display of fatherly ineptitude at supper. But she wasn't angry. Not really. The main emotion in her heart when she looked upon the fractured Caldwell family was pity.

In doing his duty to his country, George had neglected his other concern—his family. He suffered alone, but he was not the only soldier to suffer so. Red knew an entire generation of England's families would feel the tremors of Napoleon's greed as it wreaked chaos upon them, even with the war now over. The battles that remained would be fought on the home front. Much like the one currently tearing apart Oxley Park.

Eveline, bless her, was trying to cope with the loss of not just one parent but two. Little Archie was too young to understand but certainly old enough to feel. Red's heart ached for them, even as it yearned for her own family.

The Caldwell children did not need her to wipe their noses or dry their tears. They'd learned by necessity how to do it for themselves. That made Red actually consider doing it, without a hint of sarcasm or avarice.

Because no child should have to dry their own tears.

At least now they were both quiet, settled in their beds. Even Eveline's shoulders had relaxed and her breathing softened, eventually.

Red crept back to her rooms, setting her snares by habit. She did not bother with the bell on the door connecting her rooms to the nursery. She'd already be sleeping with half an ear trained on the children all night.

If anyone entered her rooms this evening, they would not find her writing in code. They would see a tired woman, curls tangled beyond repair, looking over week-old Society papers. Lord, but she did make quite an art out of spinsterhood.

If reading *Miss Plimpton's Guide for the Modern Governess* was akin to being held in the stocks, reading London Society papers must be the equivalent to being stretched upon the rack. But nonetheless, Red combed through them with a keen eye. They were her only source of news about her sisters or her fellow lady knights.

She did not begrudge Miranda's edict of no contact. It was necessary to safeguard her true identity and the ruse she was playing out at Oxley Park. But Red missed her family terribly. Thus, she was consigned to scanning scandal sheets.

The newly minted Duchess of Hartwell caused quite a stir when greeting the freshly arrived French ambassador...

Red's fingers caught in a tangle, halfway down the curl she'd been attempting to tame. She smiled through the painful tugs on her scalp as she imagined Mary Jane attempting a formal French greeting. The poor thing had never attained more than a three-year-old's grasp upon the language. Choking back a laugh, she laid that column aside for the next time her spirits were in need of lifting.

The remaining paragraphs proved devoid of meaningful

news, except—

A name snagged her interest at the very bottom of the very last sheet. It was little more than a footnote, really, a bit of information meriting a single sentence.

Mr. David Grisham, heir to the Earl of Danby, wed Miss Dominique Beauchamp in a private ceremony near the Earl's country estate in Derbyshire.

Heat prickled at the back of Red's eyes as she set the pack of papers aside. Lord in heaven, what she would not give for a swig of Jacquetta's cognac!

At least that quest had come to a happy conclusion. Dominique deserved every happiness in the world after the childhood she'd endured. As for Jacquetta, Red had no word of her quest in pursuit of the notorious Grayson Thane. Without regular communications from the Duchess of Guilford, with an ocean separating Jacquetta from her friends, all Red could do was silently pray for her friend's safety.

Her fingers caught again. There was no use attempting to untangle the ragged red mess. She'd used the last measure of her patience at that disastrous supper.

Red shook out her tresses, belted her wrapper, and untangled the snare on her door. There must be spirits somewhere in Oxley Park. Now that everyone else in the household was asleep, she'd find some to settle herself. No one was awake to judge the propriety of the governess partaking in a private nip.

Halfway down the corridor, Red realized her mistake. She'd left her rooms without a candle or lamp to light her way. She'd mapped most of Oxley Park in the first few weeks she'd been there, but if she stumbled across someone she'd look as if she was intentionally sneaking around. She paused, glancing back.

With a sigh, Red resigned herself to retracing her steps. She would—

What was that?

Red melted back against the wall, instinctively stepping into shadows.

She waited, counting the seconds. But the sound did not come again.

What was it?

It had sounded like the scraping of a chair. Perhaps pushed back as someone stood from a desk or dressing table? She glanced down the hallway toward her rooms, but nothing had moved. Besides, the sound had come from ahead.

But none of those rooms were occupied. In this corridor it was just her and the children. Sir George's chambers were around two more corners, facing the long front drive. And the late Lady Caldwell's apartments…

She'd opted to leave those undisturbed. The cream- and gold-bedecked suite of rooms was absolutely lovely. But ghosts haunted them, if only the metaphorical kind.

Red knew very little about the other woman. She'd come to Oxley Park at nineteen, wed to Sir George in an arranged match. Eight years later, she died in childbirth. The children did not speak of her. Nor did George. Red found that telling enough.

The sound was a figment of her mind, she decided. But she kept to the shadows as she edged along the corridor. The moon was full, bathing half the hallway with glowing, pearlescent light. It might have been romantic if—

Romantic?

She had never applied that word to a situation—in anything other than jest—in her entire life.

I need that drink—now.

Damn the shadows and sneaking.

Her ears pricked again.

Not a chair scraping, but a boot.

Instead of freezing, this time Red quickened her step. She moved soundlessly along the wall, her silken slippers cloaking her steps. The carpet was thick; it ought to cover all footsteps, especially if one took any level of care. But there, near the top of the stairwell, the carpet was thinner, worn away by constant foot traffic.

Red's eyes slid past the stairwell to the corridor beyond.

She was still drenched in shadow. Whoever it was could not have seen her. Which meant they'd continued on, thinking themselves undetected.

Legrand.

It might be a maid or footman sneaking off for an illicit tryst. But every instinct in Red's body said otherwise. Her rapier was back in her room, leaning against the dressing table. Her dagger was sheathed in the special garter around her thigh. She could have it in her hand in three seconds, she reminded herself. She'd timed it.

Legrand was here, and he was near. The unanswered questions were who and why. Whose identity had he assumed? Why was he sneaking around Oxley Park in the dead of night? He was an assassin. Murder and mayhem were the only realistic possibilities.

Red's heart clenched.

It was real—the threat, the quest. Some small part of her had hoped the duchess's sources were wrong. The Caldwell household did not deserve another tragedy heaped upon them.

She'd grown fond of them.

Damn.

Red could not let that fondness cloud her judgment. Their safety depended on her.

Where would Legrand go? The darkened corridor ahead or down the stairs? Down, if he was trying to flee the property. But if he was posing as a servant, as she suspected, he might make for the servants' stairwell at the end of the corridor.

She hadn't heard any of the stairs creak. It was possible that Legrand knew which steps and spots to avoid, just as Red did. But the escape of the servants' stairwell was too persuasive.

She darted past the stairs, avoiding the thinned bit of carpet. But a half step past, a flash of light flared in the periphery of her vision. She turned mid-step, catching herself on the banister. She hit the second stair with more force than she'd have liked, and the sound was too loud.

Now she had no choice. She had to move, and quickly.

As her slippered foot hit the ground floor, she used the inertia to catch the edge of her nightgown and hike it, retrieving the dagger sheathed at her thigh. The grand foyer of Oxley Park was empty. But there were mirrors—three of them positioned around the two-story-tall room. One of them must have caught the light.

Red had to pause long enough to throw her gaze upward, to calculate where the light had come from. It had been fast, like a door opening or a candle lighting just before it disappeared around a corner.

Three rooms opened from the foyer, as well as a corridor leading to the rear of the house. Legrand had to be making for the rear of the house, for safety. She lunged for the corridor, and a second later knew she'd made the right choice as she caught a flash of a dark heel in the sliver of moonlight as it rounded the corner ahead of her.

A crash ricocheted through the foyer behind her. Red spun so quickly that she had to push herself off the wall to keep from slipping. Her hand collided with a vase. She caught it, but only barely. She planted her feet hard, arms wide at her sides to steady herself.

Another split-second decision to be made: after the mysterious booted man—for that snippet of heel had told her the gender of her prey—or to investigate the crash from the study.

Could there be more than one person involved in Legrand's plan, whatever that plan might be? Had the crash been a strategic distraction?

No—he hadn't known she was there. Unless he'd heard her land on the second stair from the top. But even so, he still could not have seen her. Legrand could not know that it was the woman posing as a governess who was in pursuit. But if she went into the study to investigate, and it truly was a setup, she'd be found out.

She had to risk it. On the peripheral chance that it was Legrand himself in the study, she had to investigate.

Red bit back the curse that rose to her lips. She still had to approach with caution.

Moving on silent feet once again, she retraced her steps more deliberately to the study. No light leaked from under the door, which was why she'd dismissed it moments before in her hasty appraisal of the foyer and adjoining rooms. But there was no doubt in her mind that the sound had originated from there. It was the only one of the rooms where the doors were habitually closed—hence the slightly muffled sound of the crash-ing…whatever it was that had crashed down or over.

Reluctantly, Red dug her left hand into the embroidered silk of her wrapper until she felt the catching of her muslin night-gown. With a sharp tug, she pulled both garments up so she could conceal the knife in her garter once again. If she had any hope of playing the innocent governess, she could not be found with a dagger in her hand.

She heard the footsteps as the blade clicked back into its sheath, giving her only seconds to snap her head up as the door swung open.

He loomed over her, illuminated only by the moonlight sweeping in through the tall windows. In silhouette, he was every inch as dark and imposing as a villain of children's nightmares. With a skilled, military grace, he swung his arm upward, and the moonlight caught on the wicked blade as he lifted it above his head for that final fatal plunge.

Red acted without thought. She tightened her fist around her nightgown and wrapper, hiking the fabric up so she could level a brutal knee into his groin. The action distracted him enough, exactly as she intended. While he swept down, his aim now ruined, she ducked to the side at the same time she lifted a fist. The honed muscles of her arm powered the punch as she hit his knuckles hard, causing his grip to loosen reflexively.

She did not hear the groan when she hit him in the groin, nor the bellow as her fist connected with his. But she did register the metallic sound of the knife hitting the tiled floor. By then, her eyes were fully adjusted to the light. Another quick kick, her skirts still tight in her fist, and her slippered foot sent the knife skidding away across the floor into the corner of the room.

"Hell and damnation! What the devil are you doing? You've gelded me—"

Horror. Absolute, complete, utter horror.

"Sir George. I…" There were no words. Her mother would be horrified.

Mother? Her mother was the least of her worries. Miranda would never give her another quest. She'd be forcibly retired from the Lady Knights.

"What are you doing roaming the house in the dark? I thought you were an intruder." George didn't want for a response. He wrapped his fingers around her forearm with steely strength—a reminder that he was not the only one in this interaction made of corded muscle.

He dragged her into the study, face shadowed by the light behind him. She must be forgiven for not recognizing him. The lighting made it impossible for her to discern details of his face, even now, and he'd been holding a knife—heavens above!

But she said none of that.

Instead, she opened her blasted mouth and said: "Who would be intruding on your home in the middle of the night?"

"How the hell would I know? It is the sort of situation in which one acts first and asks questions later!" George still held her arm, tight. He'd stopped between the chairs that framed the fireplace. At least he was no longer wobbling from where she'd landed her knee against his groin.

"I… I was terrified," she managed. It wasn't entirely false. The past several moments had been terrifying. Or would have been to most women. Fear had not registered in Red's mind at all.

"You should not be traipsing around in the dark. It is dangerous." His voice was like gravel, every syllable scraping out. What had he been doing in here, alone in the dark?

"Dangerous how?" she asked, unable to resist the temptation. Maybe he would reveal his secrets, here and now, and she'd be that much closer to unmasking Legrand.

George jerked back. He released her abruptly, dropping her down onto the Aubusson-covered tiles. She had not even realized he'd held her aloft, supporting the weight of her body so she'd been balancing on nothing but her tiptoes. Holding her as if she weighed nothing. That was the sort of strength that flowed through the man before her.

"You have a lot of questions for a woman who was nearly stabbed to death," he said, voice low and even.

Hell.

Maybe it was because she was utterly out of options. Or maybe it was the thudding of her heart, the intensity and exertion of the last several minutes catching up and taking control of her better judgment. But mostly, it was the strength she sensed in him and the warmth it lit in her belly. All of those things, paired with the need to stop him from questioning, stop him from thinking.

All of those things had Red pushing up onto her toes and grabbing George's shoulders. Not to assault, but to kiss.

Which was, she would reflect later, a different sort of assault all its own.

How was this happening again?

He'd sworn to himself after that nonsense outside the summer house that he would not allow himself to lose control. It was the height of impropriety to steal kisses from his children's governess. Had it only been that morning that he'd kissed her in the autumn sun? How, then, could it feel like an eternity had passed since then? That he'd been starving for days and weeks, only to suddenly find himself seated at a feast?

Feast was what he wanted in that moment, more than anything. To glut himself on Miss Ethelreda McGovern's sweet lips, to lean her back and lift her skirts to taste her fragrant honey. He wanted her melting and willing in his hands. Just as she was now.

For even as she curled her tongue around his, her hips moved forward in a sultry invitation. George accepted it, catching her waist and pulling her against him. There was so much of her, and he wanted to touch every inch. Her nightclothes were thin and yet too much between them.

The dressing gown was already undone. He shoved it aside, sliding his hand past to the muslin of her nightgown. Nothing more than a whisper-thin barrier of fabric separated him from touching her glorious body. She jerked against him, tearing her mouth away as she gasped for breath.

George waited, giving her the chance to pull away. He would be finishing himself in his hand, but it would be a small price to pay.

But a breath later, her mouth landed on his jaw line.

She began to suck, dragging her tongue over the barest hint of stubble that had appeared since his morning shave. That was affirmation enough for him. He crushed her hips against his, fitting them together so the hard length of him was nestled between her legs. Even with his trousers on and her nightgown in place, the feeling was exquisite. She moved her hips just so, knowing how to drive him to the brink.

George threw his head back, groaning. But the separation was too much. He had to be touching her, tasting her.

"Ethelreda," he groaned against her throat as his tongue sought out her hammering pulse.

"Red," she moaned.

He paused.

"Call me Red," she said. This time he felt the entire sound as it racked through her body, in every place where her soft curves were fitted against him. Which, by this point, was nearly everywhere.

"Red," he whispered, rocking back and catching her head in his hands. He laced his fingers together at the nape of her neck, cradling that head of ridiculously wanton red hair.

It fit her, so much better than the antiquated, Tudor-era moniker. He would never tell her that he'd thumbed through two dozen tomes in his study until he found the one that listed her Christian name and its historical origins.

He had to have her—needed to bury himself within her, have her thighs wrapped around his waist, milking him for every ounce of pleasure. He backed her toward the desk, half a thought reminding him he was grateful he'd tucked away the latest draft of his treatise. Another half thought, and he'd lifted her up onto the edge of the desk.

Hell, but her bottom felt so good in his hands. When had he last held a woman who was so full? So damn perfect for him, fulfilling every statuesque fantasy?

She offered no resistance; nay, Red offered nothing but full-throated endorsement. She leaned back, bracing herself on her arms, offering herself up to him. This nightgown was a different cut than the one she'd been wearing that night he tore apart his room. This one was lower. It took only a tug of the fabric and her round, voluminous breasts popped out.

They hung low, heavy with their fullness. It was too dark for him to see, so he wondered—were her nipples the pale pink of the flush he'd seen on her cheeks at the summer house, or the coppery brown of her freckles? In any case, when he closed his mouth over one, he forgot that wondering.

And the sound she made—feral and unbridled—drove him forward. He had to be in her.

He reached for her skirts, hiking them up higher. Her hand was on his shoulder, urging him—

No. Not urging.

Holding. Tightening.

He rocked back instantly, dropping his hands away from her skirts. "What is it?"

Red's breath was coming so fast that her breasts heaved and wobbled with every gasp. He knew he was no better off. But something about the ragged quiver had him drawing back instead of diving in.

"I… Heavens, I can hardly think… I haven't," she said, trying to catch her breath but failing utterly. He watched in dawning realization as Red closed her eyes, forcing a breath in through her nostrils and out her pursed lips. "I have not done this before."

"You… You have never—" He nearly choked on the words. "You have never been intimate with a man."

He watched in horror at her red curls skimming over her exposed bosom as she shook her head from side to side.

"Hell." He stepped back, shaking his own head, catching his forehead in his hands, and raking his hands through his hair with brutal force. "I am going to hell."

Red—Ethelreda—no, Red—rolled her eyes. Those beautiful storm-cloud eyes, turned sapphire by the moonlight, rolled straight up toward the ornately carved ceiling panels.

"I am sorry," he said.

She tugged her nightgown up, tucking her glorious breasts back inside. Then she tied the wrapper, the silk dressing gown that he only now noticed was embroidered with intricate swirls of tropical plants. It was very ornate, for a governess.

"You mustn't be sorry," Red said sharply, pulling his focus entirely back to her face. "For being sorry… It would imply some deficit on my part. Which I refuse to accept."

He nearly laughed. How she could elicit such a reaction in a moment as tense as this was…incomprehensible.

"There is no deficit, I assure you. You are perfect. Too damn perfect for my own—"

She held up her hand, and he watched her teeth sink into her bottom lip. "That will suffice, Sir George."

She remained that way for several long moments, watching

him. She must have been satisfied he would not further try to compliment her, albeit ineptly, for then she lowered her hand and retreated to the door. And Christ damn him, he admired that round arse of hers every step of the way.

"Goodnight, Sir George," Red murmured, slipping out the door. She moved with such grace, wholly in command of every inch of that curvy body.

He knew then. She would be his undoing. It was only a matter of time.

Then door to the study closed with snap, and George reached for his cock.

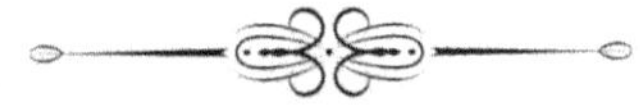

CHAPTER NINE

*T*HE QUEEN APIS *mellifera begins her mating ritual by flying high above her hive, where she is courted by a plethora of males from her own and surrounding hives. These males compete for her favor by executing a complicated dance...*

At least he was not dancing to try to get her attention. A small mercy.

The last few weeks had passed without incident. Meaning, he'd managed not to kiss or bed his children's governess. Red. Miss Trudeau, he corrected himself. But damn him, ever since she'd given him her name, he'd been unable to think of her as anything else. Red fit her so perfectly. The flaming, bright hair that bounced and swished with the vivacity of a flame, the tempest in her eyes, a blue the color of the hottest part of a flame. Red.

George may have managed to keep his hands off her, but he'd been decidedly less successful with his mind. He wrote about the way the worker bees served their queen, and he pictured the staff buzzing around her. Already she held his housekeeper and butler firmly in her thrall. The rest of the staff watched her mastery of the children with nothing short of awe.

To say nothing of the bit about honey production—which ought to have been mundane. But ever since he'd promised himself he'd sample her honey, he could think of nothing other than the naughtiest connotations of the word.

The apiaries were supposed to bring him peace and calm, the treatise a way to channel his energy into something productive but mundane. Boring, even. He needed complacency in his life.

Yet it seemed with Red in his household, such a thing was impossible.

And with each passing day, he was more and more unsure how his household would function without her.

The queen couples with multiple males during her mating flight, sometimes numbering in the dozens. Each of these drones will, shortly thereafter, die.

He shoved the quill pen back into its pot, and the force sent splatters of black ink onto the desktop and the corner of his paper.

Wonderful. He'd have to make yet another copy. This was the third iteration. The second had not survived Archie and Eveline's last visit to his study, despite the fact that it had been tucked away in a drawer.

Archie had no respect for privacy. He'd wanted a piece of paper to draw a picture of the rabbit he'd seen on his walk, and the drawers of his father's desk seemed the perfect place to look for them. Eveline, at least, was more composed.

George's heart seized. *At least.* Perhaps it was not such an advantage.

The glint of mistrust, of hesitation, in his daughter's eyes lingered whenever she looked upon him, even a full month after his return. His second return. Or third or fourth, he supposed. George had hardly been present for her childhood, sent first to America and later to the Continent. Unlike Archie, Eveline was old enough to retain clear memories of her mother.

The accusation in her eyes when she looked at him was un-mistakable.

She was entitled to it. It was his fault. All of it.

He'd been there when Eveline was born. That was the most he could say for himself, and more than he could say for

Archie…or his wife.

He was not there the night she'd died in childbed. But he dreamt of it often enough that he felt that some part of his soul had been. As he'd been bathed in the blood of his comrades and enemies, struggling for life on the battlefield at Waterloo, she fought her own battle here at Oxley Park. Only one of them had emerged alive.

The wrong one, George often thought.

For every bit of anger and frustration he held toward her, that dark-haired woman who'd altered his life in ways he was even now struggling to untangle, he wished she'd lived. If the trade could have been made, he would have done it without hesitation.

He deserved to die on the battlefield—for leaving her and the children, for what he'd done to McGovern. He deserved every bit of pain. And yet he was the one alive. While the mother of his two children lay in a grave over the hill.

George had not summoned the courage to visit her grave. Nor did he think he ever would. He could not even open the door to her apartments. Just looking at Eveline, with her dark hair and delicate features… Yes, he deserved every bit of resentment his daughter threw in his direction.

What he did not deserve was even a modicum of happiness or pleasure. He certainly did not have any right to want Ethelreda Trudeau.

So, when he heard her voice in the foyer outside his study, he resolved to keep his arse in his seat.

The children's voices were audible as well, one jubilant and the other regretful. Eveline's melodic voice bubbled through the space beneath the doors, floating through the air, only to be cut seconds later by Archie's high-pitched whine.

"But Miss Trudeau, I—"

"You say I am the one to make trouble, but—"

"Children!"

Red's voice cut through the children's arguing with military efficiency any general would admire. Just loud enough to catch their attention, but not relying on the volume at all to communicate the seriousness of her command.

George could just picture her, hands on her generous hips, a stray red curl tickling the nape of her neck. Which she would ignore, of course, because she'd be pinning the children in place with that all-knowing blue stare of hers.

"An understanding of the basic principles of music and—"

"But it looks like rain. If I do not go out now, I'll miss the fish."

Fish?

Before George realized it, he was at the door to the study. Only so he could better hear the conversation transpiring on the other side, he assured himself. He had no intention of intervening. It was in direct conflict with his determination to stay away from Red.

"Fishing is not on our schedule today," Red said firmly.

"But—"

George swung open the door, stepping into the foyer with a sharp click of his boots.

Eveline froze halfway down the corridor to the music room. But she did not turn around. Archie went wide-eyed. Red merely swept her gaze over him and then settled it on his face with a vaguely amused expression of "now what?"

He landed his hand upon Archie's shoulder. He didn't grip hard, just firmly enough to let the boy know he had his father's full attention. He watched the lad swallow, but the brave little chap raised his eyes and did not cower.

"Yes, sir?"

"Miss Trudeau sets the schedule, and you obey. I will not tolerate your sassing to her—it is not appropriate to your governess, nor to any other lady in this house." George watched the little boy's eyes widen, but he kept his voice level and clear. Scaring the child would work no better than it did on infantrymen. "Am I understood?"

"Yes, sir." Archie nodded vigorously.

"Very well."

George watched Archie relax, then dart a look to Red, whose face was now unreadable.

Ought he to demand that Archie apologize?

But Red was already waving the child away. "Off to your music lesson, the both of you. I shall see you in the nursery promptly after."

She waited until the children disappeared to round on him. "I would appreciate if you did not intervene, in future."

George blinked. "He needs to mind you."

Her eyes narrowed. "Of course he does. But he only did so just now because his father demanded it. What shall I do when you are not at hand?"

It was a good point, one he should have appreciated. He was a decorated commander, for Christ's sake. But he was not about to admit that to her. Instead, his eyes went to her arms, where she clasped several thick books.

"What have you there?"

Red's eyes narrowed; she recognized a change of subject well enough. But for the moment, she appeared willing to let this one pass. George decided not to question his good fortune.

She shifted the burden in her arms as she spoke. "Books I've sent for from the circulating library in London. You have an impressive collection here, but I would like to address some of the children's more specific interests."

"Such as music?" He nodded down the corridor.

"Yes. You gave me leave to arrange their schedule. They informed me they'd received no formal instruction in music, which I thought to remedy." At that juncture, she did look a bit reticent—full cheeks blooming with color, a hesitant glance down the hallway. "My own skills are no more than passable in this area, I am afraid. The fees are quite reasonable, but if you are concerned—"

George waved his hand. Money, thankfully, was the one thing he did not have to be concerned about in his life. "I trust your judgment."

The weight of that statement filled the foyer, large as it was.

"Though the children seemed less than enthused," he said with a moderate attempt at a grin.

Red relaxed, her own smile easy. "Archie will learn to love it, if only for the beauty of watching a beautiful woman perform. Eveline already loves music," she said, curling her arms tighter around the stack of books.

George raked a hand through his hair, a habit whose return he had no choice but to consign himself to. At least if he was busy mussing his hair, he was keeping his hands off Red. Who, of course, looked absolutely delectable in her green sprigged-muslin day gown with tiny leaves embroidered around the neckline. She'd added a fichu, which was almost laughable. As if the little wisp of fabric could hope to do anything but draw more attention to the curve of her breasts, swelling and pressing against the failed attempt at modesty.

He coughed into his hand. "You have discovered more of Eveline's likes in your short tenure at Oxley Park than I had in the entire nine years prior."

Red pursed her lips, darting a glance down the corridor to where the children had disappeared into the music room.

"Children are not so difficult," she said, then her eyes widened and she shook her head emphatically. "They are very difficult, I mean. But they are not so difficult to *understand*." When he only wrinkled a brow in response, she tilted her head. "One merely has to *listen* to them. And to listen, one must be present."

Hell and damnation, but he would not tug at his hair twice in one encounter. He shoved his hands into his pockets. The way her muscles flexed as she held the heavy stack of books, her freckles sliding across the creamy skin, had his fingers itching to touch her.

"You have made your opinion on that matter quite clear, Miss Trudeau," he said hoarsely.

"I wanted to verify again that you will notify me of any business that takes you away from Oxley Park, so that I might prepare the children." Her voice had softened a bit, free of reproval. But the steely command, as always, remained.

"I have no plans to leave."

The declaration hung in the air between them.

George had no choice but to stand under the scrutiny of her sea-blue eyes as they searched him, and hope that she would not find him lacking.

"Very well." She nodded, turning for the stairwell. "I shall peruse these while the children attend their music lesson. We shall see you for supper, Sir George."

He watched the sway of her hips, staring at the hem of her dress in hopes of catching sight of shapely ankle or calf. He could not touch her, but he could look.

She was so tired.

So damned tired that she almost missed the note tucked inside the cover of the first book on the stack. Ostensibly, it was nothing more than a receipt from the lending library in London where she'd borrowed the books, along with a quick note jotted by the librarian's assistant with the details for returning the tomes when finished.

But Red recognized it immediately for what it was.

And she was still so damned tired that all she could manage to do was tuck it back into its place on top of the stack and trudge up the stairs to the nursery.

These children were going to be the end of her, one way or another. Feral, brilliant, and utterly exhausting. First, they needed such different things from her. Poor Archie struggled over every line of text. He'd mastered his alphabet since her arriving and could read simple words, but beyond that…

Red dropped the books onto the shelves that housed the children's school materials and lowered into a chair.

They were having their music lessons just now, and thank the Lord above, because she desperately needed a moment of peace—especially after departing George's company.

Archie was sweet, at least, after he'd gotten over his initial shyness. He was trying to learn, it was only that he'd rather be playing outside. Red was inclined to agree with him. She'd much rather have instructed him in swordplay than arithmetic. Alas.

Meanwhile, Eveline's studies were advancing at such a rapid pace that she would need a dedicated tutor soon. Although her mathematics had lagged at the beginning, the girl had set herself to studying in earnest. Red sensed that Eveline did not like to have any weaknesses. Unsurprising, given the vulnerability that had been forced upon her by loss after loss in her mere nine years.

Eveline was more than ready for instruction in ladylike arts such as dancing, forms of address, embroidery, and so on. While Red was certainly qualified to teach her such things, they bored her to tears. And were the opposite of what young Archie required.

How was she supposed to manage both?

Red laid her head back against the wingback chair's upholstery and closed her eyes. As she rubbed at her temples, she decided she had a newfound respect for her own mother. Lady McGovern had managed four daughters on her own, each with profoundly different interests. No, Red amended. Her sisters were all quite tractable, though their personalities varied. Red herself had been the only true nonconformist.

Her mother had managed it all without a governess, because there was no money for one. Meanwhile, Red had two children in her charge and was ready to scream. She'd happily return to stealing documents from unsuspecting socialites' libraries and battling villains in alleyways. Playing the governess was not for her.

Which brought her attention back to the library receipt.

Forcing her eyes open, she reached up to retrieve the neat little square of paper with its clearly etched details and numerals. Even with her tired eyes, it took her no more than a minute to deduce which code the Duchess of Guilford had used for the missive she'd slipped in with the order from the circulating library.

Red paused, closing her eyes again, trying to summon to mind the different memory trick she'd created for that particular code. While Jacquetta could see something once and recall it a year later, Red had to drill her mind into remembering the minute details of her work. Finally, she landed on it—the Honeybee Code, she'd christened it.

How appropriate.

Like a hive sending out individuals to do the work of central queen, this code worked with a singular word that then pointed to individual lines, words, and letters within the greater text.

It would have been faster to pull over one of the children's school notebooks and write out the decoded message. Slower but more thorough to go back into her own rooms, set her snares, and then do the work. Instead, Red did neither. She sat in the wingback chair, one eye on the little painted clock on the mantel, and decoded the message in her mind alone.

In the end, she went through it twice to make sure she had not made any mistakes. In the distance, through the door she'd left slightly ajar for just this purpose, she heard the high-pitched voices of the children spilling from the music room into the parlor. They would be upstairs in the nursery in a matter of moments.

But it was no matter. She'd gotten Miranda's message:

Little Notley. 17th October. Mind you come dressed for our favorite pastime.

CHAPTER TEN

"HERE YOU ARE, Miss Trudeau. I apologize for the delay. I had to see to the washing as well," the maid said, curtseying while also managing to hold the freshly pressed garment aloft.

Red waved her off. "Think nothing of it. I appreciate your help; you were in no way obligated."

It was true—a governess walked a fine, awkward line between family and servant. She was not entitled to a maid of her own, which suited Red's purposes just fine. But she also would have felt like an intruder entering the laundry.

"You've done a fine job of it," Red said, fingering the skirt, which even that morning had been a wrinkled mess.

"It was refreshing to have such delicate work again." The maid smiled, brushing off the compliment. "I was the lady's maid to Lady Caldwell, you see, before."

Red had suspected as much, but it was good to hear it confirmed. The woman had been employed at Oxley Park for several years, which made her a less likely conspirator in Legrand's plan—whatever it might be.

"You are very skilled," Red said, layering on another compliment. "Are there many of you on the staff who were displaced when things...changed?" She hesitated over that last word, though there was no hesitation in her mind.

The woman's smile softened. "No, not really. Most of the staff remained in their posts. Mrs. Yates, Mr. Cross. Mr. Ellis used to help in the gardens when Sir George was away, if you'll believe it. He grew up on a farm in Dereham and knows that much about growing things. But I was the only one to be reassigned. No need for a lady's maid when there is no lady, is there?"

The maid gazed longingly at the riding habit. Red knew it was too fine for a governess, but it was the only one she possessed. Miranda had not left her enough time to commission any new clothing before leaving London. If she needed, she would pass it off as the gift of a kind former employer. She didn't dare mention her family, even in general terms.

But as she watched the woman straightening the bows on the bodice, an idea occurred to her. She recognized the forlorn look upon the other woman's face—how often had she seen it upon Jacquetta before she was recruited as a lady knight?

"If you'd like, I'd appreciate your assistance whenever you have time to offer it. In particular with this." Red shook her head of unruly hair. "I can barely manage it on my own."

The maid's eyes brightened instantly. "I've a particular skill with hair! Lady Caldwell favored the most elegant, ornate arrangements."

Red huffed a laugh. "I do not have much need for ornate, but I'd be grateful for something a bit more elegant." In truth, she'd be grateful for the help. She could manage a very simple updo, but other than that, she'd spent her life spoiled by the maid she shared with her younger sisters. "Only when you can spare the time," she added.

"I shall find the time," the maid promised.

Sara, Red remembered. She ought to start thinking of the woman by her actual name. More than the help with her hair, Sara might prove a valuable source of information. Red had ingratiated herself with the staff as much as she could, but she did not partake in their shared mealtimes, so her ability to speak casually with them was limited. But with the loquacious Sara visiting her rooms frequently…

She'd have to revisit the system of snares. But it was a small cost. And as of yet, she'd found no evidence of anyone sneaking into her rooms. It appeared that Legrand, whoever he was, was not interested in a spinster governess.

All the better.

"If you have a moment," Red said with a sheepish smile, "perhaps you'd help me with that?" She nodded toward the garments hanging on the wardrobe.

"Of course!" Sara sprang into action with vigor. "Mrs. Yates often takes her tea after breakfast is served…"

Red smiled and listened attentively. Sara would be a valuable asset indeed.

THE CHILDREN WERE reading, begrudgingly.

Breakfast had been uneventful. Or, at least, as uneventful as anything was with his children. Eveline and Archie had joined him in the dining room instead of eating upstairs with Red, who was busy readying herself for her two-day journey.

Two days.

It was enough to curdle the milk in his stomach.

She'd made the request over supper three nights before. Word had come that her godmother had fallen, fracturing her arm. Red requested two days' leave to travel to the village where the elderly woman lived in order to see that she was suitably cared for and settled with all the accommodations she would need until she regained the use of her arm. It was all perfectly reasonable.

But George could not deny the burning that began in his stomach and climbed up his chest, searing the back of his throat, as Red spoke.

Would she come back? Was this an excuse to sneak away?

No, he reassured himself for the hundredth time. Ethelreda Trudeau had not backed away from a single challenge in the time he'd known her, including the one presented by his own intractable lust. She met everything head-on. Of course, she would employ the same tenacity when it came to caring for a loved one.

But the thoughts still nagged at him. Had he done this? Driven her away with his lustful looks? He'd kept his hands off her—at the cost of his sorely abused cock. But he would pleasure himself three times a day if it meant honoring her wishes. She was a goddamned virgin. Not to mention, the governess who had wrangled his intractable children into some semblance of order. Something he'd only managed to achieve with the use of cast-iron whistle left over from his infantry days.

George cringed. He'd actually attempted to use the thing on Red. Knowing her as he did now, he considered himself lucky she had not swiped the blasted thing from his hand and shoved it up his—

"Father, how much longer?"

George straightened at his desk. It took him a moment to locate the voice. Archie had eschewed all furniture and chosen to lie on the floor between the sofa and the bookcase. His dark eyes peeked over the top of his book, imploring even from across the study.

"We have only just started," Eveline cut in, her face entirely obscured by the novel she was reading. She'd sunk deep into the wingback chair, appearing as nothing more than two hands curled around a book and a mess of blue skirts.

"I want to go fishing." Archie sat up.

"You are reading a book about fishing," Eveline said.

"Reading is not fishing!" His book hit the floor with a smack.

"Fishing is not part of the schedule," Eveline bit back.

Archie shoved to his feet. "Miss Trudeau is away—"

"Not yet!"

"You don't even like her!"

"You do not know what you are talking about—"

"Children!"

But it was not George's voice that cut through their bickering. It was Red's.

She was standing in the door of the study, which none of them had heard her open, clad head to toe in honey-colored, fine wool, a matching silk hat pinned to her head at a jaunty angle. Complete with a feather, of all things. The front of the riding habit was decorated with large bows, fashioned out of the same wool as the rest of the ensemble. Simple, elegant, heightening her red-gold coloring. She was temptation personified. And she was about to depart.

But not before she put the children to rights.

Hell and damnation, how was he going to manage without her?

However, it was to him that her accusing gaze turned, rather than her charges.

"You have the schedule I prepared for you, correct?" she asked, one brow rising in line with her stylish hat.

"Of course. Nine o'clock, reading," he recited. "They have their books."

Red's gaze swept the room, landing on where Archie's book was discarded, facedown, on the floor. He watched her mouth tighten, but the corner twitched. As if she was holding in a laugh.

Hell.

"Very good," she said, even though the entire situation was anything but good. "I shall leave you to it, then. Cross has informed me my mount is waiting."

"Wait."

Red's face softened instantly—slackened, more like—with surprise. Eveline's eyes appeared over the top of her book.

George flattened his hands on his desk to keep them out of his hair. "Mrs. Shelley has prepared you a hamper of food for the journey," he explained. "She requests that you stop in the kitchen to collect it."

Red blinked, and for a fraction of a second, George thought he saw disappointment. What—and why—that meant…he could not begin to parse. Or would not allow himself to.

"Thank you," Red said, inclining her head.

Then she swept her gaze away from him, looking to each of the children in turn. "Mind your schedule. I shall know if you do not."

Eveline disappeared again behind her novel. Archie huffed an indignant sigh, but dropped obediently back to the floor behind the sofa. The smile on Red's lips then, purely for the children, rocked George more than any she'd ever given him.

In the next breath, she was gone. George found himself thinking that perhaps it was a good thing, fortuitous, even. Because the longer that Ethelreda Trudeau spent in his household, the more he realized he did not want to ever picture it without her.

SHE HAD NOT said goodbye to George. Not really.

All the way to the back of the house, into the servants' stairwell and down to the kitchens, her heart screamed for her to turn around. It demanded she go back to the study, his study, and tell him…

Tell him what?

That she saw the longing glances he tried so diligently to hide? That they lit a fire within her that she'd not managed to douse? That, for the first time in her life, in the quiet and dark of her bedchamber, her hand had wandered between her legs? Or that it was his face, his broad shoulders and muscled arms, which she pictured as she touched herself?

For the first time, she understood what it was to want a man.

And it was damnably inconvenient.

Her quest was quite clear: unmask Legrand's identity, determine if he had any co-conspirators, and deduce why he was at

Oxley Park at all.

She knew her fellow lady knights wielded seduction to their advantage. At least, Jacquetta and Dominique did. Red almost laughed at the notion of Jane doing such a thing. No, Jane's quiet wallflower status allowed her to subvert the *ton* in other ways. But none of Red's colleagues would think ill of her if her quest required her taking the master of Oxley Park to her bed.

Except that Red could not imagine how doing so would help her with any of her three tasks. Though maybe, just maybe, if she actually bedded George, she'd be able to focus on something other than the burning heat at the center of her body.

Maybe.

That thought carried her into the kitchen, where Mrs. Shelley and the kitchen maid, Louise, were bent over the crust for the evening's steak and ale pie. The apple tarts for afternoon tea were already in the oven, filling the bustling room with cinnamon and warmth.

"Are any of those for my hamper?" Red asked, letting her appreciation show upon her face. That earned her a wide smile from Mrs. Shelley, even as the rotund woman clucked her tongue.

"You've yesterday's cherry turnovers, I'm afraid," the cook said. "If you can hold a moment, you'll have some of this morning's bread with your cheese."

Red grinned. "I'd wait all morning for your bread," she said.

Louisa rolled her eyes, earning an elbow from Mrs. Shelley, and the two women bent back to their work. The sound of footsteps heralded the arrival of the footmen, laden with empty platters from clearing away the breakfast.

"How many times have I told you lot, straight to the scullery with those," Mrs. Shelley bellowed, though she was all bark. One of the footmen was her nephew, and she made a show of being harsh on all of them to avoid the charge of favoritism.

"We smelled the—" the youngest footman, Gerald, began.

"Wash those dishes and I'll see what bits I've got for you,"

Mrs. Shelley declared.

The two lads exchanged a glance; Cross would expect them upstairs soon. But Rooney, Mrs. Shelley's nephew, slid his gaze in Louisa's direction.

Interesting, Red noted as she moved toward the other side of the kitchen. She'd have to ask Sara about those two when she returned from her meeting with the duchess. But keen as she was to appear uninterested, Red turned and let the scene play out without her intervention.

She drifted to the corner counter, where several bottles stood. Vinegars, shrubs, other concoctions that Mrs. Shelley had purchased or prepared. Even corked, some of them were fragrant enough that their scents wafted past on the breeze from the open window.

Red willed herself to melt into the wall, to disappear into the scents and sounds of the kitchen. She even turned her back on the others, toying with the bottles, the better to help them forget she was there. So they would speak freely, so she could listen. Every little morsel of information was tucked away into her growing index of the residents of Oxley Park.

She uncorked one bottle, lifting it to her nose. Rose water. So delicate, it was used only in specialty puddings. The next, cider vinegar, sharp and tangy, perfect for dressing vegetables. The third—

Her hand stilled. Her entire body went rigid in the space of one sniff.

Malt vinegar. It was meant to be malt vinegar.

But that was not all she smelled.

Dropwort—poison.

Red forced herself to relax, her hips to sway from side to side casually. She began to hum the tune Eveline had been practicing on the pianoforte the evening before. All of it was an attempt to appear normal and undisturbed as she lifted the bottle surreptitiously to her nose once again.

The second whiff was enough to confirm. She wanted to dash

the thing into the fireplace. But she could not. The scent was subtle, well disguised. Only someone familiar with the scent, trained to detect poisons, would have noticed it. Someone like Red.

Legrand had access to the kitchen.

Red did not turn, but she silently catalogued who was already in the room, even as she corked the deadly bottle and set it aside, as she had the previous two. *Louisa, Mrs. Shelley, Rooney, Gerald.*

But there were so many more who passed through this homey space. Any of the servants, really, could have switched the bottle or added the poison. It could even have been the person who orchestrated the purchase of the vinegar, if it was not one that Mrs. Shelley made herself.

Red lifted another bottle, this one a shrub with hints of lavender and plum. Her eyes drifted closed, as if she were appreciating the scent, finding it intoxicating in its loveliness. She swayed her hips again, lowered the bottle to the countertop, eyes still closed—

"Heavens! Oh, Mrs. Shelley, I beg your pardon!" Red cried as the bottle of syllabub knocked into the poison, sending both crashing to the floor.

She'd had to exert more force than normal, to ensure both bottles shattered beyond use—and hope that if the culprit was in the room with her, they did not catch on.

"Waiting for my bread and destroying my kitchen," Mrs. Shelley grumbled, but she only sighed when she lifted her eyes from the mess on the floor to Red. She pushed off the table where she'd been working, wiping her hands on her apron.

"I apologize. I am so clumsy." Red let her cheeks pinken, pinching herself hard in the thigh to draw wetness to her eyes.

"Think nothing of it, dear. It's just a bit of spilled vinegar," Mrs. Shelley replied. She retrieved a small hamper from the shelf, shoving two bread rolls inside before snapping the lid closed. "Louisa will see to it."

The kitchen maid's eyes flared, and she darted a look at

Rooney. But the footmen were stacking the last of the platters, and her sweetheart avoided her eyes. Louisa sighed with resignation and reached for a mop.

Looking duly apologetic, Red accepted the hamper. "Thank you," she said. "I shall see if I can find some grouse or pheasant to bring back, to make it up to you."

Louisa grumbled under her breath at that, but both women ignored her.

"Off you go, Miss Trudeau. Mind you don't injure yourself on the road with that clumsiness." With a pat of her arm, Mrs. Shelley dismissed her.

Red walked silently out the rear kitchen door, deciding to loop around Oxley Hall than walk through it. She could not relax her features, not yet, but the fresh air might help her think.

She'd destroyed the poison, for now. But it confirmed that the danger at Oxley Park was directed at a person, rather than an object. But who? The vinegar might have been used in any number of dishes for the staff or the Caldwell family—even for herself.

As she mounted her horse, Red was already calculating how she would obtain the menus for the household. The children's would be simple enough, as she was ostensibly in charge of it anyway. The one prepared for George... She might have to steal it. As for the servants...

She could leave them to their own devices. But no one was going to die on her watch at Oxley Park. Unless she was the one to kill them.

CHAPTER ELEVEN

THE VILLAGE WAS as quaint and quintessentially English as Red remembered, though now thoroughly in the throes of autumn rather than the final golden days of summer. She had to wonder at the Duchess of Guilford's selection of a meeting place. Yes, it was familiar to her, which was an advantage. But she was likely to be recognized, as well. The more people who saw her and asked how she fared, the more lies she would have to spin.

More lies meant more traps to fall into later.

Red avoided riding directly though the center of the village, opting instead for the outskirts, even though it meant it took her longer to arrive at the inn. Not the same inn she'd stayed at in the months leading up to her arrival at Oxley Park. That one had been situated in the center of town for maximum visibility.

The establishment she made for now was quieter. Less risk of being noticed, Red supposed. While she'd been installed here over the summer, Red had provided the duchess with a list of possible meeting points, each with a code word.

Miranda's instruction to "dress for our favorite pastime" was a reference to this specific inn, which adjoined a small stable that had horses to rent.

Sighing, Red stopped at a tavern on the opposite side of the village, tied her horse to the hitching post, and flicked the young lad on the doorstep a ha'penny to keep watch over the gelding.

Then she continued the rest of the way on foot.

At least it wasn't so damned hot, Red thought as she walked down the dirt road. Though with all the layers of wool, she was sweating between her breasts and under her arms already. Thankfully, she'd donned breeches beneath her habit—half for warmth, half for comfort.

She was half a block away from the inn when she spotted Miranda.

"How lovely to see you again, Miss Trudeau!" The dark-haired duchess swooped down upon her, brushing each cheek with her own. Red returned the gesture, but only smiled until she knew what part Miranda was playing. Surely she had not come to Little Notley as the Duchess of Guilford. "Sir Edward is gone to London again, and I've missed your company so dearly," Miranda said warmly, squeezing her hand.

Miranda was meant to be the wife of a knight, then.

"My lady, you are too kind. It is I who am blessed by your kind mentorship." Red tried to look reverent, which was not too difficult. Despite years spent working together within the Lady Knights, she always felt a touch of awe when she was in the duchess's company.

"Come," Miranda said. She looped their arms together casually. "Let's have a spot of tea and go out for a ride. The weather is lovely today."

That, at least, was true. The sun was shining even though the air was crisp, a rare sight in the gray English autumn. They walked arm in arm the rest of the way to the inn, then Red followed Miranda inside.

For an hour or so, they lingered over tea talking about everything and nothing. Red didn't try to ferret out any information. This part of the meeting was all for show, to establish background in case anyone questioned their presence in Little Notley. Luckily, Red did not recognize any of the villagers. The duchess had been astute in choosing this meeting location.

When the pot of tea was empty, the duchess inclined her

head. Red understood immediately, and together they went out and rented horses from the stable. Only when they were a half-mile away, trotting in the countryside and far from anyone else, did Miranda turn to her with purpose in her eyes.

"What have you found so far?" she asked, slowing her horse to a walk.

Red did the same with a gentle tug on the reins. "Whatever happened at Waterloo, it haunts Sir George horribly. He has night terrors—violent ones."

"That is not unusual. Many soldiers suffer so. What else?" Even as she spoke, Miranda was scanning around them, searching for anything out of place, anyone who might be hiding or trying to listen to their conversation.

Red admired her dedication, but she still bristled at the implication. "I discovered poison in the kitchen."

Miranda did not speak, merely arched her dark brows as an invitation to continue.

"It smelled of acrid celery. I am certain it was dropwort, disguised with the vinegar."

"Could you still smell the vinegar?" Miranda asked, eyes relaxing a bit.

"Yes."

"Then it would have sickened, rather than killed. A small consolation, I suppose. Whoever poisoned the vinegar either did not know the quantity needed for the dropwort to be lethal, or they meant to incapacitate the recipient rather than kill them outright," Miranda explained.

"A small consolation," Red echoed, her own mind working. "I do not know for certain whom the poison was intended for, though I cannot imagine the children being targets. So, perhaps Sir George himself."

"Perhaps." Miranda nodded. Red could see the calculation happening in her sharp mind. "Or for someone employed at Oxley Park. We do not know for certain that Legrand's presence is related to Sir George himself."

"None of the other men working in the house served on the Continent. I have already verified as much," Red said.

Miranda nodded for what seemed the hundredth time, but did not offer a further opinion. They rode on for a few minutes in silence. Red opened her mouth several times, shutting it again, debating whether she should mention her other suspicion.

Her companion solved that internal conflict for her.

"There is something else?"

Red sighed, looking out over the barren field to her left. "I do not know if it is relevant," she said. She was loath to speak about it; somehow, it felt like a betrayal. But this was her profession, and even the smallest bit of information could prove crucial. "There may be something with Sir George's late wife," she admitted. "As I said, it may not factor in at all. But no one speaks of her, not even the children."

Miranda tilted her head to the side, and the streaks of silver at the temples caught the late-afternoon sun. "There was no scandal, at least not a public one," she mused. "Continue looking into it. Even if it is not essential to the matter at hand, it may give you a better sense of Sir George, which is useful."

"Of course," Red agreed.

She knew that even as she maintained her post at Oxley Park, the duchess was in London conducting her own private investigations. Just what they entailed, Red did not know. But she knew Miranda had contacts everywhere, from Queen Charlotte's privy chambers at Buckingham House to the dungeons of Newgate and everywhere in between.

They reached a crossroads a few minutes later. Miranda steered her mount in back around in the direction they'd come, indicating that they should start back toward the village. Red followed, as always.

When they were a quarter of a mile out, the duchess spoke again. Red's hands tightened on the reins. It was a strategic choice, so that Red would not have time to argue before they were back among the villagers.

"I have no new information for you," Miranda said. "I doubt you will hear from me again. There is not much I can do to assist you until you find out more. You know how to get a letter to me if you need, and how to code it." Statements, not questions. "My only warning is this—make haste, Ethelreda. The longer you lie in wait, the stronger Legrand's position becomes. He did not become one of France's most notorious assassins by taking care for others' lives."

With those harsh words ringing in her ears, Red slipped back into the village and into her assumed identity.

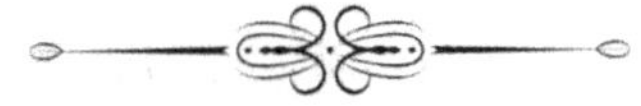

CHAPTER TWELVE

B Y NOON ON the second day, Red's schedule was in shambles and George was several pages behind on his treatise. Somewhere between the mating behaviors and the foraging strategies, he'd become embroiled in an argument about which algorithm for addition was the most efficient. The answer to which did not matter to him one jot, so long as Archie could do the computation. Eveline, however, was of a different mind.

After that, there had been the row over how to spend their afternoon exercise period. Which, he was shocked to learn, comprised most of the afternoon. What was Miss Trudeau teaching them out here?

In answer to their arguments about riding or fishing, he'd decreed an extra hour of reading. He hoped that in the silence, he might be able to make up some of the work he'd lost over the last thirty-six hours.

The hour lasted only twenty-three minutes.

As a last resort, he'd decreed they would take their afternoon tea in the summer house. Archie could play in the bushes, pretending to hunt lions and tigers to his heart's content. Eveline could read her novel—an entirely different one than he'd seen in her hands yesterday—and George could have some blasted peace in which to work.

It worked, mostly.

The children were occupied, but George once again found himself struggling to focus. Instead, he caught himself watching Archie as the boy prowled through the long grass. His hair caught the sun, shimmering with gold highlights that George had never noticed before. He'd always thought of his son's hair as dark. But all the time spent out of doors with Red had lightened it, bringing out the amber and mahogany. Archie was more like him that he'd ever realized.

If Archie was himself in miniature, then Eveline...

George forced himself to consider his daughter, sprawled across the wicker sofa, completely absorbed by her book. She was her mother in miniature.

She already possessed long, willowy limbs. Now, they made her look slightly out of proportion, but George knew that in a few years, when her height caught up, she'd have the same build as his late wife. The dark hair, fine and silky, was her mother's as well, along with the oval shape of her face and thick, unnaturally dark lashes. She was beautiful child, would grow into a beautiful woman.

But just looking at her caused his heart to ache.

For the first time, George wondered what Eveline saw in his eyes when he looked upon her. So often, he'd seen the pain and accusation in hers. Did she see his hurt, his anger? Did she think... Oh, Lord above, did innocent Eveline think they were directed at her?

"Father?"

He blinked, realizing that though he'd been lost in his own thoughts, he was staring at Eveline intensely. Clearing his throat, he shifted the writing pad in his lap and shook out his shoulders, attempting casualness.

"Are you unwell?" Eveline continued, brow wrinkling. She sat up, folding her book closed. Her eyes were sharp, calculating.

She was trying to discern if he was about to have another episode, George realized.

He forced his mouth to soften, opened his mouth to speak,

and was spared by the arrival of one of the footmen—Rooney, he thought—with a hamper of food.

"Tea, I believe. Fetch your brother," George said.

Eveline's eyes remained wary, but she stood to do as he asked. Archie came scampering in a few seconds later, eyes gleaming and practically licking his lips.

"Sit properly," George instructed them, mostly Archie.

The boy looked mutinous, but he took up a seat across from Eveline and waited impatiently, foot tapping incessantly, while Rooney unloaded the spread of food onto the glass-topped wicker table. When the last parcel was unwrapped, he turned his wide eyes up to George, all childlike, adorable imploring fully employed.

"Go on, then—"

"Have I arrived in time for tea?"

Warmth rushed through him, even as Archie squealed. Not with excitement to see his governess, mind. The lad actually fell back on the wicker chair in disappointment, causing the whole chair to tilt back precariously.

Red caught it with her hand and snapped it down smartly. Her smile widened as she tousled Archie's hair. "Oh, go on," she said. "I cannot have you expiring from hunger."

The little boy needed no further encouragement. And he was lucky both his father and his governess were too busy looking at one another to reprimand him for the way he dove into his quiche, fingers first.

"Welcome back," George said, trying to regulate his wildly ticking pulse with concentrated, measured breaths.

Red's smile was wide and so genuine, he lost count of those breaths.

"I am so happy to find you all looking so well," she said, her voice a little breathless.

Was that...concern in her eyes? But then she looked away from him, lowering herself gracefully onto the sofa beside Eveline.

"I see you are onto your next selection," Red said to Eveline, nodding approvingly to the book resting at the girl's hip. "Have you found our list satisfactory thus far?"

"Yes." Eveline took a dainty bite of scone to avoid further conversation.

Red did not push her, instead turning back to George as she poured tea for each of them. "Eveline and I collaborated on a list of appropriate novels that suit her interests and will ensure her a wide range of exposure to various authors," she explained.

"I see." Ought he to ask to peruse it? He didn't read novels; he probably wouldn't recognize most of them.

"I do wonder, Sir George." Red paused as she lifted her teacup to her full pink lips. "Where on my schedule did it specify tea in the summer house?"

George opened his mouth to remind her that he was the children's father. Or perhaps to explain that after two days he was willing to do anything to keep the children from squabbling. Or merely to tell her to bugger off.

But then he saw the twitch at the corner of her lips. Damn if he didn't want to kiss it right off her lovely, freckled face.

"This is the afternoon exercise portion of the day," he said.

Red's tongue darted over her lower lip, catching an errant droplet of cream-laden tea. "Yes, I do find reading and writing to be quite physical exertions." She tilted her head meaningfully to his discarded tablet of paper.

"Exercises of the mind, naturally," he retorted.

"And you are outdoors," she mused. "So really, you are following my edicts. Is that what you mean to imply?"

"Indeed."

Of course, he could think of other ways he'd like to exert himself with her. All of them physical. Though verbal sparring was also enjoyable. But that smirk on her face… George shifted uncomfortably, rearranging himself to avoid embarrassment.

"I am finished!" Archie declared, surging to his feet.

"The rest of us are not," Eveline said, sass imbuing every

syllable. Red's hand landed on the girl's knee, applying a steady, firm pressure.

"You may be excused this one time, young Master Caldwell. But it will not be habitual," Red decreed.

Archie set off at a trot, and George braced himself, waiting for Eveline's rejoinder. But none came. Red lifted her hand from the girl's knee and refilled her cup of tea, adding a dash of sugar, the way Eveline liked, before handing it to her. No words passed between them, but the communication was there. Silent, respectful. George was utterly bowled over.

"Have there been any excitements while I've been away?" Red asked over a scone with fresh lemon curd.

"No," George said immediately. He did not consider the rows he'd defused every hour to be exciting. Red was used to those by now. "They've attended to their studies, as you directed." That, at least, he'd accomplished.

"Excellent. I shall look over their workbooks this evening after supper," she said. "Now, Eveline—"

The scream that rent the air sliced right through every wall of protection George had built around himself, straight to his heart.

Archie.

He sprinted from the summer house, knowing he'd sent the dishes crashing, not slowing a bit at the realization. He had to get to his son. Red was right behind him—he could hear her calling Archie's name. Her hand on his shoulder steered him off the path, and together they crashed through the tall grass to the edge of the small pond formed by the autumn rains.

"Archie, what happened?" Eveline cried. George had not realized she was with them.

The boy's leg was running with blood, the gash down his calf long as a dinner knife.

George's heart stopped. His world stopped. Everything narrowed to the blood. It was pulsing, flowing so quickly, running out of Archie fast. Too fast. Death. He would bleed out then and there. George reached for him—

Except he could not move. He was paralyzed. His legs were heavy as marble, sinking into the ground, making it impossible for him to take a single step. He opened his mouth—not to call for help, no, all help should go to Archie—but to demand they care for Archie, to tell them to leave him behind, to suffer, if only to save his son.

Then he saw Red. She pushed past him, her red curls spinning in the wind she created all by herself, so fast was she moving. She dropped to the ground in the mud, tugging the child's leg to her. Behind her wide body, George could see nothing.

George. George. Colonel.

She was yelling his name. But it was nothing more than a distant echo. His ears weren't working properly either. But the pale circle of her face was fixed on him. Two heartbeats. Too long.

Then she swung back to Archie.

Eveline rushed past him, tears rolling down her cheeks. She returned what might have been minutes or hours later. George had no sense. He was trapped in his own body, his own mind holding him hostage from acting or thinking. All he could do was watch, helpless.

Still, he struggled against it. He tried and tried and tried to lift his feet, to yell and scream, to go to his son. But he could not.

Then Red was surging to her feet, Archie cradled in her arms.

By some miracle, the lad's eyes were open. His cheeks were stained with tears, but no new droplets fell. His leg... It was wrapped in white, tightly bound, no blood to be seen.

George expected Red to walk past him, to leave him to his misery. He wanted her to.

But instead, she motioned someone forward with a jerk of her chin. Rooney appeared. With absurd gentleness, she transferred Archie into his arms. George watched her mouth move, issuing instructions. Then Archie was gone, and Eveline disappeared as well. Until there was nothing left but George, Red, and the gaping hole in his soul.

She stepped in front of him and grabbed his hands.

He did not feel it—only realized she'd done it because she held them out in front of her, between them. She moved slowly, eyes wary, until gripping his forearms tightly. Tight to the point of pain.

He felt it.

He felt her nails digging through the thin fabric of his shirt, the light wool tailcoat. Her fingertips could not possibly be that strong, and yet he knew that tonight he would have bruises where each of her fingers held him tightly.

But it was bringing him back. Slowly, so slowly, he could feel each point of pain where she held his arms. Next were the sounds. Birds had begun chirping again, and the wind rustled the dried grasses. On the other side of the seasonal pond, a duck quacked defensively in their direction.

Red watched him closely, her eyes boring into his as if she could see each of his senses clicking back into use. Whether it was a blink of his eye or a tic in his cheek, somehow she knew he was ready to hear her.

"It is a minor injury," Red said, her voice perfectly calm. "Archie is fine. I've cleaned the wound, wrapped it, and Rooney is carrying him back to the house." George blinked. Red repeated herself, tightening her grip in emphasis. "Archie is fine. I've cleaned the wound, wrapped it, and Rooney is carrying him back to the house. Archie is fine. I've cleaned the wound, wrapped it, and Rooney is carrying in back to the house…"

Again and again, exactly the same, she repeated the words. Until they started to have meaning.

"Archie is fine," he echoed hoarsely, hardly recognizing his own voice.

Red eased the pressure on his arms, but did not release them.

"Archie is fine," she confirmed again. "The gash is not deep. I cleaned it with the tea. Not ideal, but better than filthy pond water. I dressed the wound in honey and bound it with some fabric from my chemise. They will call for a doctor to see if it needs to be stitched, but I doubt they will need to do much."

"Why didn't you go with them?" He was afraid to hear the answer, but he couldn't keep in the question.

"You needed me more," she said. "Can you walk?"

It ought to have been a stupid question of a grown man, an experienced soldier. But George found he did not know the answer. He had not moved an inch, even as his senses returned to him. He lifted his leg experimentally. It was heavy, but it obeyed.

Red took his arm without asking, using her considerable muscle to keep him upright. George thought he could have managed on his own, but he did not push her away. The steel within her was more comforting than he'd ever admit.

She silently guided him back to the summer house. The remnants of their tea were half scattered across the table, the other half on the stone floor. Red ignored it, hooking her foot under one of the wicker chairs and dragging it toward the open doors, near the brisk autumn air. With her customary efficiency, she lowered him onto it.

"Would you like tea?"

"Tea?" It seemed ridiculous.

"I have a bit of brandy in my saddlebag, but I don't know that it would help you just now."

Saddlebag. Yes, of course, she'd ridden in, arriving just as they sat down to tea. There was her horse—his horse, borrowed from the stable at Oxley Park—tethered over by the split in the path.

"Nothing," he said, his gravelly voice belying his statement.

But Red did not argue, and she did not seek out anything for herself. She merely sat with him, gazing out at the scenic tableau of hills and greenery that the summer house was so particularly positioned to take advantage of.

Her hand still held his, he realized. Or rather, she must have taken it up again when she returned from setting up the chairs. But now, all the command and force were gone. She held it gently but firmly, curled around his palm. He could feel her pulse under his fingers.

Steady. *Thump-thump. Thump-thump. Thump-thump.*

Gradually, his own slowed to match it. He wondered if that had been her intent.

Only when he'd felt the steady rhythm of his own pulse for several minutes did he speak. "Thank you."

Red did not meet his eyes, continuing to stare outward. But she did not pull back her hand. "It is all part of my position."

The way she said it, the resignation in her voice… He wanted to ask if there was more to that statement. But the energy to question her, when she did not want to answer… He did not have it.

"It is *my* responsibility," he said acidly instead. "To keep my children safe. It is the most basic of charges as a parent. He was bleeding, crying in pain, and all I could do was stare."

Red said nothing, but he watched her jaw work as she chewed over her next words. He waited for them, waiting for her to pronounce judgment. Because with Red, he knew there would be no mincing of words. She was forged of iron and steel.

"How often do the episodes happen?" she asked, her voice soft.

His stomach clenched. "Too often."

She did not have to turn to level him an exasperated look.

"At first, it was every now and then. I could count the weeks between them. Since I returned to Oxley Park… Every few days, if I am lucky." The truth of it hurt.

He was so much more damaged than he'd been willing to admit, even to himself. He'd always told himself that in a moment of need, his military training would win out. But it had not. He'd failed his children, the two people in the world who truly needed him.

"You have not sought help." A statement, rather than a question.

He laughed, sharp and hollow. Humorless. "What help is there? I have no physical injury. It is all in my mind."

"But you did have a physical injury, didn't you?" she asked.

His throat constricted. "Yes."

"Your leg?"

"Yes," he choked out. How could she know such a thing? Unless she was not what she seemed—

"You were unable to walk, to move your legs, when you saw Archie injured," she explained, her voice low enough to almost be lost on the wind. "Often, it seems that we reenact our worst moments."

George pressed his eyes closed, then widened them again forcefully, willing the sunlight to keep the darkness at bay.

"It was a complicated fracture, bone protruding. I could not move, could not get—" He literally choked then, on the bile rising in his throat, and a fit of coughing stole his words.

"You could not get to your men," she finished. "Just as you could not get to Archie."

"Yes."

He forced himself to look at the grass swaying in the wind, the birds that chased each other across the sky. But his pulse was hammering again, his chest constricting.

Suddenly, Red was on her knees in front of him. She pressed his knees apart, nestling herself between them, her hands on the tops of his thighs. She grasped his hands, holding them tightly as she met his gaze and held it.

At any other moment, he would have been hard with need at the sight of her kneeling between his legs. But for once, in Red's presence, his want was far from his mind. He had no room for anything but misery.

"Listen to me," she said, that command in her voice once again. "Listen to my words."

His chin dropped an inch, all the affirmation he could manage. It was enough for Red.

"Close your eyes," she instructed him.

"I can't."

"Yes, you can."

"I will see—"

"No. You will only see what I tell you to see. Now close your eyes, colonel."

The use of his military rank was grating but effective nonetheless. George closed his eyes. Before the images of gore and blood could come swirling back, Red took command.

"Imagine a door. Any door you like. The door to your study, the door to your dressing room. Do you have it?"

This was ridiculous. He opened his mouth to tell her so. Instead, he said, "The door to your rooms. With the Tudor roses."

Her hands tightened on his, but she didn't comment on his selection. It was the first one that had come to his mind, and like the fool he was, he'd said it aloud. But in this moment, it felt as if there was no room for anything but honesty between them.

"Start at the bottom left corner and draw a line along the bottom of the door. When you reach the bottom right corner, inhale." She drew her breath in loudly in demonstration. "Inhale as you trace that line in your mind up to the top of the door."

It was still ridiculous, but he did it.

"Hold that breath inside of you, let it sink into your fingers and toes, into your bones, as you draw that line across the top of the door."

He could feel the warmth of her breath on his hands as she spoke. But he did as she said, envisioning the intricately carved door in his mind.

"Now as you draw the line downward back to where you started, exhale. Keep it long—do not stop releasing your breath until you reach the bottom of the door."

His attention was wholly on his breath and the door, the white line he was tracing around the edge of it in the privacy of his mind. When he arrived at the bottom, his eyes still closed, his heart was beating slower.

Hell and damnation, she was brilliant.

"Again."

They repeated the exercise several more times, until Red

finally released his hands and rocked back on her heels.

George opened his eyes, finding her watching him, waiting.

"Where did you learn to do that?" For the first time since Archie's scream had ripped into his heart, his voice sounded halfway normal.

Red's smile was grim. "You are not the only soldier whose scars tend toward the mental, rather than physical. I have spent some time at the Royal Hospital in London."

"Thank you," he said. It seemed so small and insufficient, for what she'd done for him and for Archie.

"I have a few more exercises you can practice, to help calm yourself when you feel an episode coming on. Unfortunately, I don't have an answer for the nightmares," she said.

She braced her hands on her thighs, moving to stand. But George caught her hands instead, using his own weight to lift her up. Instead of letting her walk away, he guided her hip to his lap. Her eyes widened, but she did not protest as he gently urged her to sit on his knee. He brought her hands to his chest, above his heart, and held them as tightly as he dared without hurting her.

"Thank you, Red. For all of it," he whispered. His voice was hoarse once again.

Red's teeth worried at her lower lip, and the blue of her eyes gleamed. It might have been the sunlight slipping between the gathering clouds, or it might have been emotion. He told himself it was the latter as he leaned forward and brushed his lips against hers gently.

A thank you, without expectation or demand.

He drew back, only a hairsbreadth, to let the air between them, to let her know that he would not ask for more than she could give. That all the choices were hers. He expected her to pull away, because of the two of them, she was infinitely more likely to be possessed of control and good sense. The last hour had proven that definitively.

But she did not pull away. She shifted in his lap, spreading her palms across his chest to balance herself before she kissed him back.

It was equally soft, just as gentle. She moved her lower lip over his, testing the friction. If it had not been for her hands on his chest, moving up his shoulders, George would have thought himself still lost in his imagination. But then she murmured his name against his lips.

"George," she breathed.

That was when he realized that she wanted him as badly as he did her.

Not now; now the touches were gentle, exploratory. Her tongue grazed his upper lip, then darted away. She increased the pressure, but still there was none of the heated demand of their prior embraces. This moment was all tenderness, her baring herself in her sexual innocence to him in the same way he'd exposed his broken soul.

It felt like salvation, to have her in his lap, warm curves pressed against him. Kissing him, adoring him, even after what he would count as one of the lowest moments of his life.

He did not deserve her. But nor could he take his hands away as they sat there in the fading sunlight of autumn, letting tenderness carry them away for a few minutes more.

CHAPTER THIRTEEN

"I DO NOT like bees," Eveline said vehemently.

"You have voiced that opinion several times," Red said. "It is noted. And yet we shall continue on."

Eveline cut her a stare that told her exactly what she thought of that edict. For a moment, Red thought the girl would plant her feet and refuse to move. The bridge across Oxley Creek was as good a place as any to make her stand. But by some small miracle, her kid-booted feet kept moving.

"You like honey," Archie pointed out unhelpfully, pausing in his skipping.

Red gave his shoulder a hearty shove. For a child who'd injured his leg only days before, he was in enterprising spirits. Red had heard that children healed quickly, but if she had not seen it for herself, she would not have believed it.

She had only seen George at suppertimes since the sweet, sun-kissed moments they'd spent together in the summer house. Settling the children back into their daily routine after her short absence had been more difficult than she imagined—and reminded her that her management of them was nominal at best, despite how she might congratulate herself.

In addition to her morning jaunts to the summer house to maintain her form, she was also now making daily sweeps of the kitchens. So far, no more poison had appeared. She comforted herself with Miranda's assurances that the poison would have sickened first, before turning deadly. As such, Red watched all members of the Caldwell family closely for any sign of ill health.

None appeared. Archie was skipping toward the apiaries with unbridled joy. Eveline... Well, joy was not the word. But compliance, albeit begrudging, was enough for now.

They passed the summer house. Archie wanted to go investigate whether any of his blood was left on the ground. Red was tempted to tie him at her side with a leash. But by God's grace, they made it to the apiaries without injury.

Where they found Sir George Caldwell, scarred war hero, singing to his bees.

"Abroad as I was walking, down by some greenwood side, I heard a young girl singing..."

Even the children were silent, a true feat of improbability. It felt incredibly personal. He'd never attended one of the children's music lessons, never asked Eveline to play the pianoforte in the evenings after supper. But it was clear from the practiced tones of his voice that he possessed either natural skill or had some formal training. Or a combination of both.

The more time she spent at Oxley Park, the more layers Red discovered to the man who'd started their acquaintance by trying to train her with a whistle. She'd been trained to make solid, accurate first judgments. But with George Caldwell, she could not have been more wrong. It was disconcerting in more ways than one.

She felt a gentle tug on her arm. Glancing down, she saw that Archie had come to stand beside her, winding his arm around hers. He looked up at her with a question in his eyes. Red noted his little foot tapping in the dirt with barely contained impatience.

A smile tugged at the corners of her mouth. The little boy was duly impressed—but he was still a little boy. She squeezed his shoulder, urging him to stay quiet a few moments longer.

She waited until George took a long breath between choruses, then cleared her throat loudly.

He straightened abruptly, though he kept hold of the cover to the skep he'd been replacing. He wore a wide-brimmed hat that Red suspected was meant for a lady. It was certainly effective at shielding him from the filtered sunlight. Red bit her lip to keep in the saucy comment that rose to her lips.

"Miss Trudeau, children." George dipped his chin, brow furrowing under the brim of his bonnet. "You have never strayed this way during your afternoon exercises."

"With good reason," Eveline grumbled from half a step behind Red's shoulder.

Already, there were several bees who'd come to investigate their presence. One buzzed near Red's ear; another seemed to be doing laps around her head. Or worse, it was truly multiple bees flying haphazardly. Lord, they probably liked the color of her hair. Red did not cringe. At least not externally.

There were dozens of bees buzzing around George. They landed on his shoulder and sleeves, even a few on the side of his neck. He didn't seem bothered at all. She'd respected him before? The man was damn near fearless.

"The children would like to share with you about their recent studies," Red said, eyes boring into George, trying to make him look at her.

The furrow in his brow deepened as he glanced from once child to another. They were both too occupied eyeing the bees buzzing around them to note their father's attention.

Red cleared her throat again, finally succeeding in getting his eyes back to meet hers. "They have worked hard the past week to prepare," she said forcefully. *Give them your due consideration or I will flay you alive.*

She tried to communicate without words, moving her eyes meaningfully from George back to the two children. He blinked, setting the lid of the hive back in place.

Red decided to urge him along. "Perhaps we ought to step to the side"—she nodded to a tree at the edge of the meadow—"so that the children do not disturb the bees." It had nothing to do with her own trepidation about lingering near.

George nodded. "Of course," he said, motioning them ahead.

She caught the children by the shoulders and gave them each a gentle nudge forward. Red half expected Eveline to dig in her heels, but the girl moved. Though she did skirt around to Red's far side, putting as much distance between herself and the hives as possible. Archie seemed to be warming to the little insects considerably better. He'd already named the one perched on his lapel.

"What sort of bee is Montgomery, father?" Archie asked, tickling the bee's fuzzy behind with the tip of his finger.

"Montgomery?" George's voice floated from behind them.

"Yes, my bee."

Eveline stiffened instantly. "He is not coming into the nursery," she declared.

Red massaged her shoulder gently, suppressing the laughter in her own voice. "Of course not, Miss Caldwell."

"But he is my friend!" Archie protested.

"Archie—" Red and George said in unison.

Red glanced away, trying to hide the flush of heat and cursing herself. She was supposed to be finding a dangerous French assassin, not falling in lust with the lord of Oxley Park. Besides, she still had not cleared him from all suspicion. But her flaming cheeks seemed to care for none of those reasonable thoughts.

"The bees belong with their hives," George said, placing a firm but gentle hand on Archie's shoulder. The motion sent Montgomery buzzing away and Archie mewling in disappointment.

Red sucked in a breath, ready to soothe and comfort. It still did not come easily to her; she doubted it ever would. At least now she knew the children well enough to anticipate when it was required. But before she could intervene, George kneeled at the side of the meadow, pulling Archie to a stop with him.

Eveline and Red paused, the former rolling her eyes and continuing on to the cover of the tree. Red watched her go with one eye, noting the way Eveline swatted at the bee still around her arm. For all her complaining, Eveline Caldwell was fearless.

Archie, meanwhile, was sniffling, hardly holding back tears.

"Montgomery is a worker bee," George was saying. He did not reach out and hold the little boy's hand, as Red would have done. He did not smile or try to distract him. But his words, steady and authoritative, were comforting in their own way. "His duty is to collect nectar and return it to the hive. If he does not, his brothers and sisters will not be able to make the honey they need to survive," George explained.

Archie dragged his hand beneath his nose. "But he was my friend."

"He was," George agreed. Red could not help her smile at that. But she was several steps away from the pair, so neither noted her amusement.

"He's just one bee," Archie said.

Red wondered if George knew how perilously close Archie was to bursting into tears. She curled her hands into fists, forcing herself to stand down.

"Every bee is important to the hive. If one shirks his duty, nothing much changes. But what if it's two or three or ten? Then who will bring the nectar that makes the honey? What if the bees begin to starve? What will they feed the babies growing in the comb?"

Archie's shaky breath tugged at her heart. Blast it, when had she become so soft?

"The nursery bees need the nectar to feed the babies," Archie said, little voice wobbling.

Pride surged through Red as George rocked back on his heels. "Indeed they do," he said. "How did you learn that?"

Red stepped forward then, catching Archie's shoulder and pointing him toward the tree. Eveline had already collapsed against the trunk, book in hand. Where had she conjured that from?

"Wait for your sister, Archie," Red urged. She met George's

confused face with an enigmatic smile, nodding toward the tree.

Eveline sighed at their approach, setting aside her book but not looking very pleased about it. Red did not let her see the satisfaction that built in her chest; she knew if she did, Eveline might very well drop back to the ground just to be impudent. But instead, she came to stand beside her younger brother, tucking her hands primly behind her back.

Red raked her eyes over the pair, then nodded her approval. She stood off to the side, letting the children address their father directly. She wanted very much to give them this moment, and to fade into the background.

Of course, George chose that moment to look at her. She stabbed a finger out in the children's direction, realized she'd distracted them, and yanked it back. Heaven spare her from idiotic men.

"Begin," she told the children, before this fragile moment degraded.

Archie yelped, but Eveline opened her pert mouth and began to recite:

"Of all the bees in the hive, the queen is the largest and most important."

"She's in charge!" Archie put in excitedly. Eveline shot him a sharp look for interrupting, but continued.

"In the winter, the bees cluster together…"

George listened in solemn silence. Red was certain she saw the corner of his mouth twitch, but he stilled it with military precision. But the rest of him—he was not as successful. She watched his shoulders relax, his hands drop from where they'd been crossed over his body to hang easily at his sides. He did not even fiddle with his hair, as he was prone to do. She might have imagined it, but she thought his dark eyes twinkled brighter.

Eveline had the last word, which she punctuated with a sharp nod of her chin.

Instead of waiting for a response, she spun on her heel, marched to the tree, and stuffed her nose back into her book.

George's face darkened momentarily. But then his gaze swung back to Archie, who was still waiting hopefully. George lifted his hands high and applauded. Archie's grin took over his entire face, then he galloped forward and launched himself into his father's arms.

They were both laughing, the man and his miniature. Red didn't hold back the smile that lit her own face, but she did slide a sidelong look in Eveline's direction. Eveline watched her father and brother, for all that she was attempting to hide behind her book.

Red's heart hurt for the girl. What was it that held her back from interacting with her father? She'd wondered if it was fear of her father's episodes. But as far as Red had seen, Eveline was fearless. Or she made a good show of being so. Perhaps she was hiding something darker and more painful.

She was certainly observant. Despite Red's trained skills, Eveline noticed she was being watched. When she did, she lifted the book higher, obscuring her face entirely.

I'll leave you alone for now. But not for always, Red promised silently as she turned back to the celebrating pair.

George had Archie up on his shoulders, and they were now investigating the hive at the edge of the meadow, nearest the tree where Eveline had posted herself. Red drifted after them, the wind whipping at her hair as she stepped out of the shelter of the trees and brush. She pulled her shawl tighter around her shoulders, grateful she'd opted for wool instead of muslin. Autumn had fully descended upon Essex.

"Do you see them?" George's voice floated on the wind.

"I see them!" Archie squealed. "Why don't they sting you, Father?" he asked, voice filled with awe as George carefully lifted out a portion of comb.

"They are gentle if you are." George held up the comb so Archie could look closer.

Heat spread across Red's chest, filling her stomach and all the space around her organs. Her step hitched slightly in the soft, muddy grass. She had to temper her lust…

Except it wasn't desire that was warming her, not precisely. This was different. Still warm and pleasurable, but more subdued. Fondness, perhaps? She shivered despite her layers—fondness was more dangerous.

She arrived at the hive, forcing herself to come stand beside George and Archie, determined not to let her trepidation get the better of her. If she was stung, then so be it. George and Archie continued to speak, the latter excitedly chattering, the former's velvety syllables rolling through and around her with the smoothness of cream or chocolate.

Red's mind drifted away from the bees.

There was still so much to do at Oxley Park. With Sara assisting with her wardrobe and hair, she was learning more about the staff. She kept careful notes, all written in code and secreted away in her bedroom. But so far, there had been nothing that triggered her instincts. No one with a known connection to France or even to Waterloo. All of the men on staff were either too young or too old to have served.

She'd created a list of the servants working on the grounds, but assembling profiles of them was trickier. Especially with the weather turning—many of the groundskeeping staff would be furloughed for the winter season. But she supposed if she could wait until that happened, her list would be narrowed…

No, the duchess had been clear. Red needed to find out who Legrand was sooner rather than later. She'd already been in Essex for nearly three months. The longer she lingered, the more likely her ruse was to be discovered and the entire plan botched. Red could not allow that to happen. She could not lose her post as a lady knight.

Soft pressure on her hip dragged her attention back to the edge of the meadow. She must have wandered without realizing it—

No, the pressure was insistent. A knuckle dragged from where the gown nipped in at the side, then down along the curve of her hip.

Red's eyes flew to George, but he was still speaking with Archie, who was now at his side, holding his father's other hand. Which left one hand free. One hand that George used to covertly caress her hip, again and again, methodically and slowly. Torturously.

"Can we eat some of the honey?" Archie asked, cutting through her haze.

"Not from this hive—it is too young. But they have some to spare over there." George nodded to the far end of the row. "Run along and fetch your sister, and we shall have a taste."

Archie did not need to be told twice, galloping back toward the tree. Red could not hear him, but she would have wagered he'd have to convince his sister to give up her book. George had her full attention.

"Thank you, for the work you have done with the children," he said, eyes on the hive even as his hand continued its sensuous perusal.

"It is my duty," Red said. "And my pleasure," she added, noting how strangled her voice sounded on those last two syllables.

"Perhaps you would join me in the study this evening," George said quietly, his husky tones meant for her ears alone. "I would be pleased to share the more nuanced aspects of my treatise with you."

Red recognized it immediately for what it was—an invitation.

The pressure of his hand on her hip... He would do nothing unless she wished it.

She did wish it. Desperately.

Whatever was holding her back was quickly dissolving. She was a spinster; she might never have this chance again. Although she was a governess now, she would not be one forever. She was a lady knight. There was no risk in ruining her reputation or ability to get future positions; her work would be waiting for her. Her real life *was* waiting for her in London—her family, her friends, the lady knights.

She had nothing to lose by doing this one thing for herself. From the heat burning in her chest, she had everything to gain.

The children appeared, and George stepped away, taking Archie's hand. Red felt the loss of his touch rock through her. That was when she knew—she had to have it back. She had to sate this mad desire within her. If only because once it had been put out, she could turn her attention to the matter at hand—her quest. That was what she told herself as she followed her charges across the meadow.

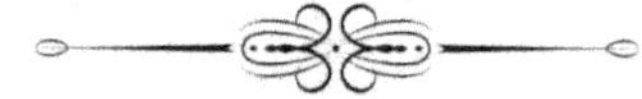

CHAPTER FOURTEEN

H E COULD NOT write a treatise while foxed.

He could still hold his quill pen. So technically, he *could* write something. He could write his treatise. He could force the nib down to the parchment and something would come out on the page. But whatever it was, it would be utter shite.

Not because of the alcohol he'd imbibed—though he'd drunk plenty. Years spent in the military meant he could hold his liquor quite effectively. But the real reason his mind had been turned to mush was soft, round, and red-haired.

Supper had finished hours ago. As usual, Miss Trudeau accompanied the children upstairs to the nursery. If the evening followed the usual pattern, he would not see her again until the children trotted down for their midmorning music lesson. But he'd invited her to his study. Ostensibly to learn about bees, but both he and Red were smart enough to know the true intent behind his invitation.

Yet he still sat there alone.

Red had not come.

Which was why he turned to drink. In theory, if he drank enough of it, his cock would soften to uselessness. He was closer to forty than thirty years old. Past his sexual prime. Two drinks ought to have been enough.

Still, he pictured her round bottom as she sashayed among

the apiaries, trying hard to mask her trepidation at the bees buzzing around her. The clever little insects loved the color red; they sought out those flowers above all others. Was it any surprise they were drawn to the woman who matched the color, not only in hair color and name, but in the shade of her very spirit?

That was the most disturbing part of this desire. It was not merely a lust to possess her body—her buxom, beautiful body. He wanted her mind as well. He wanted to tell her about his damn bees, have her read his treatise before he sent it off to the Royal Institution in London. He trusted her opinion above all others. She was wicked smart; if she approved, there was no way the intellectuals at the Royal Institution could spurn him.

He was luckier than he'd ever realized, securing her for the children's governess. How many women could provide instruction in Greek as well as French? Red could. What governess could teach one child to fish while simultaneously ensuring the other could curtsey while pressing her nose into yet another novel? Red, of course.

But if he took her to bed…he risked all of that.

Horror grabbed his chest in a vise at the thought of having to secure another governess for Archie and Eveline. He'd gone through nearly a dozen before finding Red. The children were becoming attached to her, that much was plain. Archie looked to her as often as he did his father for appreciation and validation. Eveline even more so, though the stubborn girl would surely never admit it.

George had not asked what events had transpired while he'd been away to lead to the fragile accord between the two women, younger and elder. But he had watched that relationship grow strong in the weeks since. The mutiny that had lived in Eveline's eyes in those first weeks had cooled to something more akin to respect. Certainly, more respect than those dark orbs held when she looked at him, her own father.

Could he risk damaging that?

The fact that he was already considering it proved once again that he was as terrible at the role as he'd always known. A good father did not abandon his children to go to war. A good father did not stay away when he heard of their mother's death, like a coward. And a good father certainly did not threaten the first stable relationship in their lives by taking their governess to bed.

It was wildly inappropriate. It was the reason that most wives insisted their children's governesses be old and crotchety. Bringing a vivacious, comely young woman into the house was a dangerous proposition. But Red was not so young, George reminded himself. He tried to place her age; she had not disclosed it specifically. Well past her debut. A spinster, she'd called herself more than once. Though he could not imagine she was past thirty. Not a single strand of gray was intermixed with her glowing red tresses. He knew—he'd spent an inordinate amount of time staring at them.

But he also did not have a wife.

That was his fault as well.

He did not deserve Red. His children certainly did. This was wrong.

None of it mattered, George reminded himself, because she had not come. He'd extended an invitation, and Red, being the wiser of the two of them, had opted for the safety of her own bedchamber.

It was for the best, really. No risk to the children, nor to his own peace. Or whatever illusion of peace he was living in. At least if she was here at Oxley Park, working with the children, she would continue to make his life better. To be present in it, day after day. Perhaps that was enough. It was certainly the wiser course of action.

But he'd seen the hunger in Red's eyes. Tonight, she'd said no.

If they continued to see each other every single day, he had no doubt she would grow in his estimation. He would only want her more. Though he would try to hide that, she was too smart not to know. Someday, she would say yes.

George knew that when that day came, he would not possess the strength to say no.

What if he got her with child? They were both still well within their childbearing years. His own mother had not given birth to him until she was thirty-three, his sister a few years after. Even a young, healthy woman could succumb to the perils of childbirth.

The image came to his mind, like a curtain being pulled, cloaking everything in darkness. For once, he let it come and did not fight. Fighting never seemed to help anyway. It was not real, he reminded himself. He had not been there when she died. That was part of the reason the vision was so vivid, why every cry from her throat wrenched his stomach with guilt. He had left her alone, and she had died.

Died while laboring to bring a child into the world. While he had been a continent away.

Instead of trying to force the vision away, he summoned another. A door. Red's door. The carved image of Tudor roses a momentary distraction from the exercise. Slowly, he forced himself to draw the lines as she had taught him. He dragged in a breath and then breathed it out with deliberate slowness.

The woman screaming in the bed came back. He let her come, just for a moment, before summoning the door once again. Then again and again. Until finally, his breathing was even and the darkened room did not rise to his consciousness.

He felt the study rematerializing around him. He shifted in his chair, feeling the warm leather beneath his legs. His hand tightened around the crystal glass of liquor, and his nails scraped across the etched decorations.

After several more minutes, he felt steady enough to lift the glass to his lips. He closed his eyes, letting the liquid burn down his throat, savoring the fact that he could feel it at all, that he was present in that moment and not lost in another.

Then he heard the door open.

SHE WAS TREMBLING.

Ethelreda McGovern, who'd run men through with her rapier and muscled villains through the gates of Newgate all by herself, was trembling. For a moment, she wished she had her rapier at her side. She wished she could run the pad of her finger over the intricate inlaid handle, trace the pattern until it settled the butterflies in her stomach.

But Red doubted that she would ever settle those butterflies. Or perhaps she ought to call them bees.

Not until she did the one thing she simultaneously wanted and feared the most. If she gave in, if she pushed herself, maybe—just maybe—she could quell this burning within her and be able to focus on her quest.

That burning turned to a raging inferno when she pushed the door open and her eyes landed on George Caldwell sitting exactly where she'd known he would be. Sitting behind his massive desk, even with his eyes closed as he sipped his drink, he exuded power and strength.

His shirt sleeves were rolled up to the elbow, his long forearms on display. Even at a distance, Red could see the crisscross of scars on his left arm. She wondered what they would feel like beneath her tongue.

Heavens above, she was going straight to hell. What would her mother think of her?

Jacquetta and Dominique would be proud.

She shoved lady knights and family members alike from her mind. She'd decided to do this, and she intended to share it with no one. This was entirely for herself. George was hers alone, at least for tonight.

His eyes cracked open, just a fraction, enough to watch her approach.

He knew she was aware of his watching her. Somehow, it

heightened everything. Red felt the brush of her nightgown around her legs as she crossed the room. She was all too aware of her wrapper, which suddenly seemed too tight, forcing the fabric of her night rail to rub torturously against her breasts. Her nipples were already hard, straining at the fabric. Straining to be touched, she realized. Touched by him.

She stopped in front of his desk, hands at her side, presenting herself to him.

"You came."

She swallowed, aware of how her breasts lifted with the motion. George's eyes cracked open another fraction. He made no bones about watching her now.

"I had duties to attend to this evening." It was only partially true; she'd written several letters in pursuit of a particular Greek text in its original form for Eveline. But the rest of the time, she'd been standing in front of her mirror debating which combination of nightgown and wrapper would be most enticing.

"Your duties brought you here?" He leaned forward, setting the crystal glass on his desk with a heavy thump. His eyes were fully on her now, no artifice.

"My desire brought me here," she said brazenly. She bit the corner of her lower lip to try to moor her amusement before she added, "My desire to learn about bees, of course."

"Of course."

She had to look away or risk melting under the intensity of his gaze. She glanced down on the desk, her eyes snagging on the thick stack of papers. "What is that?" she asked even as she peered closer. "George, are you writing a book?"

It was about bees. Lines and lines, paragraphs—chapters, by the look of it—about bees. Red should have been pulled entirely from the moment, but instead, a warmth in her chest began to grow to join the one already burning between her legs. The man was damned brilliant, in every way.

"A treatise," he corrected her, before clearing his throat. He grabbed the sheaf of papers and shoved it into a drawer of his desk, closing it with a sharp snap.

Red resisted the urge to tease him; the stack had been so neat, as was every line of writing. Military precision, as in all things, must govern his work on this treatise. But he'd shoved it into a drawer. Whether to get it away so she would not see it or because he was so befuddled with desire—

"Come here, Red."

She suspected she had her answer.

Red tried to slow her steps, but there was no trepidation left. Now that she'd made the decision, she was ready. Nay, she was needy. Needy for him. Which was why she did not protest at all when George caught her hand and pulled her into his lap. For a moment, surprise and confusion flashed through her. Then she realized that the hard heat pressing at her thighs, the rigid shaft her hips seemed to recognize as she strained toward him, was his manhood.

Oh, God. She was lost.

She was his, entirely. Anything he wanted, she would do, because she trusted him to bring her pleasure. His hands were already roaming over her shoulders, caressing the lace edges of the wrapper where they met her neck, thumbing them away so he could touch the skin beneath.

She shifted in his lap, reaching for the arms of the chair. She must be too heavy for him—

"If you keep moving like that, I am going to come here and now," he said in a harsh whisper from where he'd buried his mouth against her shoulder.

"I'm sorry. I am heavy—"

"You are perfect. You are heavenly. You are a goddess." His hands tightened around her waist, holding her firmly in place. "Stay where you are."

"I do not know what I am doing," she said between heavy breaths as his mouth caressed her chin. "I have not done this before."

"I will be gentle," he promised, even as he tugged her tighter against him, gripping her bottom.

"I do not need you to be gentle, I need you to..." She didn't finish the sentence. She wasn't sure how.

"Pleasure you? Ravage you?" His mouth dropped to her breasts, and his nose nudged aside the panels of her dressing gown to access the skin beneath.

She wore her one and only nightgown that did not tie at the neck, and as he dragged his tongue over the space between her breasts, she was damned glad she had. She'd never imagined...

George's fingers closed on her nipple through the thin nightgown. Only one coherent thought remained.

"Teach me," she breathed.

CHAPTER FIFTEEN

TWO MORE EROTIC words had never been spoken.

"Open your wrapper," he commanded.

She'd been trembling when she entered the room. He'd noticed it even through his lust-crazed haze. But when she reached for the tie, bunched up just below her breast, her hands were steady.

It took every bit of restraint George possessed not to throw her back on the desk and bury himself inside of her. The expanse of creamy skin that emerged from the dark blue velvet wrapper she wore was more beautiful and inviting than he'd even imagined. Once the tie was loose, he slid his thumbs beneath the lace-trimmed edges and slid the garment down her shoulders.

Her nightgown was not tied at the throat, thank heavens. This one had a low neckline and a tie just below the breasts. Simple two-inch-wide straps held it on to her shoulders. Her skin was so pale, so pure, it might have blended right into the linen of her nightgown—if it had not been for the freckles.

He was determined to kiss every one. But the sound of Red's nervous swallow brought him back to this moment. He was supposed to be showing her, teaching her. Right.

"You are exquisite. Be proud of it," he said. To hammer home his point, he lowered his mouth to her chest and ran his tongue along the exposed line of her collarbone.

"Is that my first lesson?" she asked breathily.

"Every moment, every touch, every gasp"—she did gasp as he sucked hard on her neck—"is part of the lesson," George said. He'd been a rake once. It was not so hard to remember those impulses, especially with a siren like Red in his lap.

"What do I do..." She struggled to get the words out as he nudged one of the straps down off her shoulder so he could start kissing those freckles. "What do I do with my hands?"

"Touch anywhere," he instructed her. "Touch everything."

Red, God bless her, needed no further urging. Her hands landed on his biceps, gripping so tightly that her fingernails would leave little half-moon imprints on his skin. He'd treasure each of them come the morning. When she was done with that, she slid her hands upward, past his shoulders, to the back of his neck.

As she tangled her fingers in his hair, mussing the neat club at the nape of his neck, George set his own hands to an all-important task—freeing her glorious breasts.

"I can help you—" she began, shifting as he started on the tie.

"Your job is to let me pleasure you," he said. He deftly pulled the tie free, and with the other hand tugged the gown down so her breasts were on full display. As he lowered his mouth, her fingers tightened in his hair. "You may keep doing that," he growled.

"Pulling your hair?" Red gasped when he caught one brown nipple between his lips.

"Yes," he groaned as she unintentionally tightened her grasp.

The force of her need was wearing on him. He wanted her just as badly. Nudging aside the amulet she wore on a long chain between her breasts, he dragged his tongue along the space. He cupped one breast, but the fullness of it was too big for even one of his large palms. There was so much of her to make love to, so many soft, supple inches to worship. He'd need all night. And probably several more besides.

He sucked her nipple into his mouth while he massaged the other breast with his hand. Just as her grip on his hair loosened, he lightly bit at the tender bud. She held him tight, forcing him into her breast. He could not breathe. Who needed to breathe? He needed to feast.

With that thought, another desire entered his mind.

He dragged his mouth away from her breasts, allowing himself a moment to enjoy the sight of her in his lap. Her hands were still tight around his neck, keeping her close. But a delicate flush covered her entire upper body, and her red curls bounced slightly with each heavy breath she dragged in.

Holding her gaze—were those storms in her eyes for him?—he retrieved one of her hands from behind his head and eased her off his lap. Her eyes flickered with confusion, but he held them, licking his lips as he imagined the next scene in his mind.

"What now?" she asked, standing between him and the desk, with his knees bracketing her in on either side.

"Lean back on the desk."

EVEN AS HER mouth popped open, confusion still befuddling her mind, George cupped her bottom and lifted her up easily. Every inch of the man was corded muscle, she thought with wonderment. He moved her around like she weighed nothing. Not nothing, precisely. For every time he gripped her soft curves, Red could see his eyes burning with desire.

He slid her wrapper down the rest of the way, so it fell back like a blanket over the top of his desk. When she did not move, he nudged her knees apart so he could come to stand between them and lower his lips to her ear, nudging away her curls.

"Lean back," he whispered.

Red swallowed hard, dipping her chin in a nod. But before she could actually do as he instructed, George caught her chin in his fingers and snared her mouth. Every kiss that had come before paled in comparison. Her nipples rubbed against the soft fabric of his shirt, teasing and being teased in return. Without thinking, she tightened her legs around him while his tongue curled around hers in a sensuous dance. Kissing him was absolute decadence.

Instead of leaning back, she grasped George's forearms, needing to touch him. Her fingers tried to go higher, to feel those corded muscles—but his shirt was in the way. She must have made some sound of displeasure, because George's chuckle reverberated between them before he said:

"Demanding thing, aren't you, Red?" He leaned back enough to catch a handful of his shirt, tug it free from his trousers and up over his head.

Red gulped. Then her mouth fell open. Her throat went dry. He was the most magnificent thing she'd ever seen. Not a single sculpture or painting in the British Museum could compare. More scars, she noted as her fingers spread over the muscled pectorals. George was truly a warrior, and he bore the proof upon his body.

She wanted to know the story of each one. Wanted to press her lips to the jagged line just above his left nipple. *Why not?* her mind challenged. So she did, kissing a line along the wicked slant until she was just above his nipple. Tightening her grip on him, she flicked her tongue over it experimentally.

"You're learning too fast for my own damn good," George growled, urging her back up to sit. "Let me show you."

With that, he brooked no more distractions. He lowered her back onto the desk until she was resting on her elbows, her breasts and body on full display. She did not realize she was holding her breath as George's gaze traveled over every inch of her body. Only a small bit around her waist was covered where her nightgown was bunched.

George's exhale was so slow, so carefully controlled, Red had to wonder if he was doing the breathing exercise she'd taught him in an attempt to regain control of himself. As he inhaled, he urged her hips up and pulled her nightgown the rest of the way off, letting it fall to the floor. Now she was exposed—fully.

George licked his lips, a dangerous jungle cat having caught a delicious meal. Any misgivings or self-doubts she had died as she watched him reach down and draw his manhood from his trousers, caressing himself in long strokes as he watched her.

"I could stare at you forever," he admitted. "Just the sight of you"—he drew in a ragged breath—"it's enough to undo me. But I promised to teach you, and I shall not break this promise."

With that, he released himself and reached for her. He leaned forward, pressing a kiss to her lips, then another to the space between her breasts, to her belly button, and finally to the sensitive expanse of flesh just above the dark mass of hair shielding her most private areas from view.

He tangled his fingers in the thick crimson curls at the apex of her thighs, moving through the mass at random—until one finger surged downward, nudging aside her folds with too much focus to be anything but intentional. Then that finger flicked over one spot, and she arched off the desk.

"This is the center of your pleasure," he said huskily, lowering himself back into his chair and leaning forward so his nose hovered inches above her wild mound. "When I touch it with my fingers, you will feel pleasure unlike anything you have ever experienced."

As he spoke, he touched the little nub again. This time, he rubbed the pad of his finger back and forth with agonizing slowness. Red began to whimper. Every feeling in her body, every thrill of desire he'd wrung for her, seemed to have slithered down, centering in this one place on her body.

George raised his gaze to hers, and the intensity of his dark eyes ensnared her and stopped her thoughts.

"When I touch it with my mouth, you will see stars," George promised.

He was as good as his word.

His fingers held her folds apart while his tongue swiped over the center of pleasure. Red arched and collapsed, her arms insufficient to hold her. One of George's hands came up, flattening over her belly and gently urging her down. Holding her in place.

That made it even worse. Or better. She hardly knew. All she could do was feel. A broad stroke of his tongue over her love button, followed by several quick lashes, then again. The pressure was building with every repetition. Just when she thought she was going to reach it, whatever *it* was, he dragged his tongue downward over her slit, making her feral with disappointment.

But how could it be disappointment when it felt this wonderful? Every touch shoved her skyward, toward those stars he'd promised. Then he returned to his careful coaxing, that damned repetition.

"George, please," she begged when he pulled away again. Begging for what, she did not know. Release, that was it. Release of this maddening pressure. She had to release soon or she would explode all over his desk.

"That is exactly what I have in mind," George murmured.

Christ, had she said that aloud?

It did not matter, because George set himself to the task with vigor. Repetitive, delicious vigor. When she was so close she could almost feel it, almost reach out and touch her release, he slid a finger inside of her.

She exploded then, and a rush of wetness poured from her, drenching George's face and her wrapper and everything else within several inches. Red sat straight up, her cheeks burning. "I am so sorry. I don't know—"

George caught her chin, shoving his thumb between her lips to prevent her from speaking. As he held her in place, he lifted the hand that had been inside of her and sucked two of his fingers into his mouth. Tasting her, she realized.

She almost climaxed again just watching him.

When he finally had licked away every trace of her from his fingers, he cupped her head and kissed her deeply.

"You are perfect," he said against her lips. Then, with a gentle nudge, he laid her back on the desk.

Wonder surging through her, Red watched as he reached for

his cock. It was so thick that she wondered if she'd be able to get her fingers all the way around it. She wanted to touch, wanted to know. But George was already stepping forward, resuming control.

He dragged the head down her wet slit, coating the tip in her honey. Red shivered at the contact, so gentle and also so incredibly intimate. No one had touched her there—she'd only begun to explore herself. Yet when George teased her opening, urging her wet folds apart, all she could think was: *More, more, more.*

He was in control. The thought was terrifying and thrilling. Red was a powerful woman even in her quiet moments. But with George, she surrendered. When this strict, genteel soldier took her in his arms, she was happy to follow his command. The thought actually made her wetter still.

"I am going to take you now," he said, the head of his shaft still toying at her entrance. "It might hurt, but only for a second."

Red nodded easily. She'd been trained to ignore pain. And there was no way that she'd be able to focus on anything but pleasure once George was inside of her, she was certain of that. But he did not push himself in. He was watching her intently, forcing his breathing into an even pattern, waiting. For her, Red realized.

"Yes, oh yes, George," she panted. She started to sit up, reaching for his hip, but he met her halfway. She was so wet, he had only to shift his hips slightly and he was inside of her.

Full and *right.* So very full and so very right. Those were the two words that cascaded through Red's mind.

He drew back, and she felt unfathomable loss. Until he thrust in again and she got to feel every place where her cunny clung to his cock. Again and again. If there as pain, she did not feel it. Only pleasure so intense that she thought there might be another waterfall in her future.

George seemed to know, reaching down between them to flick his thumb over her nub as he stroked inside of her. She watched his face, trying to see the pleasure there, but as soon as he realized she was looking, he caught her mouth in a kiss. His tongue surged into her depths in time with his cock. Red knew she was close, recognized the feeling a few seconds before, this time. That rhythmic pulsing of his cock inside of her, with his hand at her pleasure center, was too much. Another burst of fireworks and wetness exploded from her, covering his cock and hand.

Red was ready to collapse back, but George's speed increased. He was getting close himself, she realized. She wanted to help him, wanted to pleasure him the way he had her. He loved her breasts. On a whim, she cupped them with her hands, lifting them up until her fingertips closed around each nipple.

George's eyes glazed over with lust, and satisfaction burned through Red. In the next breath, his face contracted with pleasure and his climax took him as well.

A second before he came, he pulled away, bracing a hand on the edge of the desk as his spend poured from that glorious manhood. Red felt a pulse of loss; she'd wanted him inside of her right to the end. But she understood the necessity and appreciated it. Ever a gentleman, ever a soldier.

She gripped his hip, noting now that he was the one trembling. When he finally stilled, she leaned forward and pressed a kiss to his abdomen, to the tight muscles there. She intended to trace each one with her tongue until they were seared on her memory. But not just now.

Now, she needed to touch him.

As if reading her thoughts, George scooped her up and carried her over to the settee, settling them together so they were both comfortable, both touching in every possible place. Not touching each other seemed impossibly terrible.

She knew then that once would not be enough. Red doubted that a hundred times would suffice to quiet the need within her. But her mind was too addled with pleasure to contemplate the ramifications of that. All she could think about was the feel of

George's muscular body, curved around hers. All she could feel was the heat of his breath against her neck, where he'd buried his face in the curve of her shoulder. In a world of questions and concerns, it felt like the answer to everything.

THE FIRST RAYS of predawn light kissed the horizon as Red crept back to her quarters. She had to be behind that rose-carved door before the first servant woke, before they even stirred in their bed. Anything else would be courting disaster.

She was already courting disaster, a voice in the recesses of her mind reminded her. A voice that sounded irritatingly like the Duchess of Guilford.

Red ignored it, cinching her wrapper tight around her waist and avoiding the creaking stairs entirely, as well as the worn-down patch of carpet on the first floor. She closed the door soundlessly. But once she did, she allowed herself to collapse back against it. Her legs gave way beneath her, and her back slid down the wooden panels until she was all the way on the floor.

Instinct had her checking for signs of disturbance, even though it was highly improbable that anyone would have snuck into her rooms in the middle of the night, when the rest of the household expected her to be asleep in her bed. The bow tied around the handle of her valise was still perfect. Or rather, imperfect in the way that only Red could manage. The drawers of her dressing table were all slightly ajar, but only to the amounts that Red had left them. No one had entered this room.

Good, her weary mind whispered. *One less thing to worry about.*

Amid a hurricane of other concerns.

She could not bring herself to regret it.

Red remained there against the door in a puddle of soft nighttime fabrics, lost in her thoughts. When she heard the first soft footsteps—a maid coming around to urge the hearths to life—she finally stirred.

But instead of making for her bed to steal a few extra minutes of sleep or for her wardrobe to dress for her morning outing to the summer house, Red went to the mantel. She pulled down the book that was not a book, flipping open the pages until she found the secret compartment nestled within. She had to fish around within her gown to find the small amulet she always wore.

For a moment she simply fondled it, remembering how George had nudged it aside to get at her breasts. So committed, he was, to worshipping every inch of her body. She swallowed the lump in her throat, trying to forestall the heat that immediately ignited deep in her belly. With a well-placed fingernail, she flicked the mechanism free to reveal the key nestled within the intricate filigree.

Carefully, she inserted the delicate key into the lock and clicked open the mechanism. She pulled out the single piece of parchment secreted within. The list she'd made her first night at Oxley Park. The one she'd added to every few days as she learned more about the estate's occupants and servants.

Her hand trembled as she crossed to the dressing table, digging in the third drawer for ink and quill. As the first rays of golden light peeked through her curtains, Red crossed off the last name on the list: *George Caldwell.*

CHAPTER SIXTEEN

NO AMOUNT OF cosmetics could conceal the bags under Red's eyes. She cringed when she spotted herself in the mirror hanging in the nursery. She was thankful Sara had not appeared to help her dress; the poor former lady's maid would have been offended at the sight of her. Red tried to compensate by choosing a gown that she'd always found particularly becoming.

The dress was executed in a soft seafoam-green color that existed nowhere else in Red's wardrobe. She'd given up pastels after her second Season. No use dressing like a debutante when she was destined for a life of spinsterhood. But somehow, this particular gown persisted. It was probably the fashionable Marie sleeves. The delicate puffs cinched at regular intervals with a velvet ribbon a few shades darker than the rest of the dress were just so elegant.

Red twisted her hair up into a chignon, used several wickedly sharp hairpins—sharp enough to stab a villain, if need be—to hold it in place, and decided she could expect no better after the night she'd had. Heat flushed through her at that.

"You've misspelled 'abundance,'" Eveline said.

"Mind yourself!" Archie protested, glaring at his sister. But when he glanced back down at his workbook, his little brow wrinkled fervently.

Red rolled her eyes, stepping closer so she could peer over

Archie's shoulder. "It is an *a* in the third syllable, not a *u*." She glanced in Eveline's direction as well. "You've mistranslated the last line. He loves his brother—he is not *in* love with him."

Eveline did not snap her quill, like she would have a month before. But neither did she acknowledge Red as she blotted out the line and began again. Red glanced to the clock, counting the minutes until the children's music lesson. She would be able to return to her rooms and have a lie-down—

"Is that a carriage?" Months of instruction on decorum failed to keep Archie in his seat when he heard the steady hoofbeats of a team of horses approaching Oxley Park. Red shared his sentiment—Oxley Park was a quiet place.

When the governess was not bedding the master of the house… Or a French spy trying to do unspecified harm.

Red followed at a slower pace, Eveline not far behind. There was indeed a carriage slowing to a stop. But from the nursery, it was impossible to see who was alighting as the footman jumped down from the seat.

"Can we go see who it is?" Archie asked, percolating from one foot to the other.

"We have lessons to attend to," Red said. But she wanted to go below too. Every guest or visitor to Oxley Park was suspect and must be examined. "Each of you finish the line that you are working on, then we shall go down," she decreed.

Once again, Archie scrambled across the room, and Eveline followed at a more dignified pace. Five minutes later, Red followed them down the corridor toward the staircase, as voices drifted up from the foyer.

Red recognized George, of course, as well as Cross. There was an unknown feminine voice, laughing. For some reason, her chest tightened. How odd.

She caught up with the children just before Archie propelled himself down the stairs. With a hand on each shoulder and a gentle squeeze, she prayed they would remember their manners. If they couldn't manage themselves with company, then what was she even doing?

Catching a French spy, Miranda's voice echoed in the back of her mind.

Well, yes, of course, Red's argued back. *But if I must be a governess to do it, I at least want to be a respectable one.*

The memory of George's mouth on her breast reminded her that *respectable* was no longer a word she could apply to herself, governess or otherwise.

She shut that thought out, as well as all the other memories of the night before. Even if her stomach was doing inconsiderate flips inside her body at the sound of George's voice floating up the stairs.

Archie and Eveline, bless them, descended the stairs with even, measured footsteps. The adults gathered in the foyer did not even realize the children were there until they appeared around the curve at the bottom of the steps. That in itself was an enormous victory; they tended to cascade down those stairs in a bouncing fit of bickering.

"Are these the children?" the female voice gushed.

What a stupid question. What other children would be—Stop. She had to disentangle her emotions. She was a lady knight. She was trained to approach every situation with poise and calm, to be clever and observant so she could put any information she gleaned to use later on.

Gripping the banister, Red counted to five as she took the last few steps to come stand behind the children. By the time she was face to face with the new arrival, she was centered and ready.

But she did not speak. She was a servant. For all that George had treated her as an integral part of their household, with company in residence, she would fade into the background. The background was a good place for a spy to be—the less the guests noticed her, the more likely they were to loosen their lips. Though Red was not sure what the two women standing in the foyer of Oxley Park would have to offer her quest.

"Archibald, you are going to be as tall as your father!" the woman who had spoken first said, toying fondly with the lapel of Archie's miniature waistcoat. Very familiar, Red noted. A family member, perhaps?

"Oh, Eveline, you are the image of your mother," she continued. She reached out a hand as if to fondle the ends of Eveline's long, dark hair. But she paused just short, then retracted her hand. Red could not see Eveline's face from where she stood behind the children, but she could have drawn the expression she was sure the other woman was seeing.

George cleared his throat. Red slid her eyes to him surreptitiously. One hand clenched at his side, the other falling back into place. He'd been about to rake it through his hair, she'd wager. His eyes were on Eveline—all of their eyes were.

"*Bonjour, Tante*," Eveline said, in perfect French. "*Nous sommes tellement honorés que vous visitiez notre maison.*"

Tante. Aunt.

Red could see it now. The resemblance to George was not obvious, but she could see it in the angles of their jaws and, in particular, their eyes. But that did not account for—

"*Merci ma nièce. Vous parlez français aussi bien que moi,*" George's sister said in rapid-fire French of her own. She turned back to George with a wide smile. "You are managing better than I'd imagined," she said.

George's eyes went to her immediately. Red would not blush. She would not allow it. She thought of the first time she'd been nicked with a blade, of being stung by the bees in the apiaries— anything to keep the other thoughts that George's eyes on her summoned from taking root in her mind.

"It is all due to Miss Trudeau."

All eyes went to Red. No longer in the background.

"Janine, please allow me to introduce the children's governess, Miss Ethelreda Trudeau." George spoke with military precision, enunciating every syllable, Red noticed; she wondered if his sister did as well.

If he needed to cling to strict formality to keep his wits about him, Red could hardly blame him. Had she not just been summoning painful memories to keep her own blush at bay?

Red curtseyed, still lingering behind the children. That was her place. And if they made a useful shield for this social interaction, she was not complaining about that either.

George continued, "This is my sister, Mrs. Janine Robinson and…" He paused, looking to his sister meaningfully.

Janine, hair a few shades lighter than her brother's but with matching dark eyes, curtseyed before she motioned her companion forward. Red had noted the other woman, of course. But she'd been focused on the one talking—Janine—rather than the one standing silently off to the side. She'd noted blonde hair, creamy skin, and a white sprigged-muslin dress. A debutante, then. Or near enough.

But when the other woman stepped forward, Red realized her mistake. Quiet, perhaps. Breathtakingly beautiful— undeniably.

"My dear friend Miss Marion Abbot. My husband, Mr. Robinson, was unable to accompany me on this journey. Miss Abbot was kind enough to join me for the excursion. She has never been to Essex," Janine explained, placing a familiar hand on her friend's arm.

Miss Marion Abbot was an angel. Fashionably slim, her arms and collarbones and neck so delicate that Red wondered if she even needed stays to achieve her perfect form. Her golden hair was teased into springy ringlets that framed her face, while the rest was swept up into a neat chignon at the crown of her head. Pink bloomed on her cheeks, but not a blush. Just a hint of color to accentuate the unblemished skin. A perfect English rose.

Red felt nauseated.

Because she could ascertain exactly why Miss Marion Abbot had come to Oxley Park, even if George was still woefully unaware.

There was only one reason that Janine Robinson had brought her friend along, and it was not because she was lonely. George's sister had decided it was time for him to marry. And she'd brought along the woman for the job.

"WHAT DO YOU think of Miss Abbot?"

The tea in his mouth forestalled George's response, but only for a moment. "She seems an appropriate companion for you," he said, settling himself back on the sofa.

He was more comfortable in the chair behind his desk, especially when facing a veritable dragon. But he'd decided keeping things more casual with his sister was the right tactic. At least for the moment.

"She is lovely," Janine confirmed. She held her own teacup, but did not take a drink. "Her family's estate adjoins our own in Wessex. Her father is a baronet and her mother is the daughter of Viscount Burbage."

George nodded and reached for a biscuit. This was the sort of drivel that had always bored him to tears. Precisely why he avoided London.

"She has several younger siblings and is an absolute dream with children. Emma and Lucy adore her."

George dipped his biscuit into his tea, drawing out the chewing of it so he would not have to respond to his sister's endless prattling.

"So accomplished. Of course, she's had her debut in London and had plenty of suitors. But she prefers a quiet country life, which is why I brought her along with me on this visit." Janine still had not taken a drink of her tea.

George swallowed, and the biscuit scraped his throat uncomfortably. "I thought you brought her along because Alistair was occupied."

Janine waved her hand. "Of course, yes, that as well."

"Has he secured the remaining investors? His last letter did not say." George reached for another biscuit. The more he ate, the less he would have to talk to Janine.

"Yes, I believe so." She frowned.

"Are things going badly?" George sat up at that. He'd invested a substantial sum into his brother-in-law's new business venture. Not enough that it would endanger Oxley Park if things went amiss, but enough to warrant paying attention to its loss.

"No, no, nothing like that." Another wave of her hand. His sister was going to be the death of him. "I simply do not wish to change the subject."

George set down his teacup, feeling unease pooling in his stomach. "What subject?"

"Miss Abbot."

"Why would we need to discuss Miss Abbot—No." He stood up and retreated behind the desk. A strategic retreat, George told himself.

"No?" Her voice feigned innocence, but he recognized the determined gleam in Janine's dark eyes, the mirrors of his own.

"No, Janine. I am not interested." He reached into the bottom desk drawer, the one that was not locked.

"Not interested in what? I am merely extolling the virtues of my dear friend." Janine put her teacup down now.

"I am not interested in marrying again." He set the bottle and glass on the desktop with a thud.

Janine glared as she rose, all artifice gone now. "You must marry. The children need a mother."

"They had a mother." His chest tightened as he said the word. Time to pour the whisky.

Janine drew in a long breath through her nose before blowing it out daintily between her pursed lips. "Their mother is gone. It was a tragedy, I know, but—"

"You know nothing."

Amber liquid splashed into the glass, and then down his throat. His gaze traveled over Janine's shoulder to the open doors of the study. He couldn't very well close his eyes and picture

Red's door. But he could trace the outline of these ones without his sister noticing. Up, across, down, across.

"She is gone, George." Janine stalked to him on the other side of his desk. "Her death was tragic, we all know that. Archie was so young he cannot remember, and Eveline probably remembers just enough. And the babe…"

George didn't speak. He couldn't. A vise had closed around his throat.

"Do you mourn her, still?" Janine asked, voice just a fraction gentler.

Guilt constricted his stomach. Guilt and shame. Always the first two emotions that came. Guilt, because he should have been there. Shame, because he hadn't wanted to be.

"I mourn many things, Janine. More than you can fathom." He took another drink, still avoiding her eyes. Though he was calm now.

In the periphery of his vision, he saw his sister bite down on her lower lip. She was chewing over a thought, and he doubted she would keep it to herself. In the next moment, she proved him correct.

"What happened at Waterloo, George?"

He straightened, finally giving her back his gaze. "Her death is not the only one on my conscience. Let that suffice, sister."

Janine bit her lip again and stared down at the desk between them. Their father's desk, before George had taken over Oxley Park. His late wife had wanted to replace it when she updated the furnishings throughout the house to bring them out of the eighteenth century. He'd refused to part with it. There was some comfort, however small, in knowing he hid his whisky in the same drawer his father had thirty years before.

"I do not mean to torture you. I only think of the children's wellbeing," she said, her voice thick with emotion. "And yours."

"I am perfectly well." For the first time, it was not entirely a lie. The darkness, the nightmares—they were still there. But it had all eased, somewhat, with Red's presence. Her techniques, her gentle and shrewd management of the children, had brought a calmness to Oxley Park that had not been there before.

"What of Archie and Eveline?" Janine challenged, hands going to her hips now.

"They are fine."

"They need a mother."

"They have you, and Miss Trudeau."

Janine sighed, but she didn't retreat to the sofa or admit defeat. "I would like to see them more, it is true. But with two young ones of my own, it is not possible. Not as often as I'd like." She let one hand drop from her hips. "Your Miss Trudeau seems a capable woman. She's certainly done more with the children than you were ever able to."

Your Miss Trudeau.

Was it that obvious? No, it couldn't be.

Janine did not know. What if she did know? He wasn't regretful. Ashamed of his own lack of restraint? Perhaps. *Your Miss Trudeau. His Miss Trudeau. His Red. His.*

Hell and damnation, why did that feel so right?

"But a governess is not a mother," Janine continued. "What will happen when you leave again—"

"I will not leave again." Hell, he needed more whisky.

Janine raised a brow.

"I have resigned my commission." There it was. The words he'd struggled to voice, even to himself, even after the act was done. That part of his life was over.

Janine dropped back into her seat. "I see."

Silence reigned between them for several blessed minutes. Janine had always possessed too many opinions for her own good, and certainly for his. He needed to get her away from Oxley Park as quickly as possible, and put paid to these notions she had about marrying him off to her friend. Miss Abbot had hardly said two words to him, but that said enough.

George tipped his glass back one more time, draining the remnants of the dram of whisky, then returned the bottle to its drawer. Janine's eyes flicked toward him at the sound of the drawer snapping shut.

"You are just like Father—Is that Eveline?"

They both fell silent, listening to the melodic voice winding through the halls. A surge of pride filled George's chest. "Yes. Miss Trudeau has arranged for the children to have music lessons. Eveline must be beginning her voice instruction."

As if summoned, Red appeared outside the study. She was walking past, pretending or actually not noticing that the room was occupied. Despite the fact that he and Janine had been practically shouting at one another.

"Miss Trudeau! There you are!" Janine clapped her hands in excitement. Rather like a child, George thought, though he kept that to himself.

Red spun gracefully on her heel, walking to the threshold of the study. She lingered there, bobbing a curtsey. She did not want to get entangled in this, which meant she'd heard *something* as she crossed the foyer from the music room.

"Come in, come in and join us," his sister insisted, motioning broadly to the tea laid out before her. "George tells me you've arranged for music lessons for the children! How lovely!"

Red dipped her head in acknowledgment, coming a few more steps into the room. But she made no move to sit. "I believe every young lady should be proficient on the pianoforte and able to carry a tune, at the very least."

"And Archibald attends as well?"

"Yes. He could do with some more…refined skills."

George bit his lip to keep in his chuckle. Apparently, Red was determined to socialize his little hellion, even if she did often indulge his need for fishing and running roughshod across the estate.

"I could not agree more. Before I leave, I shall have to hear all your recommendations regarding your program—for their music instruction, particularly. I haven't found a suitable tutor for my girls, but I think I could get them started along the right path if I had a course to follow," Janine gabbed on.

George's attention was on Red. The curve of her hip through her gown, the way her curls were coming loose around the nape of her neck… Damn, she looked tired. His male pride stretched in satisfaction at that.

"I shall write up a pamphlet for you," Red said. Clearly, she eschewed the notion of spending time alone, talking with his sister. Smart woman. "If you will excuse me, I must prepare for the afternoon while the children have their music lesson."

Another flippant wave of Janine's hand. "Of course, do not let me keep you. But you must join us for supper," she said, fixing her wide smile on Red.

Red ought to look like a deer caught in the hunter's sights; that was certainly how he'd felt since his sister's arrival. But Red's blue eyes were clear of storm clouds. She bought herself time by dipping her head respectfully, giving her a few seconds to conjure a response. So damn clever, George found himself thinking.

"I appreciate the invitation, mistress. But my place is with the children," Red said, moving her hands behind her back.

The motion pressed her breasts forward, though George was sure that was not her intent. She'd looked so damn enticing that morning as she came down the stairs with the children, dressed in seafoam that brought the ocean to her eyes. She looked like a goddess of spring in the middle of winter, and George wanted to worship her accordingly. Instead, he'd spent the day enduring his younger sister's bullying.

"Nonsense," Janine said, unaware of his rapture. "You have worked wonders with the children, and you ought to be rewarded. I've asked George's cook to prepare a special feast this evening, and she has mightily risen to the task."

Red opened her mouth, her full lips ready to protest.

But Janine was a skilled hunter. "I shall not allow you to decline," she said, with all the authority of a matron twice her age. "We will dine at eight. City hours, I know, but I've just come from London and am rather in love with the habit."

Red bit her lip, clearly uncomfortable. But she inclined her head. "Thank you, Mrs. Robinson. That shall give me sufficient time to see the children settled in their bed before I join you," she said.

It was artfully done, really. Just like that, Red had managed to divert the conversation back to the children. Which meant, George realized, she was about to make her escape.

"Of course, I must go attend to their afternoon lessons," she said, somehow having made her way to the door. "Good afternoon, Mrs. Robinson, Sir George."

The children's afternoon lessons consisted of activities out of doors. Not in the nursery, which was the direction Red had disappeared. But George kept that bit of information to himself. He'd rather not submit her to his sister's presence. Especially because the longer he spent in Red's presence, the less he believed he'd be able to keep his hands off her.

What would Janine have to say about that?

A dreadful lot.

CHAPTER SEVENTEEN

RED'S HEART HAMMERED all the way across the foyer and up the stairs.

Her death is not the only one on my conscience.

The questions swirled through her head so quickly that she could not sort them out. He felt responsible for something that had happened at Waterloo—something that had resulted in the deaths of others.

This was exactly the sort of information that could move her quest forward. Whatever event had been so distressing that it sent him into fits of darkness... It had to be related to why Legrand was here in England. George must have seen or done something that the French assassin—and whomever he was working for— deemed worthy of finding out. Or worse, silencing.

The scent of the poison from the kitchen filled her nostrils, as if she were standing before it once again. But she was not, Red reminded herself. She still checked daily.

She entered her bedchamber on silent feet, tracking around the room to set her snares by habit. More than anything, she needed to sleep. If she was going to join George and his sister for supper, she needed to be in full control of her mental faculties.

After a night spent on the sofa in the study, it was a miracle her eyes were still open at all. Though it was not the sofa itself, but rather the occupant. She'd spent nights in much less comfortable circumstances. No, it was George nuzzling her neck, George nudging her knees apart, George waking her by suckling her breast… That was the reason she was tired enough to collapse.

So collapse she did, into her bed, with all the snares and traps laid to protect her for the hour of repose. Even in a deep sleep, she'd hear the children coming in enough time to detangle them. A lady knight was always listening, always watching.

As her eyes closed, two words materialized in her mind.

Her death.

Her death is not the only one on my conscience.

George's wife.

He blamed himself for her death. She'd sensed as much, from the way he avoided the mention of her. Eveline was the image of her, Janine had said. Which was why George struggled to form a close attachment with his daughter. She must remind him terribly of the love he had lost.

The babe. His sister had mentioned a baby.

Red knew his wife had died in childbirth. She'd assumed it had been giving birth to Archie. But there was another child, if her understanding of Janine's words were correct. A baby that had died with its mother.

Red's heart twisted in pain. Not for herself, but for George. And for Eveline and Archie.

But when she closed her eyes again, the picture that came to her mind was the beautiful Miss Marion Abbot. And the pain that gripped Red then was entirely for herself.

HIS SISTER WAS trying to kill him. Not only had she brought her friend along like an hors d'oeuvre to be served up for him, she'd then gone one step further and invited Red to dine with them. One disaster after another seemed to be his lot in life.

Miss Marie Abbot—or was it Marion? Hell, he couldn't remember. He didn't want to remember. He'd said no more than a sentence to the woman when she'd arrived with his sister, and then another wishing her well for an afternoon of repose in the chambers his staff prepared. Somehow, his sister had decided that was enough to herald a perfect match. It was utterly idiotic.

He was not going to marry. Not Miss Whatever-her-name-was Abbot, and not anyone else. He'd learned the hard way that the only thing that came from marriage was pain. He loved his children. Archie and Eveline were bright spots in the dark hell that had become his life since Waterloo. But even they were a source of pain in their own way; he had only to look at Eveline to be reminded of all the ways he'd failed his family.

As for inviting Red to dine with them… George sighed as he adjusted his tailcoat. He'd shared dozens of suppers with Red. Before, the children had always been in attendance. Before, he'd not had the most exquisite, cataclysmic sex of his life with his children's governess. How he was expected to sit across the table from her and keep any sort of composure was beyond his understanding.

Janine, of course, was congratulating herself on the idea. Somehow, she must think that having Red in attendance would help her suit with Miss Abbot.

His valet handed him his cravat, stepping up to knot into place, but George waved him away. "I'll manage," he insisted.

He did not dress formally much these days, but he did remember how.

For a half-second, George wondered if he ought to send a messenger to Red's room, letting her know that this would be a more elegant supper than she was accustomed to. But the grandfather clock that Eveline had famously hidden herself in rang the hour, and he realized that he was out of time.

No matter what Red wore, she'd be beautiful, he assured himself. For some reason, he knew she'd manage. She always seemed to manage. George had yet to see her in a situation in which she did not respond with aplomb and grace.

A grin tugged at his mouth. He could think of one time. On

his desk—twice, actually.

Wishing he was headed to his study to provide Red with further instruction, he instead joined his sister where she waited in the parlor. Her blonde companion lingered at her side. No sign of Red.

"Good evening, ladies," George said, inclining his head to each of them in turn.

His sister held out her hand, leaving George no option but to take it. She narrowed her eyes. She wanted him to kiss it, damn her. So he would have to do the same to her friend.

Instead, he dropped her gloved fingers as if they'd burned him.

Janine shot him a look that promised retribution, but George was spared by the sound of footsteps. He turned to see Red enter. It occurred to him that he'd never noticed her footsteps before. She always just seemed to appear. But this time, he heard them well before, and what was more, he knew it would be her.

But even so, he was not prepared for the goddess who floated into the parlor.

She'd been stunning in pale seafoam. In rich, deep turquoise, she was like a sea siren come to life. The underskirt was wider than was strictly fashionable, giving more room to accommodate her wide hips and show them off as she walked, swinging from side to side. Black lace threaded with silver overlaid the turquoise, softening the bright color. If it was meant to look matronly, on Red it utterly failed. The black gossamer puff sleeves showcased her strong arms, and the square neckline showed off those glorious breasts. She must be wearing stays, to keep them in place like that. George's hands ached to be filled with them.

Her gloves, the same color as the underskirt, reached to her elbows, so only a smattering of the freckles on her arms was in view. George missed them.

"Miss Trudeau, how lovely you look," Janine said, her words an echo behind him.

"A gift from a previous employer," Red explained, curtseying to the two other women. And to him, he supposed.

"You clearly impressed them as thoroughly as you have me," George said for her ears alone, catching her hand.

He raised her gloved hand to his lips, imagining what it would be like to make love to her—wearing nothing but those elbow-length gloves. He would happily have stayed there, holding her hand, and forgone food.

Red, however, was politer than he. She tugged her hand away, and he had no choice but to let it go. She walked past him and greeted each of the women, offering compliments of her own before they could heap more upon her.

George stalked to the sideboard and poured himself a portion of brandy from the crystal decanter, as slowly as he could manage. Fiddle with the stopper. Pick the glass. Pretend to find something amiss. Pick another. Pour a bit. Swirl. Sample. Pour a dram. Pour a bit more. Return the stopper. What else could he do to avoid joining the trio of women?

Cross, bless him, opened the door to the dining room as George turned around to face his doom.

Janine must have been watching for Cross's appearance. She jumped into action, threading her arm through Red's and whispering something that George would wager Oxley Park he did not wish to hear.

Which left Miss Abbot smiling at him demurely from below her lashes.

She was a classically beautiful woman. In every way his sister had detailed, she was the type of wife he ought to want. Except that he did not want a wife. And he'd learned from his first marriage that perfect on paper and perfect in practice were not the same thing.

But Miss Abbot was a guest in his home, so he had no choice but to offer his arm and escort her through to supper.

He caught on to Janine's ploy as soon as they entered the dining room. He was seated at the head of the table, of course. On either side were Red and Miss Abbot. Janine had positioned herself on Red's other side. Which meant that whenever Janine spoke to Red, Miss Abbot was left with no one to talk to—forcing him, the gentleman, to do so.

If he'd been close enough, he'd have kicked his sister under the table.

"I hope your journey was comfortable?" he forced out between sips of soup.

Miss Abbot blushed. Why was she blushing? *Lord above, save me.*

"How kind of you to ask, Sir George. It was very comfortable. Your sister has been most kind with her care of me," Miss Abbot said. She smiled at him, her pale skin fading into the equally pale gown she wore.

"A journey from Wessex with my sister is hardly what I would describe as comfortable," George scoffed into his wine glass. His sister shot him a look. Even as she spoke with Red, Janine was listening to him and Miss Abbot. Of course she was. She wanted to ensure her friend did well. She'd probably coached her during the entire carriage ride.

George almost felt bad about the whole thing. It was not Miss Abbot's fault his sister had lost her mind. He returned his sister's scowl, only to have his eyes pass over Red. Which was a mistake, because looking at her meant that he could not focus on anything else, let alone make meaningless conversation with a simpering debutante.

When he shifted in his seat, he found Miss Abbot staring at him, eyes wide, waiting patiently for him to return his attention to her before saying, "We've just come from London, actually."

⊰※⊱

"LONDON?" RED ASKED before sipping her wine delicately. "Do you visit frequently?"

Her heart was in her throat. Her family was in London—every single one of them. The Little Season had concluded, so there were far fewer social gatherings taking place. It was unlikely that George's sister would have encountered the McGoverns. But if she had…

The red hair would be a sure tell.

"No, I prefer life in the country," Janine said. "As does Miss Abbot." She shot a look to her brother. Miss Abbot must have missed it, busy as she was with her demure glances. But Red did not. "But my husband's business ventures have taken us to London more and more of late, so I've had to rent a house there. At least I will be well positioned when the Season comes. Miss Abbot debuted last Season," Janine continued.

Shit. Mother of God. Fuck. Hell and damnation.

Red had attended so many debutante balls last season that they all blurred together. Mary Jane had made her debut then as well, and Red had been dedicated to securing her sister a favorable match. Usually she felt a sense of accomplishment reflecting back upon it, and that her sister was now the Duchess of Hartwell. But not now. Oh no, not now.

Miss Abbot would surely recognize her. Or, at least, recall Mary Jane, who shared Red's riotous curls, if in a slightly less vivid shade of red.

Also, why couldn't Red recall Miss Abbot? That was almost more worrying. As a lady knight, she was trained to notice every mundane detail. She ought to remember the face of a woman she would have seen, at least in passing, weekly for an entire Season.

But she could not very well ask. Not directly, not without revealing too much about her own background. She was not Ethelreda McGovern, sister-in-law to the Duke of Hartwell. She was Ethelreda Trudeau, a governess of genteel background but modest means.

"How lovely for you," Red commented, her mind still turning.

Another look from Janine to George. The latter cleared his throat and turned to Miss Abbot. "Did you enjoy the opulence and excitement of London, Miss Abbot?"

"It was quite lovely," she said, tilting her blonde head. Her curls framed her face perfectly. Even her voice was breathy and sweet. Red was going to be ill.

George was already half turned back to his sister, eyes glinting.

"Unfortunately, we did not stay long. After a few weeks, I found the speed of London too overwhelming and returned home to Wessex," Miss Abbot continued, the insipid little—

She'd only stayed a few weeks. Relief flooded through Red. Miss Abbot had only been in London a few weeks and had not enjoyed herself. Janine Robinson was new to London and not regularly attending social events because of the time of year.

Maybe, just maybe, Red would get out of this meal with her ruse intact.

She murmured something insignificant and then stuffed a bite of partridge into her mouth, the better to avoid talking herself into trouble somehow. There was nothing else to be gleaned from this meal. Nothing that would help her quest. George's sister and her friend were distractions.

Perhaps she could use that to her advantage, she considered as she moved the food around her plate. She had no appetite, not now. Not when George was avoiding looking at her.

He conversed quietly with Miss Abbot. Red was not jealous, she promised herself. He had to speak with the young woman— she was a guest in his house. It would be unforgivably rude to ignore her.

After months in his employ, Red could read him well enough. The smiles she'd seen so many times did not make an appearance at the meal. He kept giving his sister glares dripping with poison, as often as he could manage. Miss Abbot was not a threat.

But nor did he look at Red. Every time his eyes went to his sister, they slipped past her. She was tempted to stab a fork into her own leg to fight the numbness spreading through her. Her body was going into protection, survival. She recognized the sensation, had experienced it a few times before. But only when her life was in danger. There was nothing dangerous about this situation… was there?

"Are you well, Miss Trudeau?"

Red blinked rapidly, clearing the clouds from her eyes. "I am feeling a bit queer. Overtired, I think. I did not sleep well last night." She didn't dare look at George as she said it. But she did push back her seat. George came to his feet immediately. Red avoided looking up at him. "I beg your pardon, Mrs. Robinson, Miss Abbot. But I think it would be best if I retire. The children will need me on the morrow."

"Of course, do rest and recoup," Janine said.

The woman had been kind to her, Red realized. She'd treated her better than most ladies would treat the governess. But still, Red found she wanted out of her presence. Away from the blushing Miss Abbot. Away from all of it.

Her emotions were not in control, and it just would not do. She was a lady knight, governed by her duty and her cleverness. Not by jealousy or fear or whatever it was coursing through her veins.

She bobbed a curtsey in George's direction and hastily beat a track for the foyer. Cross was already there opening the door for her.

Red made it two stairs up before a large, calloused hand covered hers on the banister.

She didn't reach for the dagger nestled between her breasts. She knew the scent and feel of him. She hadn't heard him behind her, which meant she was more incapacitated than she'd realized, or he had the ability to move with more stealth than she'd ever given him credit for.

"Are you truly unwell, or has my sister simply annoyed you beyond bearing?" He was right behind her, close enough she could feel the heat of his breath on her neck. That closeness… It caused the knot in her stomach to loosen, fractionally.

"Your sister is kind and cares for you deeply," Red managed.

He curled his other hand around her hip, fingering aside the folds of the gown so he could find the curve of her body beneath. The familiarity of it sent rods of heat through her.

"I am less concerned about my sister"—he paused to press a kiss to the back of her neck, just above her gown—"and more worried about why you're running away, when I've never seen you back down from a challenge."

She would not admit it. She was not jealous. It simply was not possible.

His next kiss was at her hairline, with his nose nuzzling the curls aside. Red knew she was trembling again, and that when he touched her like this, she was powerless to stop it. No amount of lady knight training would help her now.

George paused there, pressing his body into hers from behind, his face buried in her neck, simply sharing space and being close to her. Slowly, Red felt herself relaxing. Even if she'd tried, she did not think she could have resisted the comfort he offered.

She would have happily stayed there all night. But for once, it was George who remembered propriety.

"Off to bed with you," he said between pressing kisses to her neck. "I cannot properly ravage you again until you've fully recovered from our first lesson."

Red shivered but did as he said, walking up the stairs ten times lighter than she had been before. But her center was still warm and molten. She would not be going to sleep anytime soon.

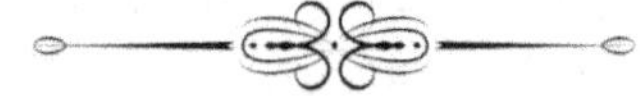

CHAPTER EIGHTEEN

THERE WAS NO chance for private trysts in the study—or anywhere else, for that matter—with his sister in residence. She was determined to shove Miss Abbot down his gullet. He was determined to thwart her. Meanwhile, Red was determined to tease him at every turn.

It all started with the fichu. The woman knew how much he adored her breasts, so the day after that disastrous supper she'd attended, she'd appeared dressed like a matronly schoolmarm twice her age. His first impulse had been to rip the thing off and toss it in the hearth. From the glint in her sea-blue eyes as she escorted the children to their music lesson, Red knew it. That, of course, had him instead envisioning tearing it off with his teeth. Which was worse.

Then there was the day she left her hair down. Honestly, it ought to have been a criminal offense. No one should have hair that glorious. As she flitted into his study to return several texts she'd borrowed for the children about local flora, she flipped it over her shoulder so the ends of the tendrils trailed over the neckline of her gown. Then she arched her back when she reached up to return the books to their shelves. Just like she had when she'd come in waves all over his desk.

But it was the sight of her in a ball gown that was going to kill him.

A governess should not possess something so fine. But she did, and she seemed to have no hesitation about wearing it. Why should she? It was clear that whoever her former patrons were—he'd have to look back at the references she'd provided upon applying for the position of governess—they'd clearly paid her well in both money and gifts.

He really ought to blame Janine for his impending death.

She was the one who'd insisted on throwing a ball. Not a ball—a quiet country dance. Just for the local gentry. The sort of thing their mother had hosted every spring. Except it was not spring, George had pointed out. To which his sister had countered that she was at Oxley Park now, and he could try to stop her but he'd likely die trying.

Janine always had been vexing beyond bearing.

But now, standing at the foot of the stairs, watching Red descend them as if she was floating on her own personal cloud summoned from the heavens, George did not know whether he wanted to murder his sister or thank her.

He supposed it depended on the outcome of the evening.

If it ended with Red finally back in his arms, he'd be plenty grateful.

If not, he'd have his sister in her carriage and on her way back to Wessex before luncheon tomorrow.

"I wondered if you would wear your uniform," Red said as she landed on the last step. She paused there, letting the two feet of space between them remain.

George wanted to drag her into his arms. Knowing his sister or her boring friend could enter any moment stilled the impulse. Instead he forced himself to speak like a perfectly normal person with self-control.

"I have retired the uniform." Suddenly, he was struck with the urge to tell Red the rest. That he'd truly retired. Resigned his commission. And why he'd done so. Not just the children, but everything else.

He staggered backward. He'd never wanted to talk about it.

In fact, he'd told himself he would take the secrets of Waterloo and his marriage to his grave. There was no one alive who would benefit from those truths being spoken aloud.

Except perhaps him.

He might heal.

For the first time, looking at this beautiful, smart, gregarious woman with a backbone made of steel, he thought he might be deserving of it.

"What is it?" Red closed the space between them immediately, reaching for his arm.

The warmth of her hand, even through the layers of glove and tailcoat and shirt, anchored him. *She* anchored him. He'd been unmoored for so long.

The proposition was utterly stunning.

"George?" She squeezed lightly. "Breathe."

His eyes found hers, calm and clear as the sea after a storm. He didn't examine that metaphor any further. Guests were already arriving—the clatter of hooves on the drive was unmistakable.

"I am well," he assured her, covering her hand with his own. "You'd best go through. There is no reason for you to torture yourself with meeting every landholder or relative of a lord who resides within ten miles."

Red's eyes narrowed, the blue clouding slightly. But the expression was gone as quickly as it had come, her brow smooth and eyes clear once more. She nodded and pulled her hand back, though she looked as regretful about it as he.

George caught her fingers before she could fully retreat. "I will find you, Miss Trudeau," he promised. "Save a waltz for me."

SHE *DID* WANT to stay and meet every landholder or relative of a lord who resided within ten miles of Oxley Park. Red could think of few things that would be as expeditious to advancing her quest.

But what she really wanted was to drag George upstairs and let him have his way with her.

The latter, she could do nothing about.

The former, however…

She felt George's eyes upon her as she drifted through the corridor toward the music room, whose doors had been opened to the adjoining hall to create a makeshift ballroom. It was modest by London standards, but Red could genuinely admire what Janine and Miss Abbot had accomplished since springing this idea on George a week ago.

Even now, as she entered the hall and accepted a glass of punch from Rooney, Janine and Miss Abbot were buzzing around seeing to last-minute details.

Janine could not have been more obvious about her attempt to install Miss Abbot as the future lady of Oxley Park. Similarly, if George had been any clearer about his distaste for the idea, he would have given offense.

It was poorly done on all counts, in Red's opinion. She'd done her share of familial maneuvering. How else would she have seen her three younger sisters so well married, with nary a dowry in sight?

But Janine was trying to force something that George clearly did not want—a wife. Red felt the way that tugged at her heart. She packaged up the pain and put it away, as she'd been trained to do. There was no room for pain tonight. Not even in this minute.

Punch in hand, she crossed the room to where Janine and Miss Abbot were pulling wilted flowers from a floral display.

"Good evening Mrs. Robinson, Miss Abbot." She dipped a curtsey and then spoke again quickly. If she left an opening, they'd comment on her dress—it was a magnificent dress—and she needed them gone. "The guests are beginning to arrive. Sir George is already in place."

"Oh dear! Well, this shall have to do." Janine shot an accusing look at the floral arrangement. "Miss Trudeau, may I beg a favor?

Will you see to these?" She held out the crumpled stems in her hands.

Perfect.

"Yes, of course," Red said, taking them instantly. "Everything looks lovely."

But her words of assurance barely registered. Janine smiled her thanks but was already leading Miss Abbot away.

Red waited until they disappeared from view before ducking into the music room. She reached for the connecting door to the parlor, only to find it locked. It seemed that someone did not want guests wandering. George? He wasn't relishing this event, but it seemed excessive for him. Perhaps Cross; he was very protective of his domain. Or Legrand...though the why eluded her.

Voices drifted from the corridors beyond. She needed to move quickly.

She dumped the wilted flowers behind the bust of Caesar. She could retrieve them later, or leave them. It was odd, but not enough for the staff to suspect anything untoward. The next bit was trickier.

One last glance around to make sure she was still alone, and Red pulled one of the jeweled hairpins from her chignon. Remembering everything Dominique had taught her over the years, she slid the pick into the lock—a simple Barron lock. It didn't budge. She needed a second pick.

The voices were coming closer. She yanked another pin out, feeling her hair coming loose over her shoulder. She'd have time to fix it later. Now with both picks, a hook and a rake, she'd be able to—

There.

The mechanism clicked and the door opened.

Red slipped through, closing it behind her. She did not have the expertise nor the time to relock it. Through the parlor, she had to dart into the hall. There was no other way. George's study had one entrance, and it was directly onto the foyer. This was the tricky bit.

One set of guests were already past the door. Through the sliver she allowed herself to open the parlor door, she could see that another spoke with George and Janine. The doors behind them, closed between guests against the autumn chill, were still.

That was it. She might have only seconds. She might have no time at all, if George and Janine did not remain where they were. But she had to take the chance.

The tall man and his reed-thin wife sauntered past. Red gave them two more steps, then she sprang into action. Her slippered feet were soundless as she darted along the wall, praying the door to the study would not creak—

There was Miss Abbot.

Not in the study. Not between Red and the study.

She was standing on George's other side, at the foot of the staircase.

Miss Abbot stood in the entryway of Oxley Park, greeting guests as if she was the presumptive lady of the house. Red swallowed down the bile that rose in her throat.

There was nothing wrong with Marion Abbot, she reminded herself. *Except that she's in the way,* her baser self retorted.

She did not have time for this.

She forced her feet to move, forced herself to open the study door just enough to slip inside, and close it behind her. Almost close it. She left it open just enough—not enough for George or anyone else passing by to notice it was ajar. But enough for her to peep out and match faces to voices.

Her gut told her that Legrand was already in residence at Oxley Park, though she was no closer to discerning who he was. She'd eliminated all the men inside the house, which meant that even though the weather was turning foul, she'd need to expand her search to those who worked outside—groundskeepers, gamekeepers, anyone in the stable. Vendors who made regular deliveries from the village were another possibility.

But none of that precluded the possibility that Legrand might be working with others. Contacts amid the gentry would be useful. Also, they were difficult to track. So many men had served on the Continent over the last decade that it was nearly impossible to manage the who, where, and when.

She must be watchful. If nothing else, the ball-that-wasn't-really-a-ball-but-was-actually-a-country-dance would provide convenient cover. The door to the parlor had been locked. It might be nothing. But her instincts told her otherwise.

Red's instincts had kept her alive more than once. Tonight, she had an entire family to protect.

CHAPTER NINETEEN

B UT TWO HOURS later, nothing of note had happened.

Perhaps that was not quite true.

Archie had snuck down and made it as far as the array of sweets in the music room before being caught. Eveline, of course, was too much of a lady for such antics. Red smiled despite herself as she sucked on an almond comfit.

But no one keeled over from poisoned punch. Red had checked it herself, as well as all the food prepared by the kitchen, during a visit earlier in the evening under the guise of bringing up samples to the children as a treat.

Nor had any of the guests or servants approached the door to the parlor. Red had watched very carefully. No one had asked her to dance, which of course made logical sense. She was the governess and knew none of these people. She did look spectacular, of course. But any interested gentleman had only to put a question to Janine to find out she was one rung above the help.

Red told herself she was not bothered. She'd never had a wealth of dance partners before this; there was no reason to expect a change now. But George… He saw her. He saw her and wanted her. He saw her and adored her.

He'd also danced with Miss Abbot. Red had eaten five almond comfits to keep the flood of feelings at bay.

When the second hour passed, she thought maybe he'd forgotten her. She hated the way that made her feel. She was a lady knight, for heaven's sake. She was not vulnerable to the whims of a man. She deceived men. She stabbed them and sent them to spend the remainder of their miserable lives in prison.

But when Sir George Caldwell started to weave through the crowd, stopping here and there to respond to a kind word, to greet an acquaintance, but making unmistakable progress toward her, Red forgot all of that.

When he took her hand and pressed a kiss against the silk glove, she was not a lady knight or a governess or an older sister. She was a woman.

"Will you honor me with this dance?" he asked, bowing.

Unnecessary, but disarming nonetheless.

"Yes," she breathed, letting him lead her to the dance floor where other couples took their places.

Next was a waltz, Red remembered. She'd seen the program for the evening. He'd waited for a waltz. The significance had her desire humming to life.

"It is time for our second lesson," George said into the air beside her head. Her curls moved with the soft breeze of his breath. Even with the help of the mirror in the parlor, she'd been unable to fully right the updo that Sara had originally created.

"I am an accomplished dancer. It is a prerequisite skill for any aspiring governess hoping to cater to the needs of proper young ladies," she recited from *Mrs. Plimpton's Guide for the Modern Governess.*

Red's mother had taught her to dance. When there'd been no extra funds for outside tutors, Mrs. McGovern had seen to instructing her daughters herself. Red's heart lurched; she missed her mother and her sisters. But she could not think of them now.

Fortuitously, George's hand caught her waist, and thinking about anything else at all became difficult.

"I hope you are. Our lesson depends upon it," he said, though the first strains of music threatened to steal his last few words. "But you've never danced like this."

Red had no opportunity to ask what that meant. In the next breath, she was whirling into the waltz.

She'd waltzed before—more times than she could count. But she'd never been interested in her partners beyond platonic or investigative purposes. Her brothers-in-law were diligent about inviting her to the dance floor. Friends of her father were kind enough to fill in her dance card. A handful of times she'd used the intervals of closeness in a dance to slip her hand inside a gentleman's coat and nick an important document or object.

But she'd never danced with a lover.

When George's hands were on her, there was nothing platonic or investigative about it. He held her too close. He spun her a bit too quickly, just so he could catch her against him. She must look a fool. She did not care.

"What are you doing?" Red demanded as they came face to face once again, hands joined. She tried to ignore George's hand at her waist. But his fingertips were kneading so torturously, and if he slid his hand even a fraction farther, it would be on her derriere.

"Teaching you a lesson."

"I feel as if I'm being punished." She was gulping for air.

"Tomorrow, I want you to burn every fichu you own." George spun her.

Red felt the wickedness of her own grin as she landed back in his arms. "That would be very wasteful."

"I demand you never wear your hair loose in sight of another man." The pressure on her hip increased, tightening, pinching, almost.

But instead of acquiescing, Red leaned her head back and laughed with delight. "I had no idea my ploys were so effective."

"You are a siren come to life, come to haunt me in my own home." George let his head drop to the side so he could nuzzle at her hand where it rested on his shoulder. Red gasped. There were people everywhere. Surely someone would see.

The pressure from her hip transferred to her hand, to where

their hands were joined. He was leading her; of course, he'd been leading the entire dance. Strong-willed as she was, Red knew that two fighting for the lead always ended in graceless disaster.

But George wasn't leading her around the dance floor any longer. He was leading her from it. She was about to question whether he'd hit his head or taken too much drink, making a spectacle in front of all his guests, when he dropped her hand.

He bowed, even though he'd cut the dance short. Red's heart hammered in her chest as she tried to make sense of what was happening. But as he brushed past her shoulder, she heard him whisper words meant only for her:

"Morning room. Do not make me wait."

Red forced herself to watch the rest of the revelers spinning around the center of the hall. She did not turn and look to see where George had gone or whom he spoke to now. As she stood there, whatever attention she'd garnered from the other guests dropped away. It may be unusual for a governess to attend the festivities, but the master of the house had not even finished their dance. Surely, that meant he found her of little interest.

George had a strategic mind, Red thought. It was no wonder he'd been such a heavily decorated officer during the war.

Finally, after the waltz had ended and the first notes of the cotillion rang out, Red murmured excuses to no one and slipped out. The parlor door remained untouched; she'd check it again later. Through the music room, into the corridor, past the study, and around the staircase to a room she'd explored only during her initial tour of Oxley Park.

George preferred his study, and the children moved mostly between the nursery, the music room, and the grounds. But she recalled the layout of the morning room, with its sunny yellow walls positioned to the east to catch the light from the rising sun. There were several upholstered chairs and a padded window seat that curved out to overhang into the gardens.

He'd chosen the window seat for his assault. Like a panther about to make his strike, or a soldier who'd scouted ahead for the best position, he lingered just within the shadows. But Red found him instantly, as if there was a string from the center of her chest to his, pulling her closer.

"I expected you to follow immediately," he growled.

Red closed the doors behind her noiselessly. "I had to give the impression that you'd abandoned me. Was that not your intent?" She moved closer, finding a bit of moonlight to light her path. To light her up. She did not need to see George's face; she heard his groan when she stepped into the silver glow.

"My intent was to get you alone as quickly as possible." He moved fully into the moonlight.

The sight of him stole her breath. For several moments, they stood at their respective ends of the moonbeam, studying one another. He was achingly handsome, his long, dark hair already coming out of its tidy queue. Other than that, his finery was in order. But the black broadcloth did nothing to hide the wide breadth of his shoulders or the slight narrowing of his muscular waist. And when he shifted his weight—Red's throat closed like a vise. She could see the outline of his cock, urgent with need and pressing against the closely cut black trousers.

"George," she breathed, her voice aching with need.

"Come here," he commanded softly, crooking a finger.

Red recalled the feeling of that curled finger inside of her and closed the gap between them in half a breath.

He caught her in his arms, folding her against him and around him with such ease. Red wondered how many women he'd loved like this before. Not for jealousy. Oh no, there was no time for jealousy. Not when she had George's mouth on her. She wanted to personally thank each and every woman who had taught him to worship her like this. She would never doubt the strength of desire again.

"Stop thinking," he said into her ear, a second before running his tongue along the freckled shell of it.

"I am not—" She caught his arms and drew back. It was harder to see his face at this angle, even though she was closer to him now. "How did you know?"

"You did not make that delightful purring sound when I kissed your neck." His lips moved past her ear to where her hair was tied up. He seemed determined to muss it again, kissing the tender hairline and weaving one hand into her curls.

"I do not purr," she cried. Surely it was a cry of annoyance and not in response to the hand that had caught her hip and was squeezing her bum.

"Yes you do, like a languorous, sated tabby." He trailed his hand along her thigh, then, taking a handful, hoisted her leg up to wrap around his waist.

"I am not a cat!"

She tried to shove him away, but that hand from her hair was now on her other leg. With another motion that he somehow made easy, he lifted her up so she was straddling him on the window seat, her knees on either side of his waist.

"No, Red, you are all woman."

Her gown was up around her waist now, her legs bare as his hands explored up and down, from rounded ankle to muscular thigh and generous bottom.

"Now you are the one purring." She laughed against his mouth.

"Call me a tomcat, then. I could die happy with you on top of me like this," he said, shifting so his cock rubbed at her center through his trousers. "Perhaps I can imagine one improvement."

Red drew back enough that she could smile wickedly and hold his gaze as she slipped her hand down between them. He might be the skilled and knowledgeable instructor in the ways of lovemaking, but she was a quick study.

She held those mysterious, dark eyes as she freed his magnificent cock, wrapping her hand around it. Releasing her hold on his shoulder, trusting the strength of her own body and the touch of his hands on her legs to keep her in place, she lifted her thumb to her mouth. The gleam in George's eyes turned feral as she dragged her tongue over the pad of her thumb, leaving it glistening with moisture.

His hands tightened on her thighs as she lowered her hand between them and dragged her thumb over the head of his shift.

"Fuck," he groaned, throwing his head back. "Red, you are—"

"Heavens above! What on—"

"Janine, what the hell are you doing here?"

George didn't shove her to the ground, which she supposed was rather gentlemanly of him. Her entire backside was exposed. Maybe not—they were blocking the moonlight pushing through the window over George's shoulder.

But none of that really helped the embarrassment as Red slid to her feet with as much grace as she could manage. George tucked himself away and straightened beside her. Red was ready for the onslaught. Even if half of her was surprised at how quickly her mind had cleared from the lust-addled haze, the other half knew it was her extensive training in action.

She steeled herself, hands curling into fists—

Except they couldn't. At least, not both of them. Because George took her hand, threaded their fingers together, and held on tight. That *had* her stunned.

"Janine," George said, voice imbued with command that Red could imagine cowing an entire regiment of soldiers. However, it was as ineffectual on his sister as it had been on his children.

"I went looking for you. Some of the older guests have begun to take their leave and wished to thank you for your hospitality." Janine did not speak to Red, but nor did she avoid looking at her.

Red braced herself for some harsh rejoinder, but none came. The other woman's brow was furrowed tightly enough that she could see it even in the dark room. But beyond that, her face was unreadable.

"I shall escort Miss Trudeau upstairs and then come join you," he said, then turned to Red, frowning. "Unless you wish to rejoin the party."

"I think it is best if I retire for the evening. The children may very well still be awake," she said, though she was thinking more of her ruined hair than Eveline or Archie. If she knew anything about those two, they would not sleep until the last carriage pulled away from Oxley Park in the wee hours of the morning.

George nodded and moved to put her hand through his arm. But Red remembered—she had one last matter to see to. "Please, I appreciate the offer, but I can manage myself." She hated to do it, but she needed George and his sister to remain here in the morning room long enough for her to sneak back to the parlor, rather than up the stairs, without their seeing her. "I think you and your sister have some matters to discuss."

The horror in George's eyes was unfeigned. She'd apologize later. Or not, she thought wickedly. She squeezed his hand and then disentangled her fingers.

As she passed Janine, she did not bother to curtsey. It seemed like it would be mocking at this point. But she did incline her head respectfully. It was not her fault that she'd brought a sedate little lamb to a lion who enjoyed spicier fare.

⇢⇢⇥⇤⇤

"I CAN SEE that my efforts with Miss Abbot have been entirely for naught."

The door behind Red had not even closed before his sister started in on him. He'd never kept any whisky in this room. It seemed uncivilized. It was the morning room, after all. It was meant for sunny breakfasts, not broody drams. But he'd never felt the absence more.

"I told you as much the day you arrived," he ground out, fists clenched.

"You could have told me you are in love with the governess."

George's throat went dry. "I am not in love."

"Ha! The drivel that comes from your mouth. You would have thought that someone nearer to forty would have some sense to his name."

"I am not in love with Red."

"Red?" She bit her lip, breathing in sharply though her nose. "Oh, dear brother. You may be the older, but you are certainly not the wiser."

"You are speaking in riddles."

She stared hard at him, her dark eyes—the twins to his own—boring into him as if she could read something written just behind the irises. But he could give her nothing. His regard for Red... He admired her above all other women. But that was not the same thing as love.

Love was folly.

Janine cleared her throat, folding her hands neatly in front of her. "Miss Abbot and I shall depart on the morrow. I do not see any sense in lingering here at Oxley Park."

George frowned. "But you've just said what a rousing success the dance was."

"Indeed. I suspect your neighbors will be talking about it for months. And expecting it to become an annual occurrence, as it once was." She gave him a pointed look from beneath her brown eyebrows before drifting over to examine the portrait above the fireplace. "Nonetheless, I came here with the hope of convincing you to wed Miss Abbot. If she did not suit, I hoped to open your eyes to the notion of remarrying, at the very least."

"You have not succeeded."

Janine did not turn to him. But George felt that if he'd been better positioned, he would have seen her eyes roll skyward.

She finished examining the portrait and turned back to him. "In any case, we shall depart tomorrow before luncheon. I have been away from my children for too long."

George cocked his head to the side. "To Wessex, then? Isn't Robinson in London?"

"Indeed he is." She nodded, smiling faintly. "But as I'm sure you're learning, dear brother, there is love...and then there is the love we bear our children. It is something else altogether."

Her words ought to have puzzled him even more, but instead

they settled into his bones and found purchase. George did not pull away when his sister reached out and grasped his hand. Then, compelled by an urge he did not understand, he tugged her forward and enveloped her in his arms.

They stood like that for several minutes, embracing for the first time since childhood. George might have felt a droplet of moisture land upon his hand. But he spared them both the agony of acknowledging it.

Janine cleared her throat again, straightening her spine and her gown. "Now, we had best return to the hall. We have many guests still enjoying themselves. As much as it pains your old bones, you must stay until the bitter end."

She held out her hand. George took it, and felt another piece of himself fall back into place.

RED HAD PRECISELY one minute to twist her hair into something presentable between the morning room and the parlor. If she encountered someone in the corridor, she'd look a mess and scurry upstairs. That was as much of a plan as she had.

But luck was with her. She reached the door to the parlor without encountering either servant or guest. She reached for the handle, expecting to find the room empty, as it had been every other time she'd peeped in that evening—

Voices.

Red's stomach twisted, but she stilled her hand just in time. The handle jiggled slightly as she swiped her hand past. She froze, waiting. The voices did not stop. Did not even pause.

She was in a terrible position. Anyone might walk out of the music room and see her lurking there by the door. George and Janine were likely only a few minutes behind her. But this exchange, this meeting—it had to be the reason the door from the music room to the parlor had been locked.

Locking both doors would have been too obvious. But by

strategically locking the one that connected directly to the party, whoever was inside the room made it much less likely their rendezvous would be interrupted. Conversely, if someone did stumble through the door that opened to the corridor, the one Red lurked behind now, the occupants were close enough to the festivities to claim they'd merely stepped away to freshen up.

Red sifted through her options. She could go into the parlor, claiming precisely the excuse that had just passed through her mind. Then she would know exactly who was inside, though she would know nothing about their intentions.

If she lingered in the corridor, she would eventually be intercepted by someone passing by. What was worse was that she could not hear a damn thing. The music from the party, drifting through the open doors of the music room from the hall beyond, made it impossible to discern anything but the fact that there *were* voices. Red could not even tell if they were male or female, or precisely how many people were engaged.

Two, her instincts told her.

But whether that was the pitches of the voices that some subterranean part of her brain perceived or complete fallacy, she could not have said.

She had to open the door. She had to risk it. Not all the way, but at least a crack.

Before she did, she shucked her slipper, catching it with one hand. Regret flashed through her at the sight of the pearls embroidered in a flower pattern on the toe. These were a favorite pair. Too bad.

With merciless strength, Red ripped apart the embroidery so the slipper hung in shreds. Now she had an excuse for when someone came up on her in the corridor. Next, the door.

She took a few heartbeats to synchronize her breath with her movement. With an inhale, she shifted her body weight forward, and on the exhale she applied faint, smooth pressure to the door handle.

It moved soundlessly beneath her hand, and the weight of her shoulder on the door edged it open just enough. The parlor was lit; she remembered that from her earlier passage through it. Good, the light from the corridor would not spill in damningly. But the music might. She hoped the increased volume through that sliver of air was unperceivable.

"…is always writing. You… nothing?" a voice demanded.

"Bees… about bees… battles."

She heard neither voice. But even if it was George himself, she'd have struggled to recognize it. They were whispering, and with the din of the music, she was only catching a few words.

"We…"

What the hell was that?

"…out of time."

"Make the report… I will… into my own hands."

"This isn't Waterloo."

Red's heart stopped. The first full sentence she'd been able to discern. Also, the one that confirmed this had everything to do with her quest.

She leaned forward just a bit more, hoping if she could get closer to the gap, she would hear what came next.

But there was no next.

There was the sound of the other door opening—the door into the music room.

Red shoved her ruined slipper onto her foot, damning herself for wrecking it beyond repair, causing her to be so damnably slow. She had to get to the music room, had to see who emerged from that door—

She froze, stomach dropping to the floor.

The room was full of people. The local magistrate and his wife, whom Red had been introduced to earlier in the evening. Several servants—Mrs. Yates, Rooney, Gerald. Even Louisa had left the kitchen, donning a housemaid's uniform to assist with the unusual number of guests. Plus half a dozen other guests that Red did not know.

She gave herself three sweeps of the room, ten short seconds, to commit all the faces to memory. Then she spun on her heel, slowing only to rip the blasted slipper off her foot and scurry upstairs. She yanked out a piece of paper and leaned over the dressing table, drawing circles for each face as quickly as she could, labeling them hastily, not bothering with code, trying to get as much down before the memory faded from her mind.

Three minutes later, she collapsed back in the chair.

Her head was beginning to ache.

She'd be trying to piece together the snippets of conversation well into the night. But the same words tugged on her consciousness again and again.

Out of time.

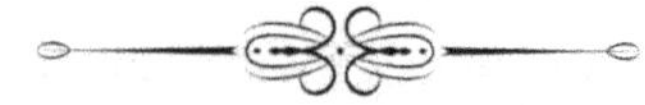

CHAPTER TWENTY

RED LAID HER trap carefully.

Even though everything in her screamed to move quickly, to take action, she did not. She watched and considered, thinking through her plan from all angles. There was a time for speed and a time for deliberation. Her training had taught her that.

Still, those whispered words haunted her.

Out of time.

Out of time.

Out of time.

If Legrand was out of time, then so was she.

Legrand had been in the parlor of Oxley Park, and she had let him go. She told herself there were many reasons why. She had not been certain it was him until the last moment, having gotten only snippets of the conversation. The house was full of guests, and though Red was an accomplished swordswoman, Legrand was an assassin in his own right. To confront him, when he was alone and there were civilians everywhere, was contrary to her brief as a lady knight.

Then there was her quest. She was not only to determine the identity of Legrand and his conspirators—now she knew there was at least one—she was to uncover why they'd come to Oxley Park in the first place. Revealing herself would have failed to accomplish those goals.

But her timeline had accelerated. She could no longer wait and watch, carefully collecting information. It was time to put things into motion, to squeeze the details she needed, from the one person who had them—George.

It took a week to arrange it all properly. She'd contacted the music instructor, asking that he begin teaching Eveline to play the harp. Of course, Red already knew that the harp was not within the current music tutor's repertoire. However, eager as he was to maintain the plum daily position, he had found someone who specialized in the harp—and only the harp.

Red would have congratulated him on his cleverness, if he had not played so perfectly into her plans. For this first lesson, she scheduled both instructors to come at the same time. The old music instructor would start with Archie on the pianoforte, and Madam Bryant would begin with Eveline on the harp. To cover herself, she'd scheduled a double lesson.

Two hours that the children would be distracted. Two hours to enact her plan.

And George, damn him, had set off early.

She stepped out the door of Oxley Park to find its master not back in his study finishing his tea, as he ought to be at this hour, but halfway to the copse of trees where the road split and led to the summer house.

He was walking. Which meant she'd have to run.

Hell and damnation.

George's favorite curses sprang to her mind as she lifted her skirts and sprinted.

She could run, when necessary. She was even reasonably fast. But she hated it. Her thighs chafed and her breasts rubbed together, with sweat pooling beneath them as they flopped mercilessly up and down. She was a woman meant for sparring, not sprinting.

He disappeared around the bend just before she would have had to slow her speed to avoid his hearing her. She darted into the trees. If she cut through, she'd beat him. With her increased speed, she should get to the summer house with enough time to get into position. And she'd be sweating profusely enough to give the impression she'd been sparring for longer than two minutes.

Red burst from the trees, her boots splashing through the mud, her pelisse flying behind her. But she didn't stop, yanking open the doors of the summer house. It was well past the time of year where she would normally be sparring with the doors open. It was cold as a witch's tit. But she couldn't let it bother her. If she closed them, there was a chance he'd walk right past her to the apiaries. She couldn't have that.

For a second, she thought she'd left her parasol.

No, there it was, tucked under her arm. She yanked the rapier free from the handle, stuffing the lacy portion under the cushions of the wicker sofa and dragging out the extra rapier she'd stashed beneath several days before.

She heard George's footsteps as she raised her arm above her into an *en garde* position.

She pretended not to hear him. Swung her arm down, threw her weight forward, and thrust. Then, with an equally quick step, she spun and parried as if there were another attacker suddenly behind her. She moved with the grace of a dancer; at least, that was how Dominique always characterized it. If anyone would know, it was the most graceful of lady knights.

George's footsteps stopped. She could not hear his breathing over her own, which was actually slowing now that she was no longer running pell-mell across the estate. But from the corner of her eye, she saw him in the middle of the path, right in front of the door she'd thrown open a bare minute before.

She pretended to notice him, dropping her sword to her waist, at the same moment he managed to get a word out.

"Red."

She swallowed, using her heaving chest to emphasize the next breath she drew. "George."

His hand immediately went to his hair. His fingers fanned out at his hairline, ready to plunge into the thick, dark waves that he'd tied back, as always. But he jerked his hand back, shoving it into his pocket instead.

If he was attempting to look casual, he was failing utterly.

But Red waited, strategically. She needed to gauge his reaction before she responded.

"Why do you have a sword?"

Red dragged in another breath through her nose. "I do have a penchant for unconventional forms of exercise."

George's laugh was dry, unsure. She still had not convinced him. He was wondering who she was—what she hadn't told him. He was assessing her with his colonel's eyes—as if she were a threat. She had to disarm him, and quickly, before he recalled the way she'd skillfully disarmed him in the study that first month at Oxley Park.

"My father was an instructor at Shrewsbury before he died. I did not have any brothers…so he taught me." She cast her eyes down, allowing color to flood her cheeks, knowing it would spread to her bosom as well. That could only help her cause; it might draw his eyes to her breasts, which would certainly distract him.

"How long was he at Shrewsbury for?" George's posture was still stiff, but he managed to soften his face. Red could have taught him to do both. But she let him come closer, willing her eyes to be clear and guileless.

"Nearly twenty years, before the palsy took him," Red said. She let her eyes flood with tears. The Duchess of Guilford had always instructed them to stay as close to the truth as possible when on a quest. It was easier to keep track of the lies you constructed. Red's father did suffer from palsy; for now, it only affected his left hand. But they all knew it would only worsen.

George was close enough to touch her now. But he didn't. Not until she lifted her chin and he saw the tears in her eyes. Then he curled his hand around hers where it grasped the rapier, dragging his thumb comfortingly over her knuckles.

"I am sorry for your loss," he said softly.

Shame washed through her at the gentleness of his voice. George had known loss—such loss. Wife and child. Here she stood, playing upon that exact pain to make sure he believed her story. For half a second, she hated her quest, the Lady Knights, and anything even tangentially related to causing this man pain. She never wanted to see him suffer again.

Shock at her own thoughts jolted her back to her purpose.

"Thank you," she said, leaning in a bit closer. Close enough to kiss, but she did not reach for his lips. Just stood there, breathing his air, for a few moments while he accustomed himself to this new part of her. "He did not want to teach me in the beginning. He wanted me to become a proper lady. But I am rather insistent."

George chuckled, and the rough tenderness rolled over her. "I can certainly imagine. Perhaps that is why you are such a natural with my little hellions."

"Because I was one myself?" She grinned.

He'd called her a natural—*with children*. Red wanted to mark it down in her secret, coded notes so she could tell Miranda sometime. Perhaps before she returned the odious *Miss Plimpton's Guide* to her.

"I have drawn on my own unconventional background to help me with Archie and Eveline," she admitted. That, at least, was the truth.

"Tell me more. What else are you hiding, beside prodigious skill with a rapier?"

Red saw her opportunity. "Prodigious skill? Are you equipped to judge, Sir George?" She stepped back, making a show of looking him over with an appraising eye.

"I am a trained infantry commander," he said, straightening and puffing out his chest. He did so without a hint of artifice. But Red did not point that out to him. Instead, she tipped her head back toward the wicker sofa and the rapier leaning against it.

"Is that from the manor?" George said, stepping around her

and grabbing it with one graceful swipe.

"Perhaps." Red did not have to feign the blush that burned on her cheeks then. "I may have borrowed it from the display case at the manor, to see how it felt in comparison to my own."

George lifted it, pointing the tip directly at her. "You are trouble, Ethelreda Trudeau."

"Shall I start giving Eveline lessons?" she teased, nudging his blade aside casually with her own.

"God, no. She'd likely run me through in a fit of temper."

"You might deserve it."

His eyes flashed, darkening for a moment. Red had half a second to decide whether to prod that wound or move on. She opted for the latter.

"Show me how much His Majesty's training is good for," she said, raising her blade.

George's mouth curved into a half-smile. In that moment, he was every bit the soldier unable to resist a challenge.

"I'm better with an infantry sword," he said, testing the balance of the blade.

"Intimidated?"

"By you, Red? Constantly." But he moved into position rather than dropping his hand. "How shall we determine the winner?"

"Touches, naturally."

"Try not to draw too much blood."

She pressed her free hand to her heart, atop her quivering breasts. "I shall do my best." Then she swung forward.

He parried easily, trying to put her on the defensive. She let him.

"Tell me more about your unconventional upbringing," he said.

Red conceded a few more steps, carefully marking the space between her and the furniture abutting the wall behind her. "A question for each touch."

She thought he would refuse. She hadn't asked any questions about his background, not really, nothing to give him any sense of what she might ask with her winning touch. It was dangerous to someone who guarded his past as carefully as George did. But the swordplay was relaxing him, just as she'd intended.

Red let him nick her arm—just a brush of the thick fabric of her pelisse with his blade. "You first, it seems."

He narrowed his eyes, evidently not fooled by how easily that first point had been. But he took his opportunity.

"Did your father teach you to wield any other weapons?"

She twisted adroitly to avoid his next swipe of the blade, huffing a laugh as she did. "No. I tried shooting once, but I was terrible at it." It had been Jane who tried to teach her, not her father.

He expected her to be off balance, talking as she swung. But he was wrong, and she landed the next touch. George was temporarily stunned. Red did not even try to suppress the victorious grin on her face.

Sighing, he lifted his blade into position once again. "Go on, then."

"When did you buy your commission?" She hoped it was neutral enough to keep him from closing off.

"The year Eveline was born." Several more moves, then she allowed him another touch. "Why did you become a governess?"

"You don't think I'm well suited to it?" she said with a thrust, landing her own touch on his shoulder.

She didn't pause, though, engaging him once again. As long as she could keep his blood pumping, she could keep the conversation going.

"I think that you are nothing like the other governesses who came—and left—Oxley Park." Beads of sweat were forming at George's temples despite the cold November air flooding in through the open doors.

"It was forced upon me by circumstances beyond my control." A truth. A circumstance otherwise known as the Duchess of Guilford. "I decided to give it my best crack, and found I was more capable than expected." She didn't need to tell him that his children had been her first and only charges. "You'd done your duty after the American war of 1812. Why didn't you resign your commission then?"

"I was able-bodied and an experienced commander. It seemed wrong to do so, even at the cost of my family."

"What do you mean by that?"

"Earn another touch."

She did, instantly.

George sighed, rocking back on his heels. "Things were not well between me and my late wife when I left for the Continent."

She wanted to press, but let him earn the next question.

He huffed out a breath, the victory softening his eyes a bit. "How long do you intend to remain at Oxley Park?"

Red sucked in sharply, nearly missing her parry for the first time. "Until my work is done." She had no more answer than that.

The tightness in her chest had nothing to do with the exertion. She fought it back at the same time that she fought forward, on the offensive. George's eyes widened. He was realizing that she'd been holding herself back, allowing him those touches. He was skilled, but not skilled enough to prevent her from scoring again.

"What happened at Waterloo that haunts you so?"

George's hand dropped to his side, and the tip of his rapier scratched the ground. "Ask a different question."

Red wanted to respect his wishes. She knew the pain he suffered, had seen it firsthand in the terrors, sleeping and waking. In a perfect world, he would have had time and peace to sort through the scars. But he had neither, even though he did not realize it.

"Sometimes, a wound is festering without us even realizing. Only by digging away at the infection can we truly cleanse and begin to heal."

George's face was unreadable. He'd retreated within himself, his blade hanging loose at his side. She knew he was replaying what had happened on that battlefield. Whether she succeeding in getting him to tell the story or not, she'd already done her damage.

"You can trust me." Uttering those words hurt the most of all.

His brows came together, cracking the veneer. "I know I can."

In the next breath, he launched forward. Red was ready, crossing her blade in front of her to protect her face—though she knew he'd never actually hurt her. He was testing her, seeing if she could handle the full force of his pain. She could. She'd been born with wide shoulders and broad hips for just this reason.

She drove him back, using the full weight of her body to push back his offensive. When he rocked back on his heels, he began to speak.

"There were two men in my command. One was from a titled family, standing to inherit, though modestly. The other—Barrow—was the son of a baker."

As he spoke, she began sorting through her knowledge of him and of Oxley Park, searching for connections. Barrow. She didn't recognize it.

"The lads argued about everything. Barrow in particular—he was salty that he was passed over for promotion in favor of someone who was gentry. He screamed foul." He thrust his blade upward, but she parried it away. A second later, he was on her again. She spun and stepped away, sure-footed and fast, leaving George panting. "I punished him for it."

They began to circle, each sizing up the other, waiting for a strike. Red knew that in this moment, she was not his lover or his children's governess. She was the war. She was the pain. She was the guilt and responsibility he carried.

He leapt forward again, punctuating each sentence with another expert swipe of his rapier. "But it all went to hell when they took a shine to the same woman. A courtesan turned camp follower, no less. Elegant manners and all that, but nothing worth dying over."

Red met him blow for blow, savoring the cry of her muscles and the sweat rolling down her back. But even as her body coursed with heat, she felt a chill begin to spread through her.

"But Barrow seemed to think differently. I watched him run the lad through with his bayonet from behind. I was pinned down, fighting—I couldn't get to him."

They were blade to blade, each pressing against the other, faces mere inches apart. Red could see the agony etched on his face. She knew what was coming even before George fell back, dropping the rapier with a sharp clang. He stumbled toward the wicker sofa, barely catching his hand on the arm to keep himself from going to the ground completely.

Red's own blade fell loose at her side, but she held her ground, letting him finish.

George raked his hand through his dark hair, loose around his shoulders from their sparring, his fingers brutally ripping through the tangles. As if he would punish himself with this little bit of pain.

"McGovern was murdered on that battlefield, and there wasn't a damn thing I could do about it."

Red froze. "McGovern."

"Young Josiah, the other soldier." George's gaze dropped to the ground, as if the weight of saying the name was too much to bear.

Josiah McGovern.

The cousin Red had lost at Waterloo.

She could not let any of it show upon her face, but her insides were storming. "What happened to Barrow?"

George dropped down to sit on the sofa, gaze still fixed on the floor with unusual focus. Red passingly wondered if he was using the exercise she'd taught him to steady himself.

"Barrow claimed that McGovern was trying to desert, that he'd been justified. I knew better, but it was my word against his, and I'd been too far away for anyone to trust what I saw enough to swear it."

Red's heart screamed for justice.

"There were a few brigades who refused to surrender and took up positions a few miles from the battlefield, along the river. I sent Barrow out alone on a scouting mission."

Red went to sit beside him. She knew what was coming next, and she wanted to be sitting beside him. She did not trust her face or features.

"Barrow was gunned down before he even made it to the river."

He'd deserved it. Barrow ought to have been hanged for murder. But she said none of that. She sat in silence as he said the words that truly haunted him.

"It is my fault. They were in my charge, my responsibility. If I'd managed them better, if I'd taken more care, Barrow would not have killed McGovern. And if I was half the man you think I am, I wouldn't have sent Barrow out. I may not have killed them directly, but their deaths are at my feet nonetheless."

Red wanted to tell George it was not his fault. She wanted to tell him that she bore the name McGovern, and she absolved him. But she could do neither. George was not in the summer house. He was far, far away in his mind. All she could do was reach out and take his hand and sit by his side while he fought his demons.

So she did.

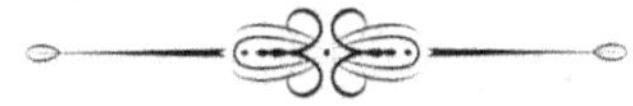

CHAPTER TWENTY-ONE

HE WAS DREAMING again. There was Red, exactly as she had been that first time she came to him in his dreams—wearing a matronly nightgown that cinched at her throat, her hair tumbling down around her shoulders, glowing like an angel.

It was a candle, some part of him noted. She held a candle as she slipped through his door. It was already burned down, as if she'd been awake all this time. What time was it? He couldn't see the clock on the table beside his bed. It was late. It might even be the morning, technically. Had she been awake all this time? No, surely not.

When she doused the candle and climbed into bed with him, he forgot to wonder.

She nudged the bedclothes back, sliding in beside him. But only for a second. She lay beside him, kissed him softly, for a moment. Then she tugged her nightgown up and swung her leg over so she was straddling him.

He'd thought to teach her? There was nothing else she needed to learn. She caught his face between her hands and dipped her tongue into his mouth, brushing her breasts against his shirt through her thin night rail. Meanwhile, her hips circled round and round, torturing his cock.

He was ready for her. He'd been thinking of her when he fell asleep. But he'd held off, drifting away to dreamland with his hand on his cock but before finishing. He'd been waiting for her, he realized. Some part of him had known she would come.

Now he had to make her come in return.

He reached between them, pausing to pay homage to her glorious breasts. She arched above him, breaking the kiss so she could pull loose the ribbon at her throat. With a graceful arch of her back, she pulled the linen over her head and tossed it aside. She glowed in the moonlight above him. So bright, she might have been a vision. But no vision could feel this good.

Those were the curls between her legs tickling the tip of his cock even now. He'd meant to tease those curls, to draw her out and help her find her pleasure. But he'd been distracted by those damn magnificent breasts. Before he could reach down and take control, she lowered herself onto his manhood, seating herself fully in one long stroke.

She knew what she wanted—what he wanted as well. She guided his hands to her breasts, kneading his fingers into the tender flesh as she rode him. He took over, rolling her nipples between his fingertips. He tried to tug her down so he could suck one between his teeth, but she was enjoying herself too much to surrender control.

Hands raised above her head, she tangled them in her hair and arched her back to get deeper, deeper, deeper.

The soft curves were a delicious and dangerous ruse, he realized. Beneath them, corded muscle hid, waiting to take its victim unawares. As her thick thighs gripped his waist and her dripping cunny clung to his shaft, he was seconds away from ultimate and unrelenting surrender.

He ought to be thinking of her. He ought to slide his hands down and massage her quivering button of nerves. But he was too lost in holding her breasts. He was still asleep. He was dreaming. He was awake. It was all real and distant and everything all at once.

She cried out, closing one hand over his. A low, feral whimper ripped from her throat as her hand tightened. He knew this—

spoke the language of need and want. He pinched the tight brown bud tight between his fingers, and then she exploded, riding him fiercely, bucking and writhing above him.

It was too much. He was going to explode. No, he was exploding. He had to—

She rolled away, only to catch his cock in her hand. She lovingly stroked the length as she plunged her tongue into his mouth and curled her leg over his. Again and again, until they were both sticky with spent desire and warm with satisfaction.

With her head tucked into his shoulder, curls tickling his chin, he fell into sleep once more. For once, it was dreamless.

CHAPTER TWENTY-TWO

THREE DAYS LATER, Red was still trying to connect George's recounting of the events he'd witnessed at Waterloo with Legrand's presence at Oxley Park. Both of the men involved were dead—including her own cousin.

She did not let herself dwell on that; she'd already mourned Josiah with the rest of her family. Like George, Red couldn't believe that her cousin would have deserted on the battlefield. Sharing that information with her aunt and uncle, or anyone else in her family—even if none of them would believe it either—would only cause more pain.

One hand went to her skirts, the other to the banister as she climbed the stairs toward her rooms. George had invited the children to spend their afternoon exercise time at the apiaries with him. Eveline was reluctant; Archie was joyous. Red was tempted to spare Eveline and allow her to read quietly in the nursery, but she'd seen the hope in George's eyes. He wanted to reconnect with his children after all the time away. He wanted to heal the wounds.

He would not be able to do that if Eveline was closeted in the nursery with her nose in a novel.

It also meant an hour or two of blessed silence for Red. Even at his calmest, Archie was constantly in motion. If not his legs running, then his foot tapping or his finger poking his sister. Red had moved through the last few days with only half a mind for whatever task was before her.

As she entered the nursery corridor, she felt herself already beginning to relax. She would set her snares, pull out all of her notes from their hiding places, and pore over everything in the light of day, rather than by stilted candlelight when she was already exhausted from looking after the children. Something would click into place, some small detail that she had been too worn out to see.

She reached her door, shrugging off the shawl she'd wrapped around her shoulders that morning and tossing it toward the bed. Fishing her key-necklace free from her bodice, she moved to the mantel to retrieve her locked box concealed among the books.

Red's heart stopped.

There was no ribbon sticking out from beneath the red leather-bound tome on the end. She'd always left it sticking out. Every time she moved the books, she always left the end of the scrap visible.

She whirled, instantly on alert.

She crossed to the dressing table, bending over to examine the drawers. She always left them out in the same pattern—one finger's width, one nail's width, one thumb's width. They were very close. But when she slid her thumb into the space left by the last drawer, she met resistance. It was just a bit too narrow.

Bloody hell.

One might be a coincidence. Two was anything but.

It was Monday. Her room was not set to be cleaned for two more days. On Wednesdays and Sundays, when the maid came in to tidy, Red always made a point of ensuring she and the children were in the nursery. That way, as soon as the maid left, she could come back in and reset all her snares.

It was just possible that the schedule had shifted. She'd have to speak with Mrs. Yates. But Red's instincts screamed foul. They'd rarely led her astray.

There was one last place to check. Her valise.

She moved toward the massive armoire in the corner where she stored her clothing. She'd stored her valise, still packed with a few items that she did not anticipate needing, inside the armoire weeks ago. There was no earthly reason for someone to look through an empty bit of luggage—unless they had nefarious purposes to mind.

Very carefully, she lifted the bag out of the armoire and set it on her bed. She had to bend around to see, but the evidence was clear. The single strand of dark hair that had been tied around the closed handles—taken from Eveline's hairbrush; Red's own was much too easy to spot—was gone.

Someone had opened her bag.

Her room had been searched by a professional. By Legrand.

The next few minutes were not about thinking—they were about verifying. She checked beneath the false bottom of the valise, inside her lockbox disguised as a book, and under the floorboard near the head of the bed. She'd pried that away during her second month at Oxley Park to give herself yet another secure hiding spot. Every document was present. The lock on the faux-book was intact, which meant Legrand either had not realized it was anything other than a book or hadn't been able to get through the tiny Bramah lock forged especially for the Lady Knights.

Legrand had not found any of her secrets.

Except the most important one—that there was more to Miss Ethelreda Trudeau than a simple governess.

Red dropped to the bed, the implications of her changed situation heavy on her shoulders.

Out of time.

Truly. She could keep up the ruse no longer. It was time to tell George who she was and why she'd come to Oxley Park.

FOR ONCE, WHEN he opened his father's bottom desk drawer and retrieved the whisky to pour himself a dram, it was in celebration rather than consolation. He'd spent three hours with his children at the apiaries.

Any way he could think to look at it, it had been a success. Archie had been stung, that was true. But the lad had learned a valuable lesson about how to differentiate between a hive that was agitated and one that was at peace. As his own father had often reminded him, education did not come for free. Archie had been nothing but smiles by the time they returned, bouncing down to the kitchen to ask for a poultice. George was sure Mrs. Shelley had stuffed him with sweets before sending him on his way.

Even Eveline had allowed a few smiles. She liked when he showed her the queen, with all her worker bees gathered around and caring for her every need. While Archie needed to follow him around from hive to hive, Eveline had been content to drift peacefully between the rows, murmuring. Singing, he realized. Just as he sang to his bees.

For the first time since he'd returned to Oxley Park, George felt that maybe—just maybe—there was a chance of peace here. There was a future in which he and his children could be happy together. A future in which Red—

He knocked back the drink.

A future in which Red was a fixture.

Sharing the horrors of Waterloo had been like the last piece of the puzzle fitting together. *Not quite,* his conscience screamed. There was one more—*Leisa.*

But telling Red about Waterloo and what had passed there, seeing the forgiveness and understanding in her blue eyes, clear of pity or judgment, told his soul that when the time came to speak of Leisa, Red would understand that as well. She would not blame him, even if he blamed himself. Because she was a woman unlike any other he'd ever met or ever would again.

A rapier-wielding, buxom lady straight from a medieval fantasy. By some miracle, she'd come to Oxley Park and taken not only his children in hand, but him.

He still sported a few bruises from their sparring session in the summer house. She was the superior swordsman. Swordswoman. George was secure enough to admit that, though he would not say so to her face. It was too much fun to torture her.

He was on his second pour of whisky when she knocked on the door. George knew it was her. He never heard her coming, but her knock was distinctive. One soft knock followed by three sharp raps.

"Come in," he called, setting aside his glass and bracing his hands on the desk to push himself up, ready to take her in his arms.

Red waved her hand. "Do not stand on my account," she said.

George wondered if he knew how badly he wanted her, just in that moment, just from a look. "Then come and sit on my lap."

A ghost of a smile flickered over her face. "Perhaps later."

George wanted to bring it back. He rifled around the drawer below him, emerging with another glass. "Whisky?"

Red's eyes widened. They were dark as storm clouds over the sea this afternoon. What did that mean? Was she worried? Or aroused? If it was the latter, why hadn't she accepted his invitation?

"Yes, please," she said emphatically, taking the crystal glass from his hand before the last drops had finished their sloshing.

She took a long sip, and her eyelids dropped closed as she savored the flavor. Even her eyelids had freckles, George saw. He'd never noticed it before. But he would know every last detail, he promised himself as he raised his glass and then took another sip himself. He would finally succeed at his goal of kissing every single one of the freckles on her creamy skin.

"I ought to have known you'd have a taste for spirits rather than claret or sherry." He chuckled as she retreated to the chaise and seated herself on the edge.

Another quirk of her wide, full mouth. Still not quite a smile.

"My father," she said, lifting her glass.

They sipped in silence for a few moments.

Her mind was occupied, that much was clear. He could ask her what it was that bothered her, urge her to share. Or he could provide her the companionship she'd so often offered to him. She would confide when she was ready. A good commander knew how to wait.

A commander no longer, he reminded himself.

A father, a lover. A friend.

After several more minutes, George set aside his empty whisky glass and unlocked the drawer that contained his treatise, pulling out the thick packet. He set it on the cleared space before him, eying it as one might an incendiary about to explode.

"Is that your treatise?" Red was leaning forward, craning her neck a bit to see the papers. He shifted them across the desk so she could see.

"*A Gentleman's Observations on the Behaviors of Resident Essex Apis Mellifera*," he read for her.

"It's quite thick," she observed, running a fingernail over the edges of the neatly stacked papers.

"I finished it a few days ago. But I have not been able to bring myself to go back and reread it," he admitted.

Red smiled for the first time. Not a wide grin, but a soft, gentle thing. Just for him. George felt that smile deep in his chest, where his heart had once been.

"Would you read it for me?"

Red's hand dropped away. "Me? I'm certainly not an authority on bees."

"You needn't be to understand it. At least, I hope that is the case. You're the cleverest woman I've ever known. If you think it's worthy, then I know the Royal Institution in London will have to accept it." He felt the conviction of his words in his heart. George slid it across the desk the rest of the way, until it threatened to fall into a disorganized heap on the floor. Unless she took it. Which she did.

"It will take me a while," she warned, flicking through the first few pages.

George stood up, stretching his arms over his head as she settled back into the chaise. "I shall ring for tea," he said.

But Red had already begun reading.

⋙⋘

MINUTES STRETCHED INTO an hour. The afternoon light turned grayer as early evening descended upon Oxley Park. Still, she read. Despite her love of novels, which she genuinely shared with Eveline, she was transfixed by the work. Page after page after page—the dedication required to construct such a thorough document. Red was more than impressed. She was in awe.

More than the facts or details, which were impressive, the level of care shone through. George clearly loved the research he'd done. He loved the bees. Not as much as he loved the children, she reminded herself with a chuckle. But the sentiment was much the same, and it oozed from every page.

"Well?"

Red jumped. She'd been so absorbed that she'd failed to realize that George was lurking just over her shoulder, tracking her progress.

"No one could read this and fail to be impressed," she said with complete sincerity.

George's hand slipped down from the back of the chaise to grip her shoulder. "You are not jesting."

A question disguised as a statement.

She reached up and covered his hand with her own. "No, George. It is more than I could have imagined. A masterpiece."

"I—"

A soft knock and the whisper of the study door over the thick rug forestalled George's next words.

"Sir, Mrs. Yates has asked to speak with you," Cross said from just inside the door.

"Yes, of course. I shall come right now." George tossed a look over his shoulder to her as he went. "Stay there. I want to hear more of your compliments—and your critiques—when I return."

Red was still smiling, even as she sat there alone in the study. She'd been granted a stay, if only a few hours. Tomorrow, she would tell him her secret. They would make a plan. They would capture and defeat Legrand together. Maybe the quest had always required the both of them to complete.

But tonight, she would celebrate George. Worship him in the same way he did her.

Her stomach jumped at the wicked ideas forming in her mind. She forced her eyes back down to the last few paragraphs.

Bees.

He'd completed a masterwork, and she could not steal that joy from him. Not tonight. She would stay awake all night to keep watch over the children. Then, on the morrow, they would plan.

Calm spread through her, new and warm, as she turned her eyes to the last page of George's tidy handwriting.

He'd written a small description about himself at the end of the treatise. Facts, mostly, and almost exclusively about his military service. *Captain, 10th Regiment of Foot, Canada, 1808. Major, 10th Regiment of Foot, America, 1812. Colonel, 5th Regiment of Foot, France, 1814.*

That could not be right.

She read it again.

He must have gotten the dates wrong. Transposed a number or some such minor error. But that was so unlike George. He lived and died for details. He'd spent half his life defining himself by his military career. There was zero likelihood that he'd written the dates incorrectly. She could count the total number of errors she'd found in the treatise on one hand.

Red stared and stared.

If those were the dates he'd been on the Continent…

The children's mother had died in childbirth in August 1815, two months after Waterloo. At that time, George had been away from England for almost a year.

Did George know? Of course he must. But he'd implied responsibility for her death. Red had assumed it was because she died trying to bear his child. But no—it hadn't been his child at all. What…what about Eveline and Archie?

Archie was too young to understand. But Eveline…

That poor girl.

Red knew she carried a heavy burden. But this… No wonder Eveline's dark eyes were so haunted.

She set the treatise back on George's desk, trying to school her face back to neutrality. When he returned, she would congratulate him and celebrate him as he deserved. Not a minute later, she heard his heavy steps on the stairs.

Her forced smile melted away when he exploded through the door, chest heaving and eyes wide with terror.

"What is it?" she whispered. All of the horrible possibilities fought for dominance in those two seconds. But hearing him say the words felt like a knife to her gut.

"Eveline is missing."

CHAPTER TWENTY-THREE

THE TERROR HE'D felt at Waterloo was nothing compared to this. Nothing to leaving his study contentment, envisioning a future with healing and happiness—only to walk up the stairs and find his world crumbling apart.

"She could be hiding," Red said, one stair behind him.

"She could," he admitted, mostly for her sake. "But she hasn't tried that tactic in months."

"Did anything happen at the apiaries?" They reached the first floor.

George raked a hand through his hair, scanning the corridor from end to end. It branched off into the two main wings of the house. "It went well, I thought. She was smiling."

Red's voice was calm as she asked, "Did you say something to upset her?"

He brought his fist down hard on the banister. "No! I am telling you, she was pleased. I was pleased. It was a success—"

Red held up her hand. "I believe you. Let's not waste any more time trying to figure out the why, at least for now. We can question her when we find her."

She was making sense. She was so calm, her face unruffled, eyes clear and bright… It was damned strange. Apparently that spine of hers really was made of steel.

"You take the nursery corridor. I will look in this one." She nodded toward the other wing. "Where is Archie?"

"In the nursery with Mrs. Yates."

Red nodded sharply. "What about the rest of the staff?"

"They've split off to their respective areas to search. Cross is organizing them." He'd managed to arrange as much as he'd run back down the stairs. A maid had taken supper up to the children, finding Archie napping in Red's bed and Eveline missing. The maid had fetched the housekeeper, who sent Cross for him in the study.

Red's eyes traveled over his shoulder and down the corridor toward the nursery. She must be considering going to Archie. But George needed her out here, searching. Archie would be fine for a while yet; he was a stout lad. Red was his best chance of locating Eveline quickly—she'd spent more time with his daughter than anyone else over the past several months.

"Go," he said, squeezing her arm. "Whoever's done first comes to find the other."

Red's eyes flicked back to him, indecision still clouding them. But when her gaze landed on his face, he watched her mouth tighten. She nodded and disappeared without a word, moving with more speed than was considered graceful. George had never been more grateful he'd fallen in love with such an unconventional woman.

EVELINE COULD BE hiding, but she wasn't.

Red checked all the usual places—that was, all the places she'd found Eveline during those weeks her father was away, when Red first came to Oxley Park. She also checked all the places she'd personally marked as potential spots should the girl try the same tactics in the future. But it was taking too long. Oxley Park was equipped with more than thirty bedrooms, many of them suites with attached parlors and dressing rooms.

Checking each one thoroughly was taking forever.

With each door she closed behind her, each empty room searched, Red realized the truth. Eveline was not hiding. She'd been taken. There was no question as to the who—only the where and why. Though Red had an inkling as to the latter.

She knew what she had to do.

Red stepped into the corridor, another room searched, as George appeared around the corner.

"The nursery wing is clear. She isn't in any of those rooms. I've searched my own room as well, but—"

"George—"

"—you haven't found her either. We'll have to go downstairs ourselves. The staff could have missed her, not realized how clever she is. I will lock her in the nursery for a week after this—"

"Colonel Caldwell." Red grabbed his shoulder, yanking him around to face her. His hand dropped, halfway to his hair, loose in dark waves around his shoulders. "I need to tell you something. I need you to listen, and I need you to not interrupt. Do you understand, sir?"

Red watched as the soldier took control. His eyes sharpened, his shoulders squared. Still her George, but with a different chamber of his mind open. One he'd tried so hard to keep locked, but she'd pried into with little hesitation.

She took a deep breath.

"My name is Lady Ethelreda McGovern, of Her Majesty Queen Charlotte's Lady Knights of the Round Table. I was sent to Oxley Park under an assumed identity as your governess in order to find and capture a dangerous French assassin by the name of Antoine Legrand. It is my belief—and that of my superiors—that Legrand is disguised and has taken up residence at Oxley Park for nefarious purposes, though the ultimate goal is unknown." Red sucked in another breath, because the next part was the hardest. "Eveline is not hiding. She has been taken, to draw me out, to draw you out—probably both."

George's breathing was ragged. But that was the only weakness he showed.

Red's heart ached. She knew the betrayal that must be swirling beneath the surface, though he could not allow it free rein now. They could sort the mess they'd created for themselves later. All that mattered now was Eveline.

"What will Legrand do now?" His voice was rough, but if he was angry, he didn't show it.

"Wait. This is a trap. Eveline is only useful as a way to get to you and me. Legrand will lie in wait for us to find them." This, at least, Red felt certain of.

George stared down at her, but it was like he did not see her at all. She could hardly blame him. She'd been a liar in his own house.

"Where?"

Red closed her eyes, exhaling slowly through her nose, feeling her whole chest move with the breath. "I do not know."

"I will take a team of servants and search the grounds. You remain here and search the house." He spun away. She'd been dismissed.

"George."

He froze, back to her.

Please turn around. Please, give me some idea what is happening in that beautiful mind of yours.

But he did not. And she could not torture him any further by asking him to do so.

"Legrand has an accomplice. It may be someone else employed at Oxley Park. Be careful." Red wished she could offer him more. It made her realize just what an utter failure this quest had been. Her charge was kidnapped, and she had almost no information to give that would aid in her retrieval.

George cleared his throat, back still to her. "Are you armed?"

Red smiled grimly, though he did not turn to see her holding up the dagger that was already clasped in her hand, concealed in the folds of her skirt while they'd talked. "I am always armed. But I will retrieve my rapier before continuing my search."

"Find her," he ordered her gruffly.

"Yes, sir."

Then Red watched the man she loved walk away, knowing that her broken heart was the least concerning casualty of this night.

CHAPTER TWENTY-FOUR

WHERE ARE THEY?

Red slammed the door to the fourteenth bedroom she'd searched. It was taking too long. Every minute she wasted—

No, she reminded herself. Legrand had nothing to gain by harming Eveline. Eveline did not know Legrand's secret. She was the trap to draw in George and, by association, Red. If Legrand harmed the child, their leverage would be gone.

She'd move on to the servants' quarters next. Legrand had been posing as a servant; Red was certain of that now. Maybe that was part of the trap—to push George and Red out of the comfortable main rooms of the manor and into the closer quarters of the servants' areas, which Legrand would undoubtedly know better at this point.

Maybe she ought to give up searching the bedrooms and go to the attics immediately. Red turned in the corridor, surveying the remaining doors, quickly calculating in her head how long it would take to search each one…

Her eyes stilled on one door in particular.

If Legrand knew anything about George at all, then that was where she would find them. Red could not believe she hadn't realized it before. The servants' quarters were narrow and unfamiliar, but both George and Red were trained fighters. There was only one place in Oxley Park that was guaranteed to set Sir George Caldwell on edge and give Legrand an advantage.

His wife's apartments.

Red regretted slamming the door. Legrand knew she was close. Still, she silenced her footsteps as she approached the set of rooms she'd entered just once in all her months at Oxley Park. With a deep inhale, rapier at the ready, she nudged the door open.

The room was empty.

At least, it would have appeared that way to an untrained eye. But Red noted the curtains billowing softly—a sign that someone had opened a window in the long-disused suite. Legrand ensuring a secondary escape route.

Senses alert, Red edged along the room, checking behind her before putting her back to the wall. There were plenty of places to hide—behind the curtains, in the shadow of the armoire. This was only the antechamber. Two doors opened on the opposite and adjacent wall. One to a designated bathing room, another to the lady's bedroom. Both doors appeared closed at first glance, but Red would have kept them just a bit ajar, to aid in a swift and silent entry. She could expect no less from Legrand.

It was the whimper from the corner that broke Red's concentration.

She moved for Eveline on instinct, not waiting to calculate the risks or rewards. All she knew was that she had to protect the child, put her body between Eveline and the volatile French assassin.

Red had at least enough sense to keep her back to the wall as she ran for the armoire. There, tucked into the space between the giant wood construction and the wall, cowered Eveline, face white as a sheet in the scant moonlight.

"Are you hurt?" Red crouched down, rapier still at the ready.

Eveline whimpered again. Red crushed the child to her side, holding her tightly, kissing the top of her dark head. The familiar scent of lavender bath soap sent burning tears to her eyes. But she didn't have time for tears. She was busy running her free hand over Eveline's body, trying to check for injury.

"Did she hurt you?" Red asked, voice as gentle as she could manage.

"She... she... she..." Eveline cried out a second after Red heard the shift in the air.

She swung out, parrying the blow with enough force to send Legrand back a few steps to regain her footing.

Red didn't give her time to recover. She lunged forward on her right foot, driving her back with all her strength. She had the element of surprise for a few seconds more, then Legrand would regain herself and fight back.

"Run, Eveline!" she commanded.

For once in her life, Eveline did not argue. Red felt her brush past, felt the air move behind her as the child ran for the door. Legrand did not try to stop her. All of her attention was on Red now.

She stalked along the opposite wall, flashing her own blade from side to side, considering Red carefully. The light in the room was scant, but it was enough for Red to do the same. For her to note the tightly bound hair, the comfortable hold she had on the blade, and the lack of deference she'd always worn so carefully.

"You've left off your kitchen apron," Red commented, flexing the fingers on her free hand.

"I thought it might hinder my movements." The assassin shrugged. "When did you work it out?"

"I could ask you the same question." Red knew the conversation was a distraction, to give George time to get there. He was the real target here.

"Oh, I've suspected you since you spilled my poison in the kitchen. You were so diligent, too, about coming down each day to check for more attempted poisonings. But once I spotted you with that rapier, I knew for sure." Legrand's eyes were on her blade even now, assessing her skill.

When had she seen her? With George, or one of those mornings she'd ventured out alone? Red hated herself for not realizing she'd been followed.

"Your turn," Legrand said, though her voice sounded almost bored. Another ruse. She was going to attack soon. Red was ready.

"Today," Red said, planting her feet. She'd make Legrand come to her. "I researched all the men in Oxley Park, but I discounted the women. A fool's mistake, given my own skills. But still, the description I'd been given was brown hair and brown eyes, medium build. It was the poison that narrowed it to you."

Legrand's eyes glittered. She swiped her tongue over her lower lip, like an animal about to pounce. Red recognized the tell for what it was. She was ready when Legrand attacked. She parried easily enough, though not as easily as that first time. Legrand's first attack had been nominal, a feint so that Eveline could escape and fetch George while she engaged Red.

Red would not make it easy on her. Her riposte was swift, forcing Legrand to give several feet of ground. If Red could drive the assassin up to the wall, she could attempt to disarm her.

"I wondered if you would be as impressive with an opponent as you were running through those exercises all alone." Legrand smiled, spinning to avoid her cut and attempting a feint.

Red was not fooled. She got her blade up in plenty of time to defeat the hidden attack.

"Quite impressive yourself. I would have expected an assassin to be better with a knife than a rapier." Red could distract, too.

Legrand had been playing the compliant kitchen maid for months. She must be bursting to be herself again, the dangerous French assassin whom no one in the entire country of England had realized was a woman. The more she gloated, the less focused she might be—and the more evidence Red would have against her to pass along to the Duchess of Guilford.

"I do prefer a knife," Legrand said, her smile wicked. She lunged, attacking with a burst of force and speed that sent Red back, giving the ground she'd claimed. Red forced her feet along the perimeter of the room, trying to get closer to the door on the adjacent wall so she had a place to retreat to if needed.

But the distraction cost her. Legrand redoubled her efforts and hit Red's hand hard, knocking the blade from her hand. Fear was a distant thing, and Red had no time for it. But she did recognize when her life was in danger.

"A knife requires you to get close to your opponent." Legrand cut up, skimming Red's arm. Red gritted her teeth against the pain. She made the decision in a flash, and then suddenly she was up against the wall, Legrand's arm across her throat. "I like to see the life leave their eyes," she whispered.

But Red had heard what Legrand had not. Footsteps.

Legrand heard them then, and loosened her hold fractionally. Red was disarmed, after all.

But her left hand was free.

She grabbed Legrand's right wrist and wrenched the blade free. Red caught the hilt before it hit the floor and shoved. Legrand stumbled backward, eyes widening to expose the whites. Red wasted no time switching the blade to her other hand; she was almost as proficient with her left as she was with her right.

When George thundered through the door, Red had Legrand pinned against the wall with the tip of her own rapier pressed to her throat.

George skidded to a stop, and his own weapon went slack at his side. He blinked in shock as he took in the two women. Legrand squirmed in place. Red increased the pressure until a tiny trickle of blood slid down the other woman's throat.

"I would rather take you in alive so you may face justice for your crimes, but you would not be the first person I have killed," Red said without hesitation.

Legrand glared defiantly, no fear showing in her eyes. Red supposed that to be an assassin, one must consider their imminent death a hazard of the profession.

George huffed out a strangled sound of disbelief.

"The… the kitchen maid?"

"Louisa," Red supplied. "Is that your real name, Legrand? The one you were born with? Or is it Antoinette, instead of Antoine?"

The assassin's eyes flashed. "I do not recall the name I was born with, though it hardly matters."

"No, I suppose it does not," Red agreed. "Don't you recognize her, George? I imagine her hair was darker—she's been lightening it with lemon or lye, I'd wager. Of course, she must have looked different dressed as a promiscuous camp follower rather than a prim and proper kitchen maid."

George shook his head. "It cannot be."

"She must have been working as an assassin even then, infiltrating the British ranks." Red was careful to keep the blade firm as she explained. She was not going to let Legrand catch her unawares. "But you suspected something was off about her, and told Barrow and McGovern as much. One of them must have mentioned it to her. Which was enough to bring her here, investigating whether her cover was in danger."

"As a kitchen maid, she would have had minimal contact with me. So I was less likely to recognize her," George finished.

Red didn't dare look at him, but she could hear the pain in his voice. Here was the woman who had not only been at the root of the conflict that had caused him such pain—she'd surely orchestrated it.

Then she'd come into his home, endangered his family, and kidnapped his daughter.

This woman could not go free. Red needed her bound and stripped, now.

"We need to—"

"Sir, we've just—" Cross broke off, his eyes nearly popping out of their sockets as he took in the scene.

"What is it, Cross?" George growled.

"The lads…" Cross mumbled. George's next growl was more animal than man. "They caught Gerald trying to flee the grounds. We did not wish to disturb Miss Eveline to ask if he'd been involved. But from the way he fought, we thought he must—"

"Who is he?" Red demanded.

Cross blinked. "I—"

"Secure him downstairs. We will be there momentarily," Red said, dismissing him. She waited until he was gone before demanding again. "Who is he?"

Legrand shrugged, a distinctly Gallic gesture for someone being held at the end of a lethal blade. "A cousin of Barrow, interested in exacting a bit of revenge."

Red felt her own temper rising. She had to get both of the captives secured before she did something rash—such as running her through. It was no more than Legrand deserved.

She jerked her head to George. "Find something to gag her with. I don't want to hear her voice ever again."

CHAPTER TWENTY-FIVE

I T HAD ALL happened so quickly. At six o'clock in the evening, he'd been sitting in his study sipping whisky while Red read his treatise on bees. That seemed like a pivotal moment in their relationship. A new trust had formed between them.

Only for everything he thought he knew about her to be torn apart an hour later.

Now, it was nine o'clock. The November skies beyond the windows had long since darkened, and he was once again in his study with Red. Though this time, they had company.

"Put him there, tied to the large cabinet," Red directed unnecessarily. He'd appraised the room as efficiently as she. While she secured Legrand to the bookcase, he did the same for Gerald.

When he was done, he stepped back to inspect Red's handiwork. She did the same, finally nodding approval and turning back to Cross, who hovered in the door. George followed her with his eyes. Poor Cross. The man had aged a decade in the last few hours, and he'd already been flirting with sixty.

"I need you to send word down to the stables. I need five riders, on fast horses," Red said.

Cross's eyes drifted over her head, which was a mess of frizzy red curls gone to madness, looking to George for confirmation. Red didn't bother to disguise her huff of frustration as her hands landed on her hips.

Cross was a braver man than George had ever given him credit for.

"Do as she asks," George ordered him. "Whatever she asks."

"Five men. Fast horses," she repeated. "Ask them to wait for me on the doorstep. I'll explain more there."

George waited for her to come back into the study, closing the door behind her, before he jerked his head toward the pair of captives. "What shall we do with them? The lads punished Gerald quite thoroughly. I could send for a physician."

Red was shaking her head before he finished his sentence. "No physicians. No one in or out of this house. Not until the authorities arrive."

"We can send for the village magistrate—"

"Not those sorts of authorities. The authorities *I* answer to."

George scrunched his eyes closed. This was all beyond bearing. He thought he'd seen the wildest—and worst—that the world had to offer while he was away at war. But this was unfolding in his own house. And it seemed like it was still far from over, despite the two villains bound and gagged on the floor of his study.

"Dare I ask who that is?" Before, she'd declared herself a lady knight of Her Majesty's Round Table. But somehow, George doubted the queen herself would be visiting Oxley Park.

Red's hand jerked to the side. "Not in front of our guests."

George sighed. "I will take the first shift. You go up and sleep." He dropped onto the chaise where he'd spent the night with Red. Just like that night, tonight there would be no sleeping.

But Red perched on the edge of his desk. "I will stand guard until the authorities return from London to retrieve them."

He blinked twice, trying to make sense of her response. Disbelief won out. "That will take a day, at least. Even switching horses."

"I'd expect someone here tomorrow afternoon."

"And you intend to stay here, in this study, awake, for that entire time."

"Yes."

Ethelreda Trudeau was the most stubborn woman he'd ever known. And that was before she declared herself a secret agent of the Crown tasked with capturing an assassin in his home.

Not Trudeau, he corrected himself. McGovern.

It might have been a coincidence. But he remembered the way her eyes had flashed while they sparred in the summer house as he told her his story. She'd known since then that he'd been responsible for her family member's death.

Who was Josiah McGovern to her? A brother? George's chest tightened painfully. Perhaps they ought to call for the physician after all.

He couldn't bring himself to ask her. Not yet. They both needed their wits about them if they were truly to stand guard for the next twenty hours.

Cross appeared a few minutes later, and Red followed him outside, spearing George with a look as she left. What she expected him to do, one way or another, was beyond him. Gerald was only half-conscious. The former kitchen maid watched them with daggers in her eyes. She might be trouble.

When Red returned fifteen minutes later, she was rubbing her eyes.

"That's all five of your men off. They should get word to London by midmorning." She dropped down into an armchair, decided she wasn't satisfied with the position, and shifted her weight around until she had a view of the door, the windows, and her captives.

He waited until she seemed settled. "Let's at least take it in shifts."

Red sighed heavily. "I assure you, I have done this before—"

"Yes. But there is no need for you to do so this time. I will not leave the room. I shall wake you in a few hours."

She cocked her head to the side, eyes rolling over him. Assessing, he realized. How many times had she turned those appraising eyes to him before, when he had not realized it? At first, he'd merely thought her clever, taking the measure of the man who had shaped the children in her care. Later, he'd imagined desire behind those long glances.

Not imagined. She could not have faked it—could she?

No. If everything else between them had been a fabrication, he at least had to believe that the desire was not. He'd seen the evidence of it again and again.

He curled his hand into a fist to keep it from trembling and willed his voice to be steady as he spoke again.

"I won't take my eyes off her." George nodded to Legrand, who showed no signs of fatigue. "I promise."

Red eyed the French assassin, reduced to nothing but her shift and stockings, hair loose around her shoulders. "I've already checked her for hidden weapons. She didn't appreciate me having a peek underneath her shift, but I assured her I was only acting as a professional." As if that stirred a thought, Red stood and reached into the pocket of her gown, retrieving something.

Many somethings, George realized, when she scattered them over the top of his desk. "Hairpins fashioned as daggers, lock-picks, so on. I think this one might even be dipped in poison." Red lifted one slightly darker pin to examine it closer, but ultimately discarded it with the others. Then she gathered them up, dumped them into a drawer of his desk, and locked it. "So she doesn't get any crafty ideas."

"Do you walk around with daggers in your hair?" George asked, incredulous. He'd walked into battle after battle armed to the teeth, but this still shocked him.

"In my corset, my garter, my boot," Red replied.

Gerald snored, startling himself. Red's softened expression closed up in a second.

She turned her hard gaze to Legrand. "I'm very good at hiding, but not as good as you. But that's all over now."

George sensed the shift in her tone. "I thought you didn't want them to overhear."

"I want them to know this." She spun on the pair, but the fire in her eyes was for Legrand alone. "Did you hear that, mademoiselle? Word has gone out across London. Everyone of importance now knows it. I would not be surprised if the *Sun* runs a column tomorrow evening."

Legrand tried to bare her teeth, but the gag prevented her.

Red chuckled darkly. "Save your theatrics for someone who cares."

George had never seen her like this, so dark and vindictive. He wondered if he'd ever known her at all.

Of course you do, his heart argued. *You know that if you had Barrow at your mercy—*

He stamped that thought out before it could take hold and burn him away to ashes.

Red was angry. She'd done an excellent job of hiding it, acting with brutal efficiency to take down Legrand and Gerald, to arrange for the appropriate parties in London to be notified. But beneath all of it, she was simmering with heat.

Not the sort he enjoyed coaxing out of her, the kind that would bring them both undulating waves of pleasure. No, this was the type of simmer that, when it boiled over, would scald anyone it could reach.

Legrand deserved every bit of that punishment for the pain she'd wrought.

But so did George.

SHE LET THE anger flow through her, let it hone her skills and keep the exhaustion at bay. But when Legrand and Gerald were loaded into an unmarked carriage and escorted away by a contingent of armed men twelve strong, Red knew the truth. The only person she was truly mad at was herself.

George stood on the front steps of Oxley Park, watching the carriage roll away down the long drive. Red recognized her moment to escape. He didn't turn his head to watch her walk away, and Red didn't look back to see if his gaze followed her inside. She dragged herself up the stairs and down the corridor.

The only temptation was the nursery. Red had not seen Eveline since she'd pulled her crying from Legrand grasp's and shoved her out the door to safety. For Archie, it had been even longer. Red wanted her bed desperately, but she wanted to hold the children and hug them tightly even more.

But George would go there next. She knew it as surely as her own name—McGovern. Oh, if only her true surname had been Trudeau. All of this would have been so much easier.

Her mind began to melt at those thoughts as she forced her feet past the nursery.

George would go to the children. He was their father, and it was where he belonged. She was nothing to them. Not even their governess. Not really.

That hurt more than anything that had come before.

Red made it through her door, not bothering with elaborate traps or snares. There were no more secrets at Oxley Park. Except, perhaps, the love she held in her heart for each member of the Caldwell family.

Even through two walls, she heard the joyous sounds of their reunion. She let their happy cries lull her to sleep as her tears soaked the pillow.

CHAPTER TWENTY-SIX

S LEEPING ON THE floor of the nursery was only marginally more comfortable than an army cot plunked down in the mud. At least he was warm. Granted, he'd had to steal the coverlet off Archie's bed to stay that way, after his children had wiggled and wormed enough that he'd given up trying to fit with them in Eveline's bed.

He would have carried them back to his rooms, where they could have piled into one bed more comfortably. But after the last two days, the only place his children wanted to be was the safety of their nursery. And he was not willing to leave them.

Never again.

They ate breakfast together the next morning, and it was such a sharp contrast to that day, months and months before, when Eveline had spilled hot tea in his lap and he'd upended the table with his knee. Eveline was smiling, for one. Archie still made a mess when he ate, but at least he punctuated his bites with "please" and "thank you."

"Is this a new table?" George asked, bending over to peer at the legs. He did not remember fitting so well beneath it. Surely, the one before had been child-size.

"Miss Trudeau had it brought in soon after she arrived," Eveline said quietly.

George's gaze was pulled toward the door over Eveline's

shoulder. The one that connected to Red's rooms. The one that had not opened, all through the night and into the morning.

"Is Miss Trudeau unwell?" Archie asked around a mouthful of eggs.

Eveline's eyes sharpened. No more looking at her plate; her ordeal seemed to have endowed her with newfound courage. She pinned him with a stare that was not a mirror of his wife or himself. It was purely Eveline.

"The last few days' events have weighed heavily upon her," George said carefully. He did not want to lie to them. Eveline, of course, was old enough and clever enough to deduce there was more to Red than a simple governess. The woman had rescued her at the point of a sword. But he had no real answers to give them. "We shall give her the time and space she needs to recover. I am certain she will speak to us when she is ready."

That was the part that was closest to a lie. He did not know if she would speak to them again. The children, certainly. Her affection for them was obvious. But him?

The attraction between them, the growing affection, the love… He'd *thought* it was love. He was in love with her. But she had been playacting, a professional lady knight sent to Oxley Park to serve and protect. George could not say for certain if what was between them had been real, or some part of her elaborate scheme.

Maybe he ought to be angry at her, for keeping it from him. But she'd saved his daughter and captured the villain. She'd followed orders. As a soldier and commander, he could under-stand that and not hate her for it.

He loved her.

But she had every reason to despise him. He was responsible for her cousin's death.

He'd managed to ask her that, during the long hours of watching and waiting for the authorities to arrive from London.

Who was Josiah McGovern to you?

He was my beloved cousin.

Not only had he allowed the conflict between McGovern and Barrow to simmer until it culminated in McGovern's murder on the battlefield, but he'd failed to notice the assassin infiltrating his ranks. Because she was a female, and until Ethelreda McGovern sparred with him in the summer house, George had never realized a woman could be such a threat.

Red had shared little about her family. What she had told him, he had no way of knowing whether it was true or not. But with Legrand and Gerald captured, the danger had passed. There was no reason for Her Majesty's lady knight to remain at Oxley Park.

⚜

IT TOOK NEARLY two days, but George finally returned to his study.

She'd been waiting for it, behind her closed doors in her self-imposed prison. At least the children came to visit. Or rather, Eveline knocked primly and then Archie came tumbling through before she could rise to her feet.

But seeing them had been a balm to her spirit. If all she had were memories of this quest, the children would be among the best of them. Damned ironic. She would never admit it to Miranda. Never.

She even caught Eveline sniffling in the corner and offered her a handkerchief. Not quite the same as wiping a snotty nose, but near enough.

But now the children were quietly occupied with their reading—or at least they had been when she left them—and she was standing outside the closed door to George's study. She hadn't been able to start packing her things, but the valise was on the foot of her bed. She'd burned her notes. The real power would be in her testimony, if Legrand ever did stand trial. Red wondered if she might be the sort to disappear in the middle of the night.

There would certainly be no one foolish enough to ask questions on her behalf.

She lifted her hand and knocked—one soft touch followed by three sharp raps.

"Come in," and then, a second later, "Please."

George was precisely where she expected him to be, tucked behind his desk. Though rather than whisky, he had a fresh cup of tea.

"Would you care for some?" He must have followed her eyes.

Red nodded, if only because it would give her something to occupy her hands as she had the most awkward conversation of her life.

She stirred in a bit of sugar and then drifted away, putting some space between them. She still had no notion where they stood. There'd been no room for talking when they were trapped in here with Legrand and Gerald. She'd seen the pain and anger in his eyes when they stood upstairs, facing down Legrand. But what portion was for the assassin and how much was reserved for her… Red could only imagine.

And she was imagining the worst.

"We have much to discuss," she began quietly.

George shifted in his seat. "Do we?"

"I… I believe so."

She never stuttered. It was not in her character. She was always self-assured. But this… She was going to muck this up.

"Do you… Are there any questions I can answer for you?" She'd tell him anything that was not strictly confidential. She'd tell him her hopes and dreams, if he asked. They were him, Archie, and Eveline. Simple.

George turned to look out the window. He could not even stand to look at her. This was a lost cause.

She stared into her tea. She would not let him see her cry. If all she was to be was a spinster lady knight, then at least she would hold on to some shred of her pride.

"I have only one," he said.

Red steeled herself.

"Was any of it real?"

He did hate her. There was the confirmation. For lying, for endangering his family, for leading him on. He probably thought she'd seduced him on purpose. But there was no point in arguing or trying to parse that out. His face may as well have been hewn from granite.

"Some of it, yes," she forced herself to say.

Pain washed over George's face. Red could not bear it any longer. She set down her untouched tea, spinning for the door.

"If you will excuse me, it is time I gather my belongings. I will leave on the morrow."

She tracked George's footsteps as they followed her out of the study, but she did not turn around. These tears of disappointment she would keep for herself.

HE WATCHED HER disappear up the stairs, wanting to run after her but also trying with every fiber of his being to respect her wishes. If she did not want to stay, if she did not love him… He could not force something that had never been there to begin with.

"I thought you were smart."

Eveline stepped out of the shelter of the staircase, where they curved and created a little pocket of shadow just big enough to hide a clever nine-year-old.

The disdain on her face was enough to choke the air out of a grown man.

A grown man like him.

"I beg your pardon?" he managed.

Eveline put her hands on her hips, the perfect mimic of Red. "You are letting her go," she accused.

George shook his head, raking a hand through his hair, pulling the entire club loose. "I… She does not want to stay."

Those dark eyes narrowed. "Did she say that?"

"No," he admitted. *But she might as well have.*

Eveline glanced up the stairs. Whether she was checking to see if Red had gone, or assessing whether she might be better off talking sense in her than him, George had no way of knowing.

"Then how do you know how she feels?"

He sighed. "Wasn't that her opportunity?"

"Did you tell her how you feel?" she asked, lips pursed now.

How was he going to manage her with Red gone? She was too smart for him, not just by half, but by many halves. He turned to go back to his study, thinking that perhaps it was time to put away the tea and get out the whisky.

"How did you get so good at arguing?" he said, settling for tea. At least while his daughter was watching.

Eveline sniffed, very ladylike. "I've had Miss Trudeau—Miss McGovern—as my governess for the past four months."

George rubbed the bridge of his nose. "Please tell me she does not consider argumentation a proper area of instruction for a nine-year-old girl."

Eveline only shrugged her slim shoulders. A deflecting technique. That was answer enough.

She walked toward the window, leaning her forehead against the glass as she gazed out. Still a child, he remembered then. Still half lost in her dreams. But apparently full of wisdom as well.

"If you let her go, Archie will never forgive you. He thinks she's meant to be his new mother."

George's hand tightened around his teacup. The vision of Red and Archie snuggled close came to him too easily. A family—that was what they might have been. What they might still be, if Eveline was correct.

He looked back to his daughter, at her breath fogging up the window. But still she looked on, a sad little smile on her face.

"I think she is too," Eveline said softly.

CHAPTER TWENTY-SEVEN

THE WHISKY BOTTLE sat before him, untouched. Not at the desk, but in the chair where Red had sat for so many of those long hours while they waited for the authorities to arrive. It still smelled of her. Like a lovesick fool, he was leaning back into the upholstery, trying to breathe her in, to etch her essence in his memory forever.

Eveline might be right. Maybe he had not really given Red the chance. Maybe he was too afraid after what had happened with Leisa. He was too ready to believe that love was not meant for him.

But if he let Red go without telling her how he truly felt, if he did not try to get her to stay... Eveline might try to kill him. He didn't think Red had been teaching her to use the rapier, but he did not doubt his daughter's ingenuity. She'd probably choose something involving bees, just to be contrary.

Aside from his daughter's wrath and his son's hopes...he wanted Red. He loved Red.

A few seconds later, he heard her footsteps.

He shouldn't have recognized them, he'd so rarely heard them before. Because she meant it that way, he realized now. She was a trained spy. She moved in silence because she'd been trained to do so. Which meant that if he heard her steps now, then maybe there was a chance that was on purpose as well.

Even if she did not realize it herself.

By the time he reached the foyer, the outer door had already closed behind her with a whispering hiss. It was cold as death outside, and he did not know where she was going. He would help no one if he froze to death while chasing her down. He forced himself to call for Cross, to have his greatcoat brought.

When he stepped outside, he could see his breath. His fingers ached instantly, but he'd eschewed gloves. He wanted to touch her again, if only once more. He wouldn't be wasting time with gloves. The stars were just emerging in the sky above, and there was a sense of promise in the air.

Snow, his instincts told him.

The same instincts that told him where to go. He could not see her, disappeared into the night. If she had a lantern, it was shielded by her body. Or she'd already made it to the copse of trees. But George knew where he would find her.

SHE HADN'T KNOWN he was following her, yet she was not surprised to see him. Or rather, to hear him. He made no effort to disguise his footsteps as they crunched over the frosty ground. An hour or two, and his approach might have been silent. Snow was coming.

Even so, she pushed the thick velvet of her heavy emerald cloak back over her shoulders. The diaphanous seafoam-green gown was almost nonexistent against the elements, but it had been the one she was unable to pack. Now, with her hair tumbling loose over her shoulders and her skin prickling from the cold, Red knew why. It was to give her the courage to say goodbye.

She hadn't thrown open the doors this time, merely slipped inside, leaving the door ajar. Perhaps part of her had known he would come. Or hoped.

He closed the door behind him, his hands fixed behind his back, just watching her as she stood in the middle of the room. All the furniture lined the walls, where she'd pushed it to accommodate her sparring.

"Is there something you need, sir?" Her voice trembled.

Instead of answering, he walked toward her with slow, steady steps. At least one of them was steady.

"You must be cold," he said, fingering one of the puffed edges of her sleeves.

His fingers were so near to touching her skin that she could feel the warmth of him. Her heart joined the trembling chorus of her pulse. "I suppose I wanted to remember the way I felt when I wore this dress, the way you looked at me."

"How did you feel, Red?"

She couldn't answer. The sound of her name on his lips was too much to bear.

George hooked his finger under her chin and slowly lifted it, forcing her to look at him.

"Adored," she breathed.

George closed his eyes, biting his lower lip as he breathed in sharply. "Red, will you ever forgive me?"

"Forgive you?" Her entire body was shaking now. "George, there is nothing—"

"I am complicit in your cousin's death. I have no right to ask for your love." He stepped away, shoving his hands deep into his greatcoat.

Was he afraid to touch her?

"Love?" She had barely dared to think it, let alone say it.

She reached out, her fingers shaking so badly she could hardly look at them. But still she reached until she touched his shoulder. For a moment, she thought he would shake her away. Then George reached up and covered her hand with his.

He turned and swept her into his arms, burying his head in the curve of her shoulder.

"I love you," he murmured into the mass of curls.

"Can this be happening to me?" A tear slid down her face as his mouth brushed across her neck.

"Please don't go, Red. The children need you. I need you." He caught her face, pressing kisses to her cheeks, her nose, her chin. Finally to her lips. "Please, say you will stay."

The tears were falling freely now. She was still shaking, but it was turning to joy. "You only had to ask," she mumbled. "I will stay. Of course I will stay. I understand if you do not wish to marry, after what happened with your wife. I will be content to stay on as the children's governess, though I would like to continue my work with the Lady Knights—"

George froze, squeezing her face a bit tighter than was comfortable. She teased his hands apart gently, and he loosened his hold immediately, but a frown still marred his brow.

"My wife?" he asked.

Red bit her lip. "I did not mean to pry. But when I read the dates of your military service... I already knew when she'd died. And the child..."

Understanding dawned in his eyes, then turned grim. "The child was not mine. Your cleverness knows no bounds, does it, Red?"

He sighed, letting his hands drop. But Red did not let him walk away—she caught them with her own and held tight. Just let him try to run away from her now that he'd told her that he loved her. He'd learn precisely how stubborn she could be.

"Leisa... my wife," he clarified, though she already knew. "Our marriage was doomed from the start. We got on well enough at the beginning. But it was an arranged match, and a bad one at that. I was dedicated to my regiment. She wanted to be in London, dancing into the wee hours. Even after the children. She loved them, mind you, very much. But when she died... It was my fault."

He stared down at their joined hands. "I left her alone for so long. What choice did she have but to turn to another for the love I could not give her? When she died... Her blood is on my hands as well."

This time, it was Red who caught him under the chin and dragged his eyes up to meet hers. "You truly believe that, don't you?"

His pained nod was her answer.

"Maybe someday I can convince you otherwise."

"Perhaps." He sighed. "But only as my wife."

Red's heart was going to explode. There were the tears again. And the damnable trembling. "I love you," she whispered.

George gathered her up in his arms, kissing her fervently. He seemed determined to kiss every inch of skin that was exposed by her dress. She finally pulled him back, demanding he kiss her lips as well.

"Red." He stroked aside a red curl. "You have saved us, in every possible way. Our lives, when they were in danger. Our hearts, when they were too broken to connect to one another. Eveline, Archie, and me—we will be whole again because of you."

Red didn't know what to say. So instead, she decided to show him. Starting with his mouth, with his hands on her breast. Until they were bare to each other in the middle of the summer house, impervious to the cold, feeling only the joy of joining and being one together.

⇢⇢⇥⇤⇠⇠

"WHAT SHOULD WE do now?" Red asked many minutes later, when the cold air finally began to sink into their bodies.

George nuzzled her ear, urging her head back up to look at him. His grin was infectious.

"Of course." Red laughed.

They both opened their mouths and spoke at the same time: "Go tell the children."

EPILOGUE

January 1818
Oxley Park, Essex

S HE WOKE WITH the dawn, as always. Except this morning, she was not sneaking out of Oxley Park to the summer house to practice her swordplay. Her parasol, with its freshly honed rapier, rested against the bed, within arm's reach. Red did not think she would be changing that habit anytime soon, especially after everything that had happened. But perhaps someday, when they returned to London.

In her mind, she heard her fellow lady knights laughing at her, reminding her that London was plenty dangerous enough and she ought to know that better than anyone. She ached for missing them. At least word had finally come that Jacquetta and Jane were well. Jacquetta was more than fine; she was a married woman returning with her criminal-turned-redeemed-lord of a husband. Dominique, too, was now married.

Red regretted she'd been unable to attend either ceremony. It seemed wrong, after all they'd been to each other. But then, none of them had attended her wedding either.

Red stretched her arms above her head, letting the slivers of early-morning light shine on her face and remind her that none of this was a dream. The bedroom was cool, the banked hearth nothing but sad little embers. A maid would be in soon to coax the flames back to life, so that when Red did deign to rise from the comfort of the coverlet, she would not freeze to death.

Except no maid would dare enter this room. Not this morning, of all mornings. There was no need for one of Red's crafty snares to hold the door closed. Not a single occupant in Oxley Park would disturb the lord and lady of the house on the morning after their wedding.

Said lord was awake, Red realized, when his hand tightened possessively around her breast.

She arched a little further, enjoying the way he moved his hand with her, keeping his hold on her breast, as if letting her go was just an impossible notion.

"Good morning, husband," she breathed as she relaxed and settled back onto the pillows.

"How long have you been awake, wife?" he murmured, rolling onto his side and levering up on one elbow so he could look down upon her. His other hand, of course, was occupied with doing very diverting things to her breast.

"Not long," she murmured, arching back her head to reveal her throat—an invitation.

George did not disappoint; he leaned forward enough to press a soft kiss to her lips before turning his attention to long, languorous swipes of his tongue along the column of her neck, followed by sucking kisses that might very well leave a mark. Red did not care. In fact, she found the idea erotic. Let him mark her. Let him show the rest of the world that she belonged to him. She certainly felt the truth of it in her very bones.

"I thought you might try to slip out for a bit of sparring." His warm breath across her neck sent gooseflesh spreading. George groaned, flexing back and admiring her breasts as her already taut nipples hardened even further.

"The only person I have interest in sparring with this morning is you," Red said, hearing the hoarseness in her own voice. From George's deep chuckle before he sucked her nipple into his mouth, she knew he heard it too.

He shifted fully atop her. Red loved the feeling of him pressed against her from top to bottom. She was grateful for the strength of her body, matched by his own, supporting one another in the most arousing of ways.

"Should I fetch my sword?" He grinned wolfishly, adjusting his hips over hers.

"You are perfectly well endowed as you are," she shot back.

Red wanted to freeze the moment in time. Paint a picture, draw a sketch—as if she had any talent at either medium. But that smile, which came so easily now, had been missing when she first met Sir George Caldwell. While the terrors remained, driving him from his sleep more often than either of them would like, they were less and less. The exercises she'd set for him, augmented with additional strategies she'd requested from Miranda, helped stave off the worst of it.

He was healing. More importantly, their family was healing. She saw it in the children's faces with each day that passed. They were becoming one.

George groaned as she shifted her hips, reminding him that she wanted them to more literally become one as soon as possible. In the next few seconds, if possible.

"You are holding me hostage," she accused, reaching for his lips and rolling her hips. Anything to entice him to quench the building ache.

He nudged her legs apart. "You will be trapped here a few months longer," he reminded her.

It was part of her agreement with the Duchess of Guilford. In order to avoid any potential scandal that could link her to the Lady Knights or Legrand, she would remain in the country with her new family until after the Season was in full swing. Only then, once she'd received word that all was calm and clear, would Red bring George and the children to London to spend the rest of the Season with the McGovern family.

"Trapped with you." She pretended to consider, spreading a

little wider so she could wrap her legs around him. "I suppose there are worse propositions."

"Are there?" George caught her lower lip between his teeth and slid into her.

Red hissed through her teeth. Just the feel of him above her, near her, was enough to make her slick and wet. She'd fallen asleep with him buried inside of her and woke with the need for him once more. Rational thought told her this euphoric lust might dim. But her heart told her their love would not.

Rising up on her elbows, Red kissed a sensuous line along his jaw to the shell of his ear. "Eventually you will have to go to London," she whispered, watching the gooseflesh rise on his neck even as he continued to rhythmically thrust inside of her.

"You are a cruel woman," George growled, his body shaking with a tremor of desire. Red felt her own beginning to take over, making clear thinking more and more difficult.

"I learned from the best," she said, dropping back onto the bed so she could cup her breasts, toying with the nipples—teasing him.

George groaned, leaning to suck a taut nipple into his mouth, just as she'd known he would. "These breasts," he murmured.

"What about them?"

"Magnificent."

"What else?"

He was picking up speed now, the rhythm of his thrusts more demanding. Red felt her own pleasure building as he alternating sucking and biting her sensitive tips.

"Your arse." George reached down and palmed one of the round cheeks for emphasis. "And these strong, thick thighs. When you wrap them around me and pull my cock inside of you—Red—" He broke off, struggling to hold back.

Red tightened her hold, using those strong thighs to hold him in when he tried to pull away. She'd taken the precautions. There would be no more children, not unless they changed their mind sometime in the future. But just now, she needed him inside of her—every last drop of him.

"Red, Red, Red," he chanted above her.

Then they were both exploding, the blankets thrown back, burning with the heat of their own climax and love. Nothing could touch them, not now that they'd found one another. There was only the future—a shared future. A family, and more love than either of them could have ever envisioned.

THE DUCHESS OF Guilford did not say goodbye. First, it was entirely unnecessary. She expected Ethelreda to remain in the arms of her new husband for the entire day. An entire week, if the looks on their besotted faces in the chapel the day before had been any indication of the depth of their desire and love.

Second, it was much too early. Only the drunk and the dead were about at this hour. It was still half dark. But Miranda's driver was used to such requests. And if there was any danger to traveling before the sun was fully up… Well, Miranda wished any assailants who attempted to take this carriage the best of luck. The excitement would at least keep her warm.

She rubbed her hands together, fighting the chill spreading in her fingertips despite the gloves, thick muff, and heated bricks beneath her feet. Her driver had pulled the shades down, to try to keep in the heat. But even with her fingers tingling, Miranda found herself raising one so she could watch the English countryside as it slowly emerged from its nighttime rest.

She'd given everything for this country. Sometimes she needed to gaze upon it, note the little thatched-roof cottages, the peaceful, rolling hills, to remind herself why exactly she'd given up everything. For peace, she repeated to herself. For all those who still slept in safety while she rode through the wee hours of the morning, contemplating deception and deadly weapons.

Three of her lady knights were now wed. One was sidelined

from action for the next several months at least. All for the better—whether Red would admit it or not, the distress of seeing one's children in danger could linger.

Miranda could not help the smile that tugged at the corners of her mouth, and alone in her carriage, she did not bother to suppress it. They *were* Red's children now. Ironic, considering Red had very proudly told her the day before that she'd burned *Mrs. Plimpton's Guide for the Modern Governess* in the hearth of her quarters before moving into Sir George's apartments.

Red had made a superb governess, just as Miranda had known she would. She would make an even better mother.

But it meant Red's role as a lady knight would have to change. Less swordplay and more carefully guarding her identity. Miranda filed that problem away to be dealt with later. Red and her new family would not come to London for several months. There were more pressing matters.

Such as the imminent return of the other three lady knights. By the time she reached London, Jacquetta, Dominique, and Jane would all be there as well. Miranda would send word ahead to her calligrapher to begin working on invitations. Another of the Duchess of Guilford's famed balls was in order—she needed her lady knights around the table.

A shiver slid down her spine. Miranda told herself it was from the cold January air. The sun was hardly even up.

What was coming would require all of their talents.

But as she thought back to the dossier carefully concealed in her boudoir, behind the false panel in the walls and locked within a safe, only one face came to her mind. Her most skilled and clever lady knight. The one who was the most like her. The one who could get this done, if anyone could.

Jane.

About the Author

A lifetime reader of romance, Cara put pen to paper (or rather, fingers to keyboard) in 2019 and published her first book. She hasn't slowed down from there. Cara is an avid traveler. As she explores new places, she imagines her characters walking hand-in-hand down a cobblestone path or sharing a passionate kiss in a secluded alcove. Cara is living out her own happily ever after in Seattle, Washington, where she resides with her husband, daughter, and two cats, RoseArt and Etch-o-Sketch.

Instagram: caramaxwellromance
Facebook: caramaxwellromance

www.ingramcontent.com/pod-product-compliance
Lightning Source LLC
Chambersburg PA
CBHW070336200726
48294CB00003B/685